THE LAST GASP

Also by this Author:
Better Red than Dead
Jake's Tale

Look out for Mike's next book:
Zoe and the Duke

THE LAST GASP

MIKE HODGKINS

About the author

Mike Hodgkins is a retired fire officer, having worked in both the north and south of England as a firefighter. Mike is married to Carol, has two children and six grandchildren. Mike lives in Chesterfield on the edge of the Derbyshire Peak District and retains his interest in walking and climbing. He also paints, turns wood and writes poetry. He is currently writing a book based on Chatsworth House, a work of fiction, as well as a crime novel and several short stories. Mike is also kept busy giving talks to groups and organisations about the life of a firefighter and the life of a writer.

First published 2017 by DB Publishing, an imprint of JMD Media Ltd, Nottingham, United Kingdom.

ISBN 9781780913094

Printed and bound in the UK

INTRODUCTION

This book, the third in the series which completes the story of Mac and his men at Graveton fire station, moves the story along about Jake and his love Antonella; we also see Janet the Ranger make changes in her life. We follow the lives of Jim and Maddie, Pete and his girl, and of course Mac, whose career closes down and a new life beckons. Writing these books has been a journey for me, enabling me to express my love of the Peak District and the respect I have for my former colleagues in the Fire Service, along with the Peak Rangers and the Mountain Rescue Service. It has been a delight and I hope that you, the reader, extract as much pleasure from reading my imaginings as I had in writing them.

Mike Hodgkins, March 2016

ACKNOWLEDGEMENTS

Writing any book is a hard, lengthy process, made easier by having the support of friends and family who from time to time have to put up with my – sometimes obsessive – need to get to the computer to put down in words a thought I have just had, whilst maybe driving the car or being out on a walk. I would also like to thank my ranger friend, Andrea Pedley, who has given me valuable information on procedures, et cetera. The Peak District Mountain Rescue Service, who have been generous with their time and advice. My friend Mimma Cardullo, who in the early days of my writing was a great support. To all the people who have acquired my books and been most complimentary about my writing, this has been a great help and motivator to keep me focused on my love of writing. Thank you to all.

CHAPTER 1

The day was hot and dusty; the air was filled with the heady aroma of molten tar as it softened on the road in the heat of the day; the boy sat on the grimy pavement, his feet in the gutter, playing marbles with his best friend Freddie.

'Do you want to swap that blue one for this twister?' he asked. Freddie nodded enthusiastically. He didn't really like the blue one anyway and he was sure his pal Malcolm wouldn't swizz him. They swapped a lot of things, especially comics. They were best pals. In the summer holidays they'd play together all day. Malcolm loved wrestling and was stronger, so he'd usually win, but it always ended up with them both laughing, to the point where they'd have to stand and pee in the privet hedge. That was the problem with the long, hot summer days and no school – what to do? Malcolm was restless, always on the move, scouring the nearby woods for adventures, climbing trees, hunting for birds' nests, building hideouts in the bracken, making pea-shooters and having their own versions of wars or cowboys, where there was a lot of shooting and crashing to the floor in spectacular death falls. The days seemed to last forever. Freddie was more introverted, more of a thinker. He would certainly think, and think hard, before following Malcolm on some of his riskier adventures.

As the light began to fade, their parents would come out onto the street calling, 'Come on in Freddie, bedtime.' To be followed a few seconds later by, 'And you, Malcolm.' The boys would dawdle reluctantly back to their homes, their skinny bodies caked in grime, scraped shoes and backsides worn out of their breeches telling the story of their day's adventures. Mac's younger sister, Wendy, would already be in bed. 'Don't forget to wash your neck, Malcolm,' his mother said as he leaned over the old pot sink trying hard to wash with the minimum use of water, the red soap smelling horrible. He'd look down and see the dirt ring around his wrists, where the effect of the water had ceased, and the layer of black scum on the surface of the tepid water.

'How on earth do you get so dirty, Malcolm? Here, let's just have a look at you.' She'd twist his head towards the gas light to get a better view.

'Well, son, you missed your neck again, there's still a tide mark there and it doesn't hurt you know if you wash your arms as well,' she'd say, and then add more hot water to the sink from the geyser on the wall.

Malcolm's dad, Bill James, would sit in his rocking chair and chuckle at the nightly ritual his wife Doreen had, trying to get their beloved son to wash properly. Wendy would be washed first and got off to bed by his mum before he would have to go.

'Leave him alone lass, he's alright. He'll only get mucky again tomorrow,' he would say to her through the fog of smoke from his pipe. To Malcolm his dad was his hero. He was a fireman in Sheffield. Malcolm already knew that was what he would do when he grew up; be just like his dad. He loved it when dad came home from work, he could smell the smoke on his clothes, he'd sit and tell him about the fires that he'd been to that day, and the things that happened on the fire station. He was stationed at Division Street in the city, a busy fire station. Malcolm had been there many times. Every year they had a Christmas party; Father Christmas would arrive by sliding down the pole with his sack of presents across his shoulder, to the sound of excited cheering from all the children. His dad would let him sit on the fire engine and put his fire helmet on and let him ring the bell. From this early age, Malcolm was steeped in the fire brigade, and he already knew a lot about being a fireman even at seven years old.

'Off you go to bed now son, you've got to be strong for tomorrow,' he would say. They didn't kiss, that was what sissies did. He loved it when his mother hugged him, almost drowning him in her large bosoms. His dad would walk him up the narrow stairs and tuck him up in bed and tell him stories of the war and the fire station. Before he drifted off to sleep his dad would ruffle his hair, and say, 'Goodnight, sunny Jim.' He didn't half love his mum and dad, but nobody in their house ever said those words.

Malcolm's dad had been in the war. He'd been injured, so he left the army and joined the fire brigade. Malcolm knew that his dad had been to a place called Dunkirk, but wasn't sure why or what it was.

It was 1949, and Malcolm and Freddie were at school together. Freddie

10

was clever and could do adding and taking away easily, and he could spell really well, Malcolm was impressed because Freddie taught him how to spell BEAUTIFUL. They loved their teacher, Miss Snell; she was very pretty but quite old. Malcolm thought that she was nearly thirty. She taught them Religious Education and the songs that are sung to God in church, and she was in charge of PT. They weren't sure what PT was, but it meant they could play football or cricket; all the boys loved that, but not many girls; they played rounders and did lots of skipping and stood on their hands against the wall, the boys thought it was stupid. The girls all wore green knickers, this made the boys giggle behind their hands. Malcolm wasn't clever; he liked football, climbing trees and getting into scrapes. Most of Malcolm's time in the classroom was spent imagining he was shooting Germans in the woods or with his dad fighting massive fires.

Mister Bruce was Malcolm's nemesis, he was from Scotland. He had his eyes on Malcolm after he caught him laughing when he came to school one day wearing his kilt.

'James,' he would shout, 'if you're not interested in what I have to say, you can go and stand in the corridor.' Malcolm would happily leave the classroom and look out of the window at the birds and the occasional car driving past the school. The worst thing about it was when Mister Bruce made him go back into the class, assuming that Malcolm had somehow learned his lesson. Malcolm knew different. He sat at his desk and dreamed of fields and hills, guns and fire engines; he was completely immersed in his other world, the voices in the room seeming to be distant echoes. Then the impact of a hand across the side of his head would quickly bring him back to reality.

CHAPTER 2

Mac woke with a start. Sunday morning, and the heat in the conservatory had made him drowsy.

'Wakey, wakey. Do you fancy a cuppa?' his wife Val asked. 'Who was Old Bruce you were just talking about? Isn't he the teacher you had at primary school?'

'Oh, old Bruce,' Mac laughed, 'yeah, he was my old teacher; we had an understanding when I was in his class. He didn't like me; and I knew it.' Mac chuckled. 'When I dozed off there I was dreaming about when I was a kid at school, he was always sending me out into the corridor.' Mac smiled to himself. *The good old days*, he thought. 'He was a big fella, a Scot with a broad Glaswegian accent. He used to say to me, "Ifn ye dinni work hard now James yee'll never dae anything with yer life." Of course, I never took any notice of him, and he was probably right.'

Mac smiled, and stood up and looked out of the window across the garden. 'It's sad, really. Later on we got on better. I think he realised I wasn't the studying kind, he let me go my own way to some extent, then he was killed, he got trampled by a bull when he was up on his father's farm in Scotland. Surprisingly it upset me quite a bit. I think, really, I liked him.'

The sun burned through the conservatory window, its brightness casting deep shadows across the lawn. Mac and Val sat having their customary hour reading the Sunday papers.

'Phew, it's hot here. Shall we go out?' Mac suggested.

'Well that sounds like a good idea, where do you fancy?'

'I need to practise my map reading, so do you fancy a gentle wander across Big Moor?'

Mac pulled up the car in the lay-by near to the access to the moor. There was just a gentle breeze and the sky was dotted with small, unthreatening white clouds. The moor was lit up by the bright sun, with just the odd shadows as the clouds moved slowly across the sky. They walked along the grassy bridleway;

the land fell steeply into a deep gulley to their left where a shallow stream flowed. In the middle of the moor was a huge grey boulder, which sat alone in the centre of a vast area of boggy ground inhabited by large tufts of bog grass. Mac looked and then looked again; sat on the rock amid the bog were what appeared to be two middle-aged walkers, serenely eating their sandwiches. *What a strange place to stop for lunch*, Mac thought. They walked, passing a small stone circle. Mac thought at the time: *I ought to know something about that, I'll ask Janet when I see her.*

It was quiet as they traversed the moor; there were no other humans in sight, just the occasional sheep calmly chewing the rough grass. They descended to the stream and found a narrow crossing point, then climbing steeply up the rocky bank on the other side until they reached the gently sloping heather-clad moorland.

'What's that do you reckon?' Val asked, as they came across a narrow pillar of deeply scarred rock.

'Well, according to Janet the Ranger, they're guide posts. Some of these on the moor apparently were used for target practice in the war, so it's lucky they've survived. Let's wander over to Lady Cross; I was over there the other day, I've got a little exercise in mind,' Mac said enthusiastically, quickly unfolding the map and setting his compass. 'I reckon it's about two miles, so we'll contour round the moor, it should be a nice gentle stroll,' he said, leading off with Val following him.

'Look at that, Mac,' Val whispered as they crested the slope.

'What am I looking for?' Mac asked.

'Just keep low and look over there, and shush!' she said, pointing slowly. 'The stag's there with the deer,' she whispered as they knelt down and peered carefully over the crest of the rise. About two hundred yards ahead, and as yet unaware of their visitors, the group of deer stood quietly nibbling at the gorse. Then, without warning, the stag pricked up his ears and the herd turned and trotted away and out of sight.

Val smiled. 'That's made my day,' she said. 'How long have we been walking on this moor? Years. It's the first time we've ever got close, that was fantastic.'

Soon they were standing by the Lady Cross, a large rectangular chunk of grit stone. Where the cross had once been located all that remained of the original cross was a stone stump, around two feet in height; Val sat on a nearby rock and took off her jacket. 'Phew, it's warm. Let's have a breather, shall we?'

Mac checked his map, 'That was not bad, I'm happy with that. Hit it spot on. I'm improving,' he said as he folded the map and shoved it into the top of his rucksack.

Val sat on the flat-topped rock and mused. 'Haven't the times flown?' she said. 'It doesn't seem like thirty years since you started in the brigade, and suddenly it's nearly over, your last tour of duty coming up.'

'Yeah, I'm not quite sure how I feel about it yet,' Mac replied. 'I'm sure I'll miss it but I'm looking forward to doing something a bit different, I think the rangers will bridge the gap to some extent.'

Just then, some movement in the gorse caught his attention. 'What was that?' he said.

The movement had been just a small sound, or something that just caught his eye. He moved over to the place where he'd seen the gorse shift. He peered into the dense growth and suddenly stepped back.

'Whoa, it's an adder,' he said with some surprise in his voice. 'It's beautiful Val, come and see,' he added in a low whisper.

Val moved away quickly. 'You must be joking; you know snakes scare me to death.'

'It won't hurt us; it's trying to get away from us,' Mac insisted.

'Say what you like, matey, I won't be looking at it. I'd rather walk the other way on the path, thank you very much.'

Mac laughed.

CHAPTER 3

Antonella sat in her small apartment in London. She was tired. It had been a tough couple of months, with regular performances at the Barbican and an exhaustive series of concerts; she loved her work and appreciated how lucky she was to be living and working in this fantastic city. She hadn't the energy to watch the television, so sat with the radio on low. From her window she could see the lights of the city twinkling in the dark of the late evening. The highlight of her life at the present time was the young man from the north of England who she'd met only a few months earlier. He'd rescued her from an attack by a thug on Oxford Street. Somehow they'd clicked, and now she would wend away hours of her time thinking of that young man, Jake in Sheffield. She expected him to call her soon, as he did most nights. They would chat about the day's events, just chit-chat, whiling away their time, keeping in touch. So far they had met only once since the attack, his mother had engineered the opportunity for them to be alone together. They'd walked and talked until the dawn broke over the city. They'd kissed and promised that they would do everything possible to allow them to spend time together. However, it hadn't worked out like that. With the complex hours she was required to work as a violinist with the orchestra, and Jake's fire brigade duty system, it had become a matter of some frustration for both of them.

The phone rang. Antonella instantly picked it up.

'Hiya Nella.' It was Jake. 'How are things with you, I've been thinking about you all day?'

'Hello Jacob, it is very nice to hear you again. I'm very well, but I'm missing you a very lot of the time.'

Jake laughed – her use of the English language, whilst improving, always made him smile. 'I'm missing you too, Mum sends you her love.'

'Tell her thank you and I send her my love also. And I send you my love Jacob. When will we be able to be together again?' she asked, a tinge of sadness in her voice.

'Hopefully it will be soon. Mum has asked me to ask you if you would like to visit us in Sheffield, when you get some time. You can stay with us, it would be a change from London.'

'That would be wonderful, I will see when I have some time and when you have the time I would very much like to do that.'

When Jake spoke to her on the phone he had this perfect vision of her when they first met, he'd been enchanted by her face and in some ways he found her as-yet undeveloped sense of English very charming. For her part, she always saw in Jake, a young but a very masculine person, a man who would always protect her.

'What are you doing this week?' Jake asked.

'Well, tomorrow and the day after I will be practising and rehearsing, we have a concert in the middle of the week so it will be for that that I have to work. What will you be doing?'

'I'm back to work tomorrow. I'm looking forward to that, and it's my boss Mac's last tour of duty. I'm not looking forward to that at all, I'll be sad when he leaves.'

'I enjoy our conversations Jacob very much, I hope that we will be able to meet soon. I have to go to bed now, I have to get up early to go on the tube to my practice. Goodnight my Jacob, I'm thinking of you.'

'And me too. I'll talk to Mum and see if we can work out a time for you to visit.'

'Thank you, I will be looking forward to that, goodnight. I think I'm dreaming of you tonight again.'

CHAPTER 4

Janet Clark steered the car carefully along the rough track. The lane was narrow, bounded by semi-derelict dry stone walls heavily covered by bright green sphagnum moss with heavy branches hanging precariously across the track, making travel difficult. Janet had been searching through her OS maps looking for new territory to explore. She took her job as a part-time ranger seriously – too seriously, some might say – but throughout her life she had always been the epitome of organisation, and applied the same set of rules to everything she did, including shopping, something that Duncan her husband had, on many occasions, commented on. Walking was her main interest, and being a ranger was the perfect vehicle for her to utilise her love of her hobby, but also to delve deeper into her other fascination: that being the history of the Peak District. Today she had decided to formulate a new walk, one not done before, off the usual beaten track. Part of her duties as a ranger was to lead guided walks in and around Brunts Barn, which was her base, close to the railway station at Grindleford. She had had her fill of the usual walks over the years; she'd walked the vast majority of the paths and tracks on her patch. Her search of the map had indicated that a disused track led diagonally across the woods, formally an old drover's track, which by a circuitous route linked with other old tracks culminating close to the well-known spot close to Curbar Gap. The route, she reckoned, was about six miles over rough, overgrown country; hence the four-by-four, to get over the problems the terrain might pose.

The day was sunny and warm. Janet wore only slacks and a T-shirt, and still she was too hot even with the windows of the car wound down. The car's air conditioning hadn't worked since she'd acquired it. The track was boulder-strewn, and where, years ago, it had been used to move sheep and cattle around, the surface undulated violently making her weave, where space would permit, around the worst of the track. There were some parts where the track was so overgrown that the daylight was almost completely cut out.

'This will be fantastic,' she said to herself, 'it'll sure make them sweat. I don't think anyone's been along here for years.' In the twenty minutes she'd been driving along the track, she guessed she'd covered maybe a mile. She looked ahead, and across the track lay the branch of a rotten old tree. She drove slowly and pulled the car to a halt just short of the obstruction. She climbed out of the car and tugged at the branch; it moved slightly, but Janet quickly realised that it was going to be too big for her to move on her own. She was going to need help.

'Oh bugger!' she shouted at the top of her voice. *What the hell do I do now?* she thought, as she stumbled around the car; the ground was far too rough for her to consider reversing all the way back. She sat and pondered for a few minutes, bemoaning her position, albeit self-inflicted. A few minutes ago she was revelling in her new discovery, now she was well and truly stuffed. *Ah!* she thought, *mobile phone. I'll ring Jack, he'll sort me out*. She switched on the phone and waited. 'What a bugger,' she shouted at no one in particular. 'No damned signal, thank you very much Mister-bloody-Orange, if you ever need me, don't bother calling, I'll be out.'

Janet was normally calm in all circumstances, but for some reason her situation had knocked her out of her usual placid place. *There's no choice*, she thought. *Shank's pony, see if there's anybody around who can help*. She started to walk. It felt strange; she knew the area she was in very well, but there was this odd feeling of isolation. No one knew she was there, and this was an almost untouched piece of ground, at least for the past sixty years, she reasoned. She walked slowly, her footwear not suitable for the terrain; the heat began to make her sweat heavily. She ducked under the blanket of low-hanging foliage. After about twenty minutes the trees began to thin out. She looked north and could see the brown crags of Froggatt Edge on the skyline. She cocked her head; in the distance she could hear the familiar rumble of what sounded like a tractor. Her morale lifted. *Tractor equals farmer, equals machinery including chains,* she rationalised. She continued forward, keeping her ear strained to gauge where the sound was coming from. She passed a small, dense copse then a stone cottage, and then there were fields in which there was a tractor, which by pure good fortune was being driven slowly and directly towards her. Janet breathed a sigh of relief.

The farmer looked down from the seat of the tractor at Janet, who by now had gathered several small pieces of foliage in her hair and managed to get several green marks from the moss on the branches of the trees on the white T-shirt, which clung to her body, bathed in perspiration.

CHAPTER 5

The first day of Mac's last tour of duty

Brian had pressed his uniform trousers and was ready to go. This was the usual weekday routine; he'd drop Jane off at her office, then Jill at school, then he'd head off to the fire station. Mac was already on the road, the twenty-minute drive to work was so much a regular part of his day that it often barely registered with him. But this week was different, his last tour of duty. He felt slightly nervous about it. It had been a part of his thoughts now for months, ever since his friend – and number two – Ray's heart attack, and then his premature exit from the brigade, had brought their long-standing working relationship to a close. There had been many highlights and some lowlights over this period, but he had in some way prepared the ground ready for his retirement with the plan to involve himself in the Ranger Service; and he knew his two daughters were bound to keep him busy. As he drove he saw the still-derelict site of the series of shops which had been severely damaged in a fire, where young Jake had got involved in rescuing an old man who sadly didn't make it. He'd renewed his contact with his old pal George Collier from Central. George had been a pal for years, but of late they had not had much chance to get together; their meeting at the fire had somehow revitalised their friendship.

He pulled into the fire station yard and parked his car alongside those of the night shift, and wandered into the station office. The officer in charge of White Watch, Alan Shaw, was sat at the desk writing out a fire report.

'Have you had a busy night, Al?' Mac asked, as he peered over Alan's shoulder looking at the fire report.

'No, it was pretty quiet, after midnight we had nothing.'

'What did you have, anything interesting?'

'We had a house fire about ten o'clock. Vandals set fire to a rubbish bin that spread through the back window of the house, it was lucky there wasn't anybody home, but it was a decent BA job, we contained it to the ground floor.'

'That's interesting, we seem to have had a few of those recently. I see they were all on the West Side Estate, we'll have to bear that in mind.'

Jake pulled his car into the yard and parked alongside Mac's Volvo. As always he was bursting with energy and enthusiasm. Since he'd become a firefighter, after a slow start he had been involved in some serious fires, and he felt that he was beginning to earn his spurs and the respect of the guys on the watch. He couldn't remember driving in today, though, he'd been thinking of Antonella and what they had been speaking about last night. Somehow this young woman had woven herself into Jake's heart and he spent much of his time just thinking about her.

Mick Young had walked the two miles into work; he had determined that using his car at every opportunity was making him lazy, and this was his attempt to remedy this. It also gave him the time to reflect on his life. Before he'd been a firefighter he'd been a soldier, a job which he loved and to some extent he'd doubted that the fire service would be able to compensate. He now knew he'd been mistaken. What he got out of the job had surprised him: the comradeship, the excitement, and latterly a new girlfriend who he liked a lot.

Gavin Maclean – or Jock to his watch mates – was proud, his son Fraser was due to play his first game for the Blades first team. He was excited, over the years he'd sacrificed so much to help his son to be the best at whatever he wanted to be. When he was ten years old he wanted to be a tennis star, then he loved rugby and swimming, also having a go at golf; every time, Jock was there giving him support. Jock eventually gave up his spare-time job as a doorman to devote his time to getting Fraser to games. Jock didn't mind, he bathed in the glow of his son's success. He'd do whatever he could to help Fraser succeed.

Taff Evans parked his car and strolled over to the station. The rest of the watch were milling around the watchroom. Taff yawned loudly.

'Are you alright Taff, you look knackered?' Brian commented.

'Yeah, I didn't get a lot of sleep last night,' Taff replied.

'Oh, why's that, the missus keeping you up?' Brian asked with a laugh in his voice.

'I should be so lucky,' Taff joked. And smiled inwardly – little did they know.

Pete Jacks came into the watchroom looking very tired.

'How are things with you today, Pete?' Mac asked.

'I'm alright. I'm still not sleeping very well, the boys are missing Trudy a lot, they wake up pretty much every night, calling out for her.'

Pete's wife had died a couple of months earlier, having lost her long battle with illness. She'd been sick for a long while but her death still came as a massive shock to everyone. The watch had done their best to give him the support he needed, but he was still finding it hard to manage everyday life and keep his sons' spirits up.

'Brian – I've things to do in the office, you do the parade and sort the lads out, then pop up and see me, alright?'

Mac sat at his desk and dialled a number.

'Hello, DC's secretary.' The honey voice of Claire Huchings came over the phone.

'Hi Clair, I need a word with the DC, can he spare a minute?'

'Hang on Mac, I'll see for you.'

'Hi Mac, what can I do for you?' Ian Blain's voice, sounding energetic and confident, bellowed out of the phone.

'Well boss, I'm a bit concerned about one of my boys, Pete Jacks. He lost his wife a while back, as you know. Well, he's struggling, most of the time he's exhausted and stressed. I was just wondering if it would be possible for the brigade to do something to help him out.'

'How do you think he'd he take to seeing the brigade councillor?' Ian asked.

Mac thought for a second.

'I'm not sure boss, but I'll speak to him about it and come back to you.'

'Good Mac, let me know and we'll see if we can get him seen as a priority, we can't do with him doing this on his own.'

Mac sat back in his chair. He was always concerned about the welfare of the boys on his watch, but this had really got to him, it had been a tragedy that Pete had lost his wife and been left with his two boys. Brian knocked on his office door.

'Come in, Brian,' Mac called. Brian came into the office and sat down opposite Mac. 'I don't want any fuss, but just so that you know, I've noticed that Pete seems to be going through a bad patch at the moment. I've just spoken to the DC and he's going to try to get him some counselling, but in the meantime let's see what we can do to take some of the worry out of his life.'

Brian sat up in the chair. 'Well, I have to say Mac, I've noticed that he seems down a lot lately. It's not surprising really. Have you got any ideas, I'm sure the guys on the watch will be happy to do anything to help?'

'Well I'm no expert, but I reckon between us all we can give him some support, maybe get him and the boys out into Derbyshire doing some things may be appropriate – first I need to talk to Pete, see what he reckons. How are the lads today?' Mac asked.

'They're fine, raring to go,' Brian replied, getting up from his chair.

'Good, let's go down to the canal and get Jake doing a bit of pump operating.'

Paula Townsend had arrived on time at her office in the Fire Service Headquarters building. She'd just finished the cup of coffee that her partner in crime, Angie Webster, had made for them. She stood and carried the small stack of Fire Safety files that she had systematically worked her way through over the past couple of days to re-file them. She peered at herself in the mirror on the wall at the side of the grey filing cabinet, and noticed that her long, brown hair was getting ready for a session at the hairdresser's. Paula wasn't tall and willowy like her friend Angie, she was maybe five feet two, but she was noticed, she was attractive and had the type of figure that brought many male visitors to her office, many of the visits being spurious to give the men a chance to attempt chatting Paula up. She spent a good portion of her day deflecting – for the most part unwelcome – offers of meals and discos or dates. She had no need of that. She had a boyfriend, her man, Mick Young, they'd been going out for a couple of months and she really liked him, she had told him so and showed him on a few occasions how she felt. She knew he liked her a lot, she thought he was funny and serious at the same time, he had some depth to his personality, an ex-soldier who had experience of life beyond the city of his birth. They spent time together when he was off duty.

CHAPTER 6

Maddie had had a busy night shift; one of her patients had passed away, an old man that Maddie had come to know well during his lengthy spell in her ward. He'd lost his wife a couple of years earlier but had regular visits from his children and grandchildren, all of whom were at his bedside when he died. Maddie finished her shift with a tinge of sadness in her heart.

Maddie's boyfriend Jim was at his workbench, in the early stages of training to become a plumber. Today it was pipe-bending and soldering, yesterday had been the theory of a central heating system. Jim loved it; his previous job had been as a security guard. It paid his rent, but it was boring, it numbed his brain. Now that brain was being tested and he loved it. He also loved Maddie, his girl, a nurse, the love of his life.

Janet looked up at the young farmer with an almost loving admiration for the man who would be her saviour.

'Hello there,' he said, his tanned face giving Janet a quizzical examination. 'You look a bit the worse for wear.'

Janet was hot and dirty and not at all comfortable. Being in a position where she needed help from a stranger was not something she was used too.

'Yes, I think I am a bit worn and grubby. I've got my car stuck about half a mile back along this track,' she explained.

The young farmer smiled. He looked at Janet, and despite her dishevelled appearance he thought her to be very attractive.

'I don't think I've ever seen anyone come down that track, even on foot, before,' he said almost jokingly.

'Well, now you see me,' she joked, her mood now lighter. Despite herself she liked the look of him. She guessed him to be in his mid-thirties, broad shouldered with powerful arms and hands weathered by many hours working outdoors, his short blond hair draped across his weathered forehead. She noticed his pale blue eyes and felt a shiver run through her body.

'I do see you, how can I help?' he said, climbing down from the seat of his tractor.

'Well, I was OK until I met a tree blocking the track. It's too big for me to move, and I wondered if you could help.'

He looked her in the eye. He towered above her, and she guessed him to be about six foot three tall.

'Here, climb up,' he said, motioning for her to climb into the tractor with him. She stood on the step and held out her hand. He took hold of her and gently hauled her in alongside him.

'Right, let's go and see what we can do, shall we? So tell me, what are you doing coming up the old Saltway?'

Janet thought for a second. *Yes, a good question, what was I doing, you idiot?*

'I'm a ranger. I had a look at an old map and it showed the old track, and I'm always interested in new routes on my patch so thought I'd have a look at it, hence, here we are,' she said, looking mildly embarrassed.

'Ranger, hey? You'll know Jack Gregg then?'

'Know him? I love him, he thinks he's my dad sometimes.'

'I'm not surprised at that,' he said, 'you know he lost his daughter a few years back?'

'Yes, I knew that, but he never talks about it.'

'Yeah, she was in her early twenties, got into drugs and OD'd. It broke his heart, she was a lovely young lass as well, you look a lot like her.'

The tractor chugged noisily across a couple of fields, disturbing the tranquillity of the sheep which stood and stared as they drove slowly along the edge of the fields.

'I reckon I'm stuck just over the wall somewhere around here,' Janet guessed.

The length of the wall was almost solid scrubland, thick brambles and bushes with the occasional tree leaning crazily, covered in a thick layer of moss. The farmer pulled the tractor to a stop close to the spot Janet had indicated.

'OK, let's take a look then,' he said as he jumped down from the tractor cab. Janet climbed down more carefully; he waited and offered her his hand, she took it and stepped lightly down to the ground.

'Thank you,' she said, having noted the moisture on his skin and the manly aroma of someone who has been working hard.

He leaned across the wall, parting the dense curtain of growth. It was the first time in years that he'd looked into the track.

'OK, I see it,' he said. 'It's about fifty yards further back; I'll get across and have a look and see if I can move the tree.' He struggled and eventually forced his way through the brush. 'If you wait here I'll see what I can do.'

Janet stood and waited. After a few minutes she could hear movement and see the undergrowth shaking, a couple of loud grunts followed by a few expletives – then the track went quiet. Janet peered through the bushes, worried that he'd injured himself. He appeared with a broad smile on his face.

'Phew that made me sweat a bit. Problem solved, it should be OK for you to drive out now, but you take care, it's very rough in there.'

Janet offered him her hand as he climbed back over the wall. He took it and hopped easily back into the field.

'I'm very grateful for the help,' Janet said, breathing a sigh of relief.

'Think nothing of it. I'd not got anything else to do other than milk the sheep and shear a couple of cows,' he said, laughing. They stood and looked at each other, both smiling nervously. Janet felt hot and her heart raced. She thanked him and leaned forward and kissed him on the cheek.

'Thank you,' she said again. 'If there's anything I can do for you, you know where to find me.'

He stood tall with his arms across his body. 'Funny you should say that, there is something.'

Pete Hackett woke up slowly and painfully. The night before he'd had a skinful of lager and a few shorts for good measure. The taxi had dropped him off in a semi-conscious condition outside his block of flats on the Parkside Estate around midnight. He couldn't remember how he got into his flat or into bed. But today he had a meeting scheduled with his dealer; he was low on supplies and getting ready for another shot. He fell into his old Mondeo, the need for drugs taking precedence over the need to sleep off the drink which still circulated around his body and his drug-addled brain.

He drove fast out of the estate and headed towards the city; his car slewed around the roundabout, almost colliding with a delivery van. The van driver shouted an obscenity at him from his window, but nothing was registering with him. His brain buzzed, his vision was sporadically blurred as he trod heavily on the car's accelerator, the car radio blared, and he slumped back in his seat, his mind in another world. He hit the roadside kerb and mounted the pavement, swerving violently; he tried to focus his mind but it was blurred. He swung the wheel left then right and sideswiped a parked car, before running nose-first into a garden fence. He heard momentarily the crack of timber but felt nothing as the windscreen of his car shattered and a ragged section of the fence entered the car and penetrated his neck. There was no pain and no cognisance of what was happening. Peter Hackett was dead.

The engine of the lightweight pump roared as Jake slammed down the throttle, attempting to prime the pump and deliver water to the aluminium branch pipe which Taff was holding, ready to deliver a jet of water across to the other side of the canal. He pushed down the priming lever and the water inside the primer came into contact with the hot exhaust, causing a vast cloud of steam to erupt from the pump. He heard the engine tone change and the sudden drop of the suction hose as the water was lifted into the pump. Jake watched his gauges; they moved and told him he had a lift, so he carefully opened the delivery valve and simultaneously reduced the engine revs, a skill practised at training school and now being perfected. Taff raised his hand.

'Water on number one delivery, a branch working at ground level, four bars pressure,' he called at the top of his voice, ensuring that Jake clearly heard the order; Jake heard and repeated the order.

Jake increased the revs on the pump and checked his gauges again, repeating Taff's order; he spun the delivery wheel and fed the water smoothly along the hose to Taff, who felt the reaction of the water as it powered out of the nozzle. He braced himself, ensuring he had full control of the branch, directing the silver stream of water back into the canal.

'Knock off make up,' Mac shouted. The crew responded immediately. Jake flipped up the throttle lever which left the engine idling and then closed down the pump, then sprang the hose coupling from the delivery. They hauled on the line which held the heavy suction hose in the canal. Taff threw the hose over his shoulder and passed it quickly backward to aid the removal of the water from the hose, before Jock rewound the hose and put it back in the locker.

'OK that was fine, get re-stowed and let's get back to the station,' Mac instructed.

Taff pulled on the steering and turned the machine into the main street leading down towards Graveton. Control came onto the radio.

'Control to Alpha 010, over.'

Mac picked up the handset.

'Alpha 010 go ahead, over.'

'Alpha 010 proceed to Park View Road, RTC. Persons trapped, over.'

'Alpha 010 your message received, proceeding to Park View Road.'

Taff gunned the machine. The crew, already rigged in their gear, hung on to anything at hand as Taff threw the machine with the lightest of touches around corners and bollards. Jake marvelled at his relaxed but fast style of driving.

In the distance, they could see the traffic backing up. Mac hit the wailers and cars and trucks pulled into the side of the road to give the machine a clear run at the incident.

'Control from Alpha 010, in attendance Park View Road, over.'

'Pull in here, Taff,' Mac instructed. 'Right, let's get the gear off. Jake, get the first aid kit and salvage sheets; Taff, get a hose reel out. OK, let's go.'

Mac quickly surveyed the job. A single car had skidded and hit a timber fence. The car had slid and turned onto its passenger side, its engine still running. The occupant of the car was slumped, held by his seat belt.

'You get in there, Pete, have a look and tell me what you reckon,' Mac instructed.

The driver was pale and motionless. Pete managed to scramble into the car through a broken window; he soon got to the driver. He looked at Mac and said, 'He's had it. Drunk I reckon, he reeks of beer.'

Mac looked, peering in through the broken screen. He could see Pete was correct, a long shard of timber from the fence had penetrated the driver's neck just below his Adam's apple and exited from the back of his neck. There was very little blood. Pete had checked for a pulse, there was none evident.

'OK Pete, leave him. The police will want pictures, then we'll do the business,' Mac instructed. The police quickly coned off the incident and marked the road with chalk, ran out tapes and gathered the necessary evidence.

The traffic officer spoke to Mac. 'The doctor is on his way, so is the recovery truck, so it shouldn't be too long now before we get the road clear and you can get away.'

Mac put his hand on Brian's shoulder. 'Get the boys to put some sheets around the job; don't want any casual pictures appearing in the local paper.'

Ten minutes later, the doctor had confirmed the driver was dead. Pete was back in the car, and with the crew they quickly removed the body of the young man. Along with help from the police they put the car back on its wheels, ready to be towed away.

'Control from Alpha 010, stop message. From Sub Officer James, stop for the same address one motor car in collision with garden fence. Driver code one. Removed from vehicle and transported via ambulance to the city mortuary, alpha zero one zero mobile to home station and available, over.'

'010 your stop message received, control out.'

Taff pulled the machine away from the roadside and accelerated towards Graveton.

'Good job boys, let's get back for tea and toast,' Mac said, praising them for their good work.

Mac sat in his office whilst the rest of the crew were sorting out the gear and the food for tea break; he leaned back in his seat and closed his eyes.

Janet stood looking at the farmer. He'd rescued her and she was very grateful, but what was he about to ask?

He looked down at his feet, his hair damp with sweat from the effort of moving the tree. 'I don't suppose you'd fancy going out for a meal with me, would you? It's OK if you don't want to?' he exclaimed nervously.

Janet's heart quickened. She almost reacted instantaneously and said 'yes please'. But being married, the long-held morals instilled in her from her childhood made her hesitate.

'I'm very flattered by that,' she said, her lips not saying what her mind was telling her to say. 'But I'm sorry, I can't,' she said, holding out her left hand and displaying the ring on her finger.

'Oh, you're married, I'm sorry; I didn't want to embarrass you,' he said, looking again at his wellington-booted feet.

'No, don't apologise. I like you, you seem like a nice man, and I'm grateful for the help you gave me. I hope we can meet up again sometime. What's your name?'

'Don. Don Maddern. What's yours?'

'Janet Clarke. And thank you, it's been good meeting you.'

They both stood, an invisible wall of uncertainty surrounding them. Don suddenly spoke.

'Right, let's get you over the wall and to your car, shall we.'

He climbed the wall first and then held the undergrowth apart, allowing Janet to climb easily through.

'Right, there you are,' he said, pointing down the lane to where he'd cleared the tree away. 'I'll hang on here until you get it moving and make sure you're OK.'

Janet climbed into her car and started the engine. She was aware that she was breathing heavily and her heart was beating fast. She was aware of feelings inside her that she hadn't felt for a long time. She depressed the clutch and put the car into gear, slowly moving forward taking care to avoid the deep holes in the track.

He stood leaning casually against the wall. As she passed he raised his hand slowly and smiled. Janet returned his smile; something inside her was telling her that they would meet again.

Malcolm sat in class; the history teacher, Mister Nevin, was talking to them about William the Conqueror and 1066. History was a subject that Malcolm really enjoyed. There were stories of ancient wars. There were the Athenians and the Spartans, whose dead bodies would be carried back to Sparta on their shields. There was Roland and Oliver, French heroes, King Charlemagne's knights who gave their lives for their comrades. Mac, as a thirteen-year-old, identified with them; he thought if he had the chance he would have been a Spartan and died a hero's death. He liked Mister Nevin, he told the class about his exploits as a Spitfire pilot in the war, he'd shot down loads of German planes and to prove it he had a large scar on his forehead from when he crashed in France, and was almost captured by the Germans, but managed to escape by swimming back to England. He told them that he thought that it was the first time that anyone had swum the channel in flying gear, he kept his flying boots on because he knew that the beach at Dover had lots of pebbles and they would hurt his feet.

Then there was the diminutive Miss Brownlow, who Malcolm led a merry dance by fooling around in her class, but secretly he really liked her. In fact, he thought about her a lot, he though one time that maybe he loved her, she was pretty but quite old. Malcolm guessed her to be about thirty-five, she had long brown hair and very small hands, he thought she was married because she had some rings on her fingers. She also spoke with a strange accent, he had heard that she came from a place called Dorset; he wasn't sure where it was. Freddie said he thought it was about five hundred miles away in the south of England.

Then he was in the playground with the other boys in his class and some girls who were just at the point of developing into young ladies, the boys had noticed and frequently tried to bump into them and touch them quite by accident. There was much tittering and risqué talk amongst the boys, who were also just becoming young men. Then there was a scuffle and Mac was wrestling roughly with a boy one year older; he had Mac in a headlock and was shouting at him. Mac felt the anger rise in him, unplanned and natural; it seemed to give him added strength, something maybe his dad had told him. He grabbed the boy's fingers and twisted until there was a yelp of pain and a high-pitched crack. The boy let go and began to cry. Mac stood back and punched him in the side of the head. The commotion had alerted the teacher on playground duty, who arrived on the scene just as Mac delivered the blow.

The headmaster's office was filled with books and files, his desk was a sea of papers. Malcolm looked across the room to the wall behind Mister Jennings' seat, where a long, thin, black cane hung, ready, as if to say, 'I'm here waiting for you'. Malcolm had made the acquaintance of Black Bess on more than one occasion.

'Well, young James, we meet again,' he said, a resigned smile crossing his lips. 'What is it this time?'

Malcolm could almost feel the sting of the cane on his hand as he spoke.

'I've been fighting, Sir.'

'Oh, so the last time you were here it didn't register that fighting isn't allowed, if you fight you get punished? That was the lesson last time and I think that should be the lesson this time, do you agree James?'

'Yes, Sir,' Malcolm said reluctantly.

'Tell me James, I'm interested. Why do you like fighting? I don't think I have ever known anyone get so involved in fisticuffs the way you do, and it's always bigger, older boys. Why is that?'

'I don't know, Sir. I don't like fighting, but they sometimes grab me and call me things and slap me so I just fight back.'

'Don't you think it would be better, James, if you ignored them and walked away?'

'Probably Sir, but my dad told me to stick up for myself; he says if you let them do it, then they'll keep doing it, so I do, I fight back.'

'Yes, very commendable James, but from what I understand you stick your fists up for anyone who asks you.'

'I try not to, Sir, but sometimes I can't get out of it. My friend Freddie, he can't fight, and they try to hit him so I have to help him.'

'Now look here James, I want you to take this as a final warning. I'm not going to turn Black Bess on you this time,' he said, almost as though he felt some sympathy for Malcolm, 'but do not tell anyone that I let you off, and I *don't want to see you up here again, do you understand?'*

'Yes Sir, thank you,' Malcolm said with relief echoing in his voice. To escape Black Bess was a real achievement, almost unique in the history of the school.

'Right, off you go, and do not tell anyone that you didn't get the cane,' Mister Jennings reiterated, then he sat back in his upholstered chair and watched Malcolm leave his office. Mister Jennings' face split into a broad smile.

'Mac, tea's ready.' It was Brian.

'OK Bry, I'll be down in a second,' Mac replied. He sat and thought about Mister Jennings; he was a proper human being, Mac remembered with affection. He thought about his friend Freddie and the awful memory came back to him. He gulped and felt the painful ache in his chest again as he always did when he remembered his friend; he took the handkerchief out of his pocket and wiped his eyes before walking slowly down the stairs to the mess room. The mess room was busy with loud conversations and laughter. Mac loved to hear this; it reinforced his view that he had a good watch. The best watch, he often thought. But then he remembered many of the other men he'd worked with over the years. In his mind, he had loved them all. There was Tom Jackson, one of his friends from the early days when he joined the job. Tom was as honest as the day is long and eminently trustworthy. But he had a flaw. Money worries drove him into gambling and the problems escalated, so did the risk taking, gambling his wages in an attempt to recoup his losses. It killed his marriage. At thirty-five years of age it all became too much. His wife left with their two children. Tom cracked and was found floating in a canal a mile from his home.

Then there was Jim Watson, one of the old hands he worked with as a young firefighter. He was tough as leather, fearless on the fireground and no respecter of rank or authority. He often found himself at odds with his station officer, who tried his hardest to keep Jim onside. It was only when Jim received a serious injury fighting a fire in the steelworks that he mellowed and began to listen to his crewmates. From his watch at Division Street there was his pal Dick Blackburn, who had spent hours with Mac and Ray Swift, doing people's gardens to earn extra cash. When Dick was killed attempting the rescue of a family from a house fire it was one of Mac's saddest days.

CHAPTER 7

'So, young Jake, tell all. What were you up to this weekend?' Mick Young enquired playfully.

Jake was settled into the watch, now he knew and respected every one of the men he worked alongside. He realised that he still had a lot to learn about fighting fires and all the other sides to the work they encountered, but he had also become aware that the job was so varied that you couldn't plan for every eventuality, and what was required was experience and nous. Jake had learned early in his career when common sense, rather than rules, had decided the actions they'd taken to do the job. Now he could speak, without his sense of inferiority or lack of experience dictating that he kept silent.

'What did I do? Well, it was a really exciting weekend. On Saturday I took my mum to town and we did some shopping at Sainsbury's. In the afternoon, I did some studying.' Jake paused, smiled and waited for the comments he knew would come.

Pete Jacks spoke.

'So Jake, you shopped and studied. That's very exciting. Anything else? We're all busting to know the gory details.'

Jake sat back in his chair and sipped the tea from his mug. He took a bite from his cheese sandwich and began.

'Sunday, went to church with mum. It was really exciting, we sang some great hymns. Then we said some prayers.' Suddenly there was a shriek of laughter as Brian jumped up and got Jake in a headlock.

'Methinks, young Jake, you're telling us porky pies. Spill the beans young Higgins, or I'll eat your cheese roll.' Jake feigned semi-collapse and laughed.

'Look guys, I have a pretty boring life, running mum about, church, working with you lot – it's enough to drive a man mad. So I rang my friend in London, she's my only bit of excitement.'

'Yeah and what did you talk about?' Taff asked. 'You know, the nitty gritty, the sexy stuff.'

'Give over, Taff. You know me: as yet untried, pure, saving myself. And anyway, why should I have to liven up your dull lives?'

'Yeah, alright. So when are we going to see this girl? We've not even seen a picture of her yet, is she so gorgeous that you're worried one of us will take her off you?'

Jake grinned; he loved this gentle joshing he got regularly from his mates.

'Leave it out. She's young, you're all old – why should she fancy you lot?'

'Because we may be old and a bit on the well-worn side of life, but we have experience, women like that you know,' Taff laughed.

The alarm actuated, they all jumped up from the mess table. Brian ripped the message from the printer.

'We've got a chip pan fire,' Brian shouted as he jumped up onto the machine.

The crew got themselves rigged en route to the job; Jake remembered what he'd been taught at training school about the dangers of chip pan fires. The talk had finished off with a demonstration of what happens when the hot oil comes into contact with water: the water instantly turns to steam, which expands to over one thousand seven hundred times its volume, potentially throwing out the boiling oil over the unfortunate householder. Jake was amazed that there still seemed to be a lot of people who didn't appreciate the dangers.

Fortunately, the traffic was light and Taff was able to make good progress, and they arrived quickly at the incident. The job was in a small, terraced house and it was obvious which house was involved, as all of the windows were open and smoke was issuing from them all.

'Jake, you get the fire blanket,' Mac instructed.

Jake threw up the locker and took out the red-packaged fire blanket, and dashed down the garden path to catch up with the rest of the crew.

A young woman stood amid the smoke, her face smudged with soot, her hair hanging untidily around her face. She sobbed aloud. 'We only had the kitchen fitted last week, my husband will kill me,' she said, wailing and wringing her hands.

'Pete, take the young lady outside will you, while we clear up.' Mac looked around the room. 'Jake, leave the blanket here, check out the rest of the house, open any windows, and let's get some cross-ventilation going.'

Pete stood in the small back garden with the young woman.

'Are you insured?' he asked, attempting to be sympathetic and supportive.

'No,' she replied, 'the mortgage kills us; just paying for the kitchen has been a struggle. God knows what he'll say when he sees this,' she said, struggling to hold back the shaking in her voice.

'Well, if I were him,' Pete said, 'I'd just be grateful that you were OK.'

'Well that's not my Frank, he'll be really peed off,' she sobbed.

Mac and the crew cleaned up the best they could, checked the house out for any small pockets of fire, removed the chip pan to the garden, and prepared for their return to the fire station.

Mac spoke to the young woman and got information for his fire report.

'I hope you don't mind,' Mac said, 'I couldn't help but notice that you haven't got a fire extinguisher of any kind and more important, no smoke alarm. If you could manage it get yourself a fire blanket we'll come along and put it in the right place. And we can supply you with a smoke alarm free of charge.'

'Oh thank you, I'll do that; thank you,' she said, 'I'm very grateful.'

'OK, well, consider it done. We'll get somebody to bring it and fit it for you.'

'*Alpha 010, stop message. From Sub Officer James, stop for the same address. Chip pan fire, extinguished before arrival, premises ventilated. Kitchen severely damaged by smoke and heat, remainder of the house slightly damaged by smoke, alpha 010, over.*'

'Right Taff, back to the homestead, and don't spare the horses,' Mac called over the sound of the appliance engine.

Taff pulled the machine to a halt under the canopied wash down at the rear of the station.

'Right guys, clean the machine off. Brian, you can do the fire report for this one.' Mac walked slowly up the stone stairs back to his office, every step seeming to make him think that he wouldn't be doing this for very much longer. He felt sad; this had been his life for thirty years.

He sat quietly in his office; he could hear Brian next door, rummaging through the filing cabinet looking for the fire report. There was a light tap on his door.

'Come in.'

It was Jake.

'I've brought you a cup of tea, Sub.'

Mac looked up and smiled at Jake, his protégé, the young man who had, purely by fate, been in the right place at the right time to help Mac out on the moors – who then was inspired to join the fire service, and who almost died before he was trained, attempting the rescue of a girl from a house fire. Subsequently, at the end of his training, he had received the silver axe for becoming the top recruit of the year.

'Thanks, Jake.' Mac sipped his tea and once again his mind returned to past times. Maybe it was some form of treatment, an automatic response by his mind to alleviate some of the stress from his body, with his forthcoming retirement in four days' time.

It was 1956, he was fifteen years old; he'd left school with no idea of what he would do to fill the gap between now and the future, when he would be old enough to join the fire brigade. He'd asked his dad.

'Don't ask me, son, it's your life. Have a look around and see what takes your fancy.' Mac reflected that in those days school leavers had a choice, unlike today.

Freddie was alright, he'd stay on, he was clever; he wanted to go to college. He thought he wanted to be a scientist or an astronomer. When they left school, that final day there had been a mad dash for the school gate with a rash of cheers from the pupils who wouldn't be returning, eyes bright and looking to the future. Some had already decided that their days would be spent working in the Sheffield steelworks, the girls seemed mostly to be hell-bent on becoming nurses or hairdressers. Mac hadn't a clue. He just knew it had to be something he could do with his hands, something to put him on until he was eighteen. He had always had a knack of being able to repair things. Many of his pals brought their bikes round to his house to fix broken parts. He sometimes serviced his dad's car; Mac was happy to lift the bonnet, and managed to sort out the problem. Mac's dad was a practical, physical man but he had little ability with the mechanical side of things. His abilities lay in his garden and allotment, where he grew vegetables, sufficient to feed the whole street.

'I'm going to miss you, Malcolm,' Freddie said as they left the school gates behind and started the one-mile walk to their homes.

'Don't worry about it, Freddie, we'll still see a lot of each other.'

'I know, but it just seems like the end of something; you know, we've always been together, when I go off the college, we won't see each other for ages.'

Mac looked at Freddie. He'd always known that he was a sensitive boy, and to some extent that had always been Malcolm's problem; he seemed always to be defending Freddie from bullies who taunted him because he was vulnerable. The problem was that they only did it when Malcolm wasn't around, realising the consequences if they were caught attacking him.

Freddie looked at Malcolm. 'You've been a good friend to me, Malc. I hope we always will be like that.'

Malcolm saw Freddie's eyes begin to fill up. There was never any self-consciousness between them, they were what they were, and there were no secrets.

'You know, Malc, I'll miss you when I'm away. I ought to tell you something, I hope it won't spoil things between us.'

'What do you mean, spoil things? We're mates, unbreakable, blood brothers. Remember when we cut our fingers and shared each other's blood? That's us, we're always friends, no matter what.'

Freddie looked nervous. 'I think I'm a homosexual,' he blurted, half turning away, trying to hide his embarrassment.

'What! Don't be daft, you're not, you're my mate,' Mac reassured him.

'I'll always be your friend, Malc, no matter what, but I'm sure.'

'How can you be sure?' Malcolm said, confusion covering his face.

Freddie was perspiring heavily, somehow the stress surrounding this admission was frightening him.

'I didn't want it to be like this, Malc, and I've always liked you a lot as a *friend, and what I'm saying now isn't directed at you. But I like boys; I can't say I like girls at all.'*

Malcolm was shocked, but tried not to show it.

'Say something, Malc. I don't look at you like that,' he emphasised, 'you're my best friend.'

Malcolm gathered his thoughts, realising that this was an important point in their friendship.

'Well, Freddie, let me say this: I like girls. I don't know what they call that, but that's me. I can't say I understand what being a homosexual is, but it won't make any difference to how we're friends. Blood brothers, and always will be.'

Freddie sobbed almost in relief, wiping his sleeve across his face. 'I've known for ages and hidden it; I was worried how you'd feel about it. And, you're a heterosexual, just in case anybody asks you. You shouldn't worry though, Malc, it doesn't mean I fancy every boy I meet, I like you like a brother.'

'Freddie, I like you like a brother as well, but let's not tell anybody shall we?' Malcolm laughed as he grabbed Freddie and held him in a head lock. 'Do you give in?' he laughed, as they stumbled down the street together.

Brian tapped on the office door and walked in; he noticed that Mac was looking thoughtful.

'How are you doing, Mac?'

'Yeah, I'm fine. Just mulling a few things over, it's getting a bit close now.' Mac spun round in his chair. 'Sit down, Brian; let's have a chat for a minute.' Brian pulled up a chair. 'How are all the arrangements going for the do?'

'Everything is on track. Maybe you should have a glance at the guest list and see if there's anybody missing that you'd like to come?'

'Maybe I'll do that, will you let me have it before the day's out?' Mac sat up and tied his tie around his neck. 'I've been thinking, Brian. I need to have a talk to the boys. Will you get them all together before we go off tonight? Also, I need to talk to Pete before I leave tonight, will you tell him? I'll see him after the changeover tonight.'

'Course I will, anything else?'

'Yes, I need to have a chat with you before I go also,' Mac said. 'How about tonight down at the Brown Bear, we can have pint, and a chat. We've not had a drink together for ages.'

'Yeah, OK. What do you reckon, about half seven?'

'That will be fine.'

The reminder of the day was routine: no more calls, the watch got on with their tasks, and cleaned the machine and mopped the appliance room floor.

Brian tapped on Mac's office door. 'The boys have cleared up, I've got them all up on the mess deck.'

'OK Brian, I'll be straight there.'

Mac walked down the concrete steps and into the mess room. The watch were sitting around in an informal group. Mac sat down opposite them. He cast an eye over them and felt the pride of a man who had moulded a good unit of firefighters.

'Well, here we are,' Mac said. He hadn't prepared anything special to say, not wanting what he said to sound like a lecture. 'I needed to have a quiet word about a few things before I leave, and I didn't want to say it on the retirement night. I didn't want to embarrass you all, or myself. As the week goes on, things might get a bit busy, and I wanted to just spend a few minutes with you all in peace and quiet.' Mac sat back in his seat. 'Things are going to change here soon. I retire and you'll have a new officer in charge. Brian will probably be leaving for the Training Centre before too long, I think.' Mac paused and sipped his water. 'However, I know that there are some things that won't change. You're the best group of men I've known, and I'm sure that after we've left you'll still be the best. I know who my replacement is and you'll find out soon enough, he'll be fine.' Mac sipped from the cup that had been put on the table in front of him.

Jock spoke up. 'Mac, I think I'm the same as the rest of the lads: you won't be getting rid of us that easily. We'll be testing the hydrant near your house most weeks, I reckon.'

'Yeah, Val said that to me some time ago. You'll always be welcome to drop in for a cup of something, for a small charge of course.'

The shift drew to a close and the crew drifted away to their respective destinations. Mac hung back to have a word with the sub officer in charge of the night crew. Pete had also stayed back, he was in no hurry to get home, and he'd been told that Mac needed a word with him; the boys were OK, they were at home being looked after by a helpful neighbour.

'Are you OK, Mac?' It was Pete, who'd hung back after parade.

'Hi Pete, thanks for hanging on, I just needed a quick word.'

They strolled slowly across the drill yard.

'Pete, after what you said earlier about how you're coping with things, I wondered if there was anything we, meaning the brigade, could do to help. So I had a quick word with the DC and the station commander. They said they'll do whatever is possible to help out. We all realise it must be tough for you and the boys, but you don't have to do it on your own.'

'I'm sure I'll be OK, Mac, I just have bad days, and this morning was one of them. I'm OK now.'

'Well, I wanted to say that there is a brigade counselling service, we wondered if that would be any help to you. They're good, and it might help.'

'Thanks for taking the trouble, but I reckon I'll be OK. It's just a matter of adjusting, I guess. You know going home isn't my favourite thing these days, so I wondered if you thought it would be OK for me to take a smoke alarm round to the house where we had the fire today. Nothing like striking while the iron's hot, and it's not out of my way at all?'

'Well, if it's no problem, yeah, go for it. And give what I've said some thought; if not for you, for the boys.'

CHAPTER 8

Pete pulled his car up outside the house. All of the windows were still open. He walked slowly up the flagstone path to the front of the house and tapped lightly on the door.

'Who the hell is that?' the rough voice from inside shouted. Almost instantly the door opened. A short, broad man of about thirty years of age appeared. He had a shaven head and an earring dangled from his right ear. 'Yes.' The man's voice crackled aggressively at the sight of Pete standing by the door.

'I'm from the fire brigade; I've got a smoke alarm for you.'

'It's a bit late now isn't it, pal. That bitch has soddin' wrecked the bloody new kitchen.'

Pete looked beyond the broad shoulders of the angry man and saw the young woman he had spoken to earlier in the day; she sobbed in terror and masked her face with her hands.

Pete felt the blood in his head begin to pound.

'Excuse me, sir, I know fire is damaging and traumatic, but at least your wife survived uninjured. Fires happen from time to time, and this will help,' he said, waving the box with the alarm in it in front of the man's face.

'She needs a bloody good hiding, stupid cow,' he shouted, looking back at the obviously terrified woman.

Pete felt his heckles rise. He knew he shouldn't interfere, but something within him rebelled, against his better judgement.

'I shouldn't do that, sir. She's just a small young woman, your wife. She's alive, you should be grateful.'

'Why don't you butt out and mind your own business, you overbearing dickhead. Piss off and leave us alone.'

'I can't do that, I'm sorry. I lost my wife not long ago, I miss her and I have to tell you it makes me angry to see you threatening your wife, she's done nothing to deserve that.'

'What I say and do is none of your business, so just get off my property before I thump you as well,' he shouted, his face seething red.

'Well, I suppose thumping me is better than thumping your wife,' Pete retorted, all fear now having dissipated. Pete then felt the impact of the man's right fist on his temple and he slumped to the floor, stunned. When he recovered his senses the door was shut, he could hear the man shouting abuse at his wife.

When Jake arrived home, his mother was sat in her chair, knitting something for the local charity shop.

'Hello, Jacob. How was your day?' she asked, sounding very cheerful.

'It was good, we had a nice little fire and Mac had a chat with us about his leaving party at the weekend. I don't know, mum... it's all going to change, and I've only just started.'

'Well, Jacob, I have some good news.'

'Oh yes, what's that then?' Jake asked.

'Well, Jacob, if I were to ask you if you could see anyone you liked this weekend, who would it be?' she said, a broad smile crossing her face.

'Well, you know who that would be, but she's working, she's got a concert.'

Jake's mother smiled broadly, barely able to conceal what she was about to say.

'But it can't be Antonella, mum,' he looked, tilting his head to one side questioningly, 'can it?'

His mother laughed. 'Jacob, yes, she's coming this Friday night for the weekend, she rang to say she couldn't wait any longer and would it be OK for her to visit. I said yes, so she managed to talk to her boss, he's given her the time off. She gets in at half past nine on Friday night and can you pick her up at the railway station.'

Jake laughed an almost uncontrolled nervous laugh.

'I don't believe it, I can't wait. It'll be great to see her again.'

'I know, son. She can sleep in the spare room, and you'll have to think of some things to do whilst she's here.'

'That shouldn't be difficult, we've got Mac's retirement do on Saturday night.' He smiled.

Mick Young sat in the armchair, his leg stretched over its arm, the television playing unwatched with the sound turned down. He laughed silently as he spoke on the phone.

'So are you going to come with me on Saturday then?' he said, a smile crossing his lips. 'OK, that would be good. What about afterwards then?' he paused and smiled again. 'How about we come back here to my place? OK then, that's fine, I'll look forward to that. I'll be very interested to see how you do that.' A huge grin creased his face.

'Bye then, will speak again tomorrow.' He put the phone back in its cradle. He looked like a very happy young man. He couldn't believe the turn of events that had so affected his life. He'd gone from years of semi-solitude to almost the opposite; he now had a girl that he liked a lot, who it seemed couldn't get enough of him. He smiled the smile of a truly lucky man.

The daylight had gone and darkness now covered the town. Mac walked the half mile to the pub where he had arranged to meet Brian. The pub was the place where Mac had had his first legal drink; it was a dark comfortable space to be in, its small panelled rooms with upholstered bench seats surrounding the bar, the subdued lighting giving it a warm, cosy atmosphere. Mac and his dad had used it as their local for years prior to his father's death. Mac's visits to the Brown Bear since then had been only sporadic. When he walked into the taproom Brian was already there.

'Hiya Brian, what can I get you?' Mac asked above the drone of voices around them.

'A pint of bitter, thanks,' Brian said, licking his lips.

They sat opposite each other behind a small wooden table, half covered with beer mats. The room was poorly lit and comprised of only very basic furnishings, a typical Yorkshire drinking pub.

'Well, Bry, it's a long time since we've done this, ten years I reckon.'

Brian scratched his head, 'I reckon you're about right, I don't think we'd got Jill when we last went out.'

'I thought that, as my time's coming to an end, we ought to have a little meeting away from work. I mentioned Pete. I think for his sake, and the watch, he needs some support, he's a nice lad and with the kids it's hard. When I'm gone I'll still keep in touch with him, but day to day he's gonna need you guys a lot.'

'You can be sure we'll do that Mac, he's done well, and despite his dodgy start he's come on great. He's a really good fireman, he just never had the chance or motivation to express it before.'

'Yeah. And that other thing we spoke about, you moving on into training. I spoke to the BTO on the phone and he reckons there'll be a vacancy within a couple of months, so start girding your loins, get back into the manuals, you'll need them.'

'You know, Mac, if anyone had told me about this last year I'd have laughed at them, but now I'm looking forward to it: the challenge, and being on permanent days, having more time with Jane and Jill, will be good.'

'Your round, I believe,' Mac exclaimed. 'One more and I'll get off.'

Pete got home and parked the car on the drive. The boys were already home, being watched by the woman next door. Pete had arranged for her to keep her eye on them and give them something to eat before he got home. Pete had tried to sort out some form of payment but she was adamant she didn't want it.

'I was a friend of your good lady, and I'm doing this because it's only right I do it. I'm sure if I ever need anything then you'd help me out, so just forget it Peter,' she said earnestly.

'OK, Brenda. I'm very grateful, you know you only need to ask.'

Brenda, his neighbour, was a couple of years older than Pete, and had been divorced for about five years. She and Pete's wife had spent many hours together whilst Pete was out at work or doing his part-time job for the local taxi company. They had developed a good neighbourly friendship. Pete didn't know her very well, as most of his time was spent at work or sleeping.

Pete settled the boys down in front of the television and had a shower. He told the boys that he'd banged his head on the door frame at work. He looked in the bathroom mirror, and could see a dark bruise appearing on his left temple and spreading into his eye socket. It wasn't too bad, it didn't hurt too much, so he didn't worry.

CHAPTER 9

Dave Blakely and Dennis Alder had stopped off in Hathersage and spent a short while in the climbing shop chatting to the staff, most of whom were rock climbers. They usually had a couple of drinks in the pub before they headed up to Stanage Edge to bivouac for the night. It was quiet as they sat drinking the cold beer and talking about their plans for the next day, when they were going to get an early start on the rocks. They could have just slept at home and driven over the next morning, but to sleep at the rocks somehow made it feel a more like a Boy's Own adventure. They'd sleep in one of the caves, and get the Primus stove going and cook a simple breakfast of bacon and eggs before they got going on the serious matter of the new route they had planned.

They walked slightly fuzzy-headed up the steep hill in the dark, heading for the edge. Leaving the road they climbed again, steeply up the bracken-choked hillside, finally arriving at the base of the crags. After a short struggle in the dark they climbed up onto the broad ledge, where Robin Hood's cave sat waiting for its latest visitors. Over the years, thousands of temporary residents had availed themselves of its free accommodation. Their visit to the pub had turned into a proper session and both had drunk more beer than planned. They scrambled blearily into their sleeping bags, which lay on the dirt floor of the cave.

'You know what, Dave?' Dennis slurred.

'What mate?' Dave replied sleepily.

'This is the life. I love you mate, we'll have a good day tomorrow.' He slumped down and was almost instantly snoring.

The bleak early morning light began to penetrate the entrance of the cave and Dave's bladder was fit to burst. 'I've got to pee,' he cried out as he struggled to free himself of the sleeping bag, which somehow during the night had wound itself tightly around his body. Eventually he staggered out on to the balcony and relieved himself of the now painful pressure of the beer consumed the previous night. A Ringed Plover stood silently on the rock opposite, and looked curiously at this side of human behaviour it hadn't seen before.

Dave rummaged around in his rucksack and pulled out the Primus and folding rectangular pan. He threw in some rashers of bacon and a tin of beans and allowed the contents to bubble away, while he attempted to bring his brain into full focus.

'You gonna shake a leg, Den?'

There was no response.

'Come on, I've got breakfast on the go, you lazy git.'

The rushing noise from the Primus was making Den's head hurt. He buried his head inside the sleeping bag, trying to minimise the painful effect the booming, rushing sound that the burning butane made.

They sat in silence, eating the undercooked bacon and beans.

'This food is crap,' Den managed to say, through lips which seemed to have a mind of their own.

'Well, Dennis my old fruit,' Dave retorted, 'if you can do better, I will be very happy to sit and watch you do the food next time.' He tried hard not to laugh at the distorted and still intoxicated features of his friend.

'You know, Den, climbing in this state is going to be a bit risky.'

'Nah, it'll be alright, I sometimes climb better when I've had a few.'

Den was a brilliant climber; when he was sober he took risks, but to have a section of your brain operating under the influence of beer could be a problem, as the line between a calculated risk and a stupid move could become blurred.

'Well, Den, I think we should delay a bit, just until your head's on the right way round. If what you say about this route is true, you're gonna need to be at your best,' Dave said, trying his best to get his friend to see the logic of his argument.

Jack Greenstock had gone to the Mountain Rescue headquarters as usual. It was something he did every day. He lived within spitting distance of the base, so his level of commitment to the service wasn't any inconvenience. It gave him the opportunity to keep up to date with the paperwork and keep the vehicles tip-top. Often after a late night call the other team members needed to get back to their beds, to catch some sleep before going off to work. Jack was retired, he'd given up on his job as an accountant five years before. He sometimes leathered the vehicles and checked the kit was OK before he left to get some sleep. Time was a thing that Jack had plenty of since he had lost his wife. The Mountain Rescue Service was a big part of his life.

'Are we going to have a go then, Dave?' Den said, chomping at the bit.

'I think not, my friend; I think you need a bit more time to clear your head before we have a proper go at that route,' Dave replied. 'Why don't we go for a little walk along the top of the edge? It'll give you time to get your head sorted out, we'll get some fresh air and it'll get the blood moving round your head.'

Den looked at him questioningly through bleary eyes.

'You know mate, if you're gonna do it you'll have to be on the ball. Half an hour's delay won't kill you, but if you go into it under par, the climb just might.'

'Yeah alright,' Den agreed, 'I suppose you're right. It's just that this purple patch can't last forever, I need to do it while I'm in the best form of my life.'

'Yeah, I understand that, but I reckon in about half an hour you'll be nearer your best than you are now. So get your boots on and we'll go for a walk.'

Jack sat leafing through the log book, looking at some of the jobs they'd been to recently. He turned the page and saw the details of the call where the team had brought several young Scouts off the Kinder Plateau in the middle of the night during a snowstorm. He recalled the feeling he got talking to the young Scout leader on the radio, and advised him when he was in desperate need of it. The success of the operation gave Jack and his team a buzz which was an important factor in his continuing devotion to the Mountain Rescue team.

Dennis and Dave strolled slowly along the rough track which followed the line of Stanage Edge. It was a nice day, they were clad only in T-shirts and shorts, ready for the climb.

'You know you said a bit back that you might have a go at joining the fire brigade? You've not mentioned it recently,' Dave asked, 'have you gone off the idea?'

'No, I still fancy it, but being on benefits… well, it's a nice comfortable set-up: go to bed, get up when you like. If I had to work, the climbing would suffer.'

'Yeah, I know that, but what about your own self-respect? You know, improving yourself? You're not daft, you've got loads of O levels, and despite your best efforts you're pretty bright. I reckon you should go for it, the wages are half decent they say; I might even try myself.'

Den looked at Dave and smiled. 'It's time we walked back, you're getting too serious. I feel fit enough now I've got the cobwebs out of my system.'

Pete Jacks scrambled out of bed. The alarm clock hadn't gone off and he was half an hour behind schedule.

'Come on boys, we're late; out you both come. I'll put your cereal out, we've got to get a move on or we'll all be late.' After gulping down their breakfast, Pete bundled them into the car and dropped them off at school.

'See you tonight, boys,' he called to them, as they made their way into the school yard.

Jack sat in the small canteen of the Mountain Rescue Service HQ, drinking his cup of coffee. He heard the door open and footsteps. He guessed it was one of the lads coming in to see what was happening.

'Hi Jack, how's things?' Danny Thorpe, one of the younger and keener team members, asked.

'It's all quiet on the western front, not expecting much. It seems to have gone a bit quiet, which is a good thing. The water's hot in the teapot, make yourself a cuppa.'

The dark grey rock soared above them into the almost cloudless sky; it was unusually quiet on the crag.

'For God's sake, Den, do you reckon it's possible?' Dave said, looking bemused as he scoured the slab, which appeared to be almost completely devoid of holds.

Den looked at his climbing partner of five years. 'Do you really think I'd be stupid enough to try to climb it if I didn't think it was possible?'

Dave began uncoiling the rope, which he meticulously laid in a random pile on the grassy bank. 'Den, I've been watching you do daft things for the past God knows how long, so yeah, I reckon you would.'

'Well, you're wrong, I think it will go. Look, it's not all overhanging, there's a crack there,' he said, pointing to a small section about fifteen feet from the ground, 'and look, there's a little ledge there over to the left,' again pointing in the general direction of a slightly darker, greener part of the rock.

'I have to say, Den, I think it's going to be a struggle. That last one nearly saw you come off. You said then that it was about at your limit, well this looks a lot harder,' Dave said with real conviction in his voice.

'Don't be a wuss, Dave; you know what they say about the faint heart.' He turned away and laughed. 'What's the worst thing that could happen?'

Dave looked at him, grim-faced.

'Well, if you mean other than killing yourself... You could come off and do yourself some serious damage. Look at the rocks here on the floor, you hit them at speed it'll be goodnight Irene.'

Den gave him a determined look. The effect of the beer still circulating around him was making him irrational. 'Look Dave, I'm gonna do it. If you don't want to be here, then go, I'll just solo the bloody thing, or get some other guy to hang on to the rope. It's up to you.'

CHAPTER 10

0830hrs – The second day shift of Mac's final tour of duty

Pete Jacks pulled the car into the station yard. He'd become accustomed to being the first to arrive on the watch, but today he would barely make it in time to prepare in his usual way for the parade. He was disappointed with himself for this lapse. This was something which, a few months ago, would not have troubled him at all; now it was different, better, he now enjoyed his work, he liked the company of his watch mates and he had grown some self-respect. He took pride in his appearance; something which the men on his old watch had noticed and had expressed surprise at. They had always seen Pete as a nice guy, but one who didn't care too much about himself, his work or his workmates; he was seen as a self-contained man, whose only goal in life was to be with his family.

Stanage Edge

The route was about forty feet high and the slab, which varied in trajectory between the vertical and the overhanging, had a series of bubble-shaped bulges at mid-height which looked as though they would compound the severity of the climb.

'Well at least rope down and have a close look, and maybe put a bit of protection in and clean it up a bit. Don't go at it cold.'

'Nah, it'll be alright, I'll manage.' At this point, Dave was sure that his mind was still being distorted by the alcohol from the previous night.

'Well, if that's what you think it's your neck,' Dave said finally, having given up trying to talk Den out of it.

Den looked to be getting angry. 'Dead right, it is my neck, now if you're staying, get hold of the rope. Otherwise, sod off.'

Dave was worried; his fears for his mate were real, so he figured it would be better to be here, just in case something went wrong.

Edale Mountain Rescue Station, Hope Valley

'I expect a few of the other guys to be here in a few minutes, when they do get here let's get loaded up and get out on the vehicle and see what's occurring.' Jack Greenstock had that feeling, a feeling he'd had many times before. Almost like a premonition that they were going to be needed.

Graveton Fire Station, 0900hrs

'Red Watch, fall out,' Mac called to end the morning parade. He folded his fire kit and placed it in the front of the appliance, then walked up the stairs to his office.

Brian came in. 'Morning, Mac.'

'Ha, glad you're here, Bry. What do you make of the bruise on Pete's head? He reckons he banged it on the door at home. Sounds like a likely story to me,' Mac said, expressing his concern. 'And to cap it off, I got a call from the police when I got in first thing.'

Brian screwed his face up. 'Yeah, I've got a funny feeling about it, he's not a very good liar.'

'I'll tell you what, Bry, get him up here. We'll have a chat with him in private.'

Stanage Edge, 9 a.m.

Den tied the loop through the ring on his nylon harness, wiped his rock shoes on a towel spread on the floor, dusted his hands with the chalk from the bag which hung from the waist of his harness. He stood at the base of the rock. He figured that it was straight up for about six feet, then he'd have to trend left and look to get near the crack to gain some protection should he come off. The rock there was just on the vertical so it would be hard on the arms. At forehead level there were a couple of shallow holes, almost like the remnant of some long-ago fired bullet just sufficient to place the end of a finger in. There was nothing for the feet at all, just a slope barely under the vertical. He would have to hope that his rigid, sticky-soled rubber boots would to live up to their reputation. First his right foot just twelve inches off the ground, the sole flat against the rock, then the other foot; they stuck. Den stood twelve inches off the ground with the end of one finger sitting in a small indentation; neither point of contact offered him the opportunity to move upwards. Den felt around with his free hand. Over to his left was a small lump. If he leaned across and laid his left hand on the lump, he could maybe move one of his feet.

'You were right, Dave, it could be impossible,' he said, his voice already strained.

Dave smiled to himself. 'Look, Den, if you're going to fall off this would be a good time to do it, so go for it. As you say, the faint heart and all that.'

'That's easy for you to say. I could do that without moving my lips if I wanted.'

'True, but I can see your next move if you've got it in you, and if the beer hasn't stunted your undoubted brilliance.'

'Stop messing about; tell me what to do before I fall off,' Den said hurriedly, his voice sounding strained. The crackle of tension in his voice telling Dave that his friend could soon find himself in desperate trouble.

Graveton Fire Station

Pete tapped on the office door. 'Come in, Pete,' Mac called. Pete tentatively opened the door to the office. He saw that both Mac and Brian were there.

'Sit down, Pete; we just want a quick word.'

Pete looked uneasily at them.

'It's nothing to worry about, but we wondered how you got the bruise on your head. And has anybody had a look at it?' Mac said, trying to allay Pete's obvious nervousness.

'No, it's OK, it's not a problem, I'll be fine.'

Mac noted his body language and surmised that he wasn't telling the truth.

'Pete, you delivered the smoke alarm to the Jenkins house last night on the way home?'

'Yeah,' Pete said, squirming on his chair.

'And there wasn't a problem at all?' Mac said, trying to appear nonchalant.

'No,' Pete responded, looking even more stressed. Mac looked at Pete and felt an empathy with this man whose life was so hard.

'It's just I had a call from the police this morning, telling me that they were called to that house last night. A neighbour heard a disturbance and a woman crying. When they arrived she was in a bit of a state but wouldn't make a complaint, so it seems the husband Frank Jenkins, who has a record of violence, will get away with it.'

Pete looked up and into the faces of Brian and Mac.

'I'm sorry, I was embarrassed. I delivered the detector. He said she deserved a slap, I said to him that he shouldn't do that, he should just be happy his wife was unhurt. Next thing he gave me a right-hander.'

'Would you tell that to the police?' Mac asked.

'No, I've got enough problems keeping my head straight as it is, without getting involved with that idiot.'

'OK Pete, we'll leave it at that then,' Mac said, feeling less than happy but also understanding Pete's stance: he really didn't need the hassle and the worry.

Mountain Rescue HQ

'OK Donald, let's go.'

Don Perkins, the driver, looked at Jack. 'Yes leader, where to?'

'I've got a feeling in my water that Stanage would be a good place to be. There'll be a few up there today, taking advantage of the wonderful Peak District weather.'

The group of five mountain rescue volunteers headed out from the Hope cement works, where their headquarters was based. As they approached Hathersage they could see small knots of climbers on Millstones Edge, high up on the hillside. 'It looks like there's a few out today,' Jack said to the other guys in the truck.

Don steered the vehicle up to the left and climbed rapidly as they headed up towards Stanage. They soon reached the top of the steep roadway, and the length of Stanage was spread out before them.

'Where do you want to park, Jack?' Don asked, as he pulled the truck sharp right and headed along the narrow, metalled road, which was inhabited by large numbers of sheep intent on performing the duties of traffic calming.

'We'll head up to the popular end and park up there; it'll give us good access if we need it.'

Don pulled the vehicle amongst other cars left by their owners, who had gone up the half-mile track to climb to the escarpment. They took off their jackets and sat on the wall, idly talking and taking in the scenery. A warm breeze made for an idyllic setting.

Stanage Edge

Den was now four feet from the ground and struggling. Still without a hold, he had defied gravity using pure friction, but the energy output for him to continue wouldn't be sustained unless something worthy of being called a hold could be found. Den grumbled and swore. He'd reached the part of the climb where the slab began to overhang. Without something substantial to cling to, Den couldn't see any chance of forward or upwards progress.

'Can you see anything, Dave?' Den pleaded.

Dave looked carefully. 'If you can slide a couple of feet to your left, just around the side of the bulge there's a thin, vertical crack that may help.'

Den was now living on friction. He transferred his weight slowly to his left foot; having established that the foot would stick, he slid his right foot across to the left, and repeated the process. He could feel his legs begin to shake, the muscles in his arms were burning but he doggedly convinced himself it was possible. He leaned left and slid his left hand around the side of the bulge.

'You've got it, Den,' Dave shouted triumphantly.

Den fumbled around, trying to find an edge he could wrap his fingers around. Behind the flake was a shallow recess but to Den it felt fantastic. He slid his hand along the flake and carefully selected the best position; he knew he couldn't linger, he was very close to his limit. He grasped the edge of the flake and swung his body to the left, his whole weight now supported on his shallow grip on the flake. He twisted his body to make room enough to turn and get his other hand on to the flake, and he got it. He flailed around with his feet, frantically searching for a placement.

'Den, listen to me; put your right foot up a couple of feet.'

Den acquiesced immediately.

'There, that's it.' There was a small depression in the rock, just sufficient to allow the toe of his boot to fit and gain some purchase.

Den gasped, 'I know why it's not been climbed yet, it's a soddin' nightmare.'

'Sounds like a good title to me when you've done it,' Dave laughed. 'Where are you gonna get some protection in?'

'Dave, don't be a prat. When am I gonna be able to take a hand off to put the protection in? Even if there was somewhere, I couldn't do it.'

'Then you'd be as well falling off now, before you get too high to survive the fall,' Dave said. In his heart he knew this was going to beat his friend.

'No, it's not going to beat me,' he said unconvincingly, as the sweat poured from his head and he fought to keep his fingers sufficiently dry to maintain a grip on the flake.

Jack scanned the edge, more out of curiosity than any sense that anything was wrong. Suddenly something caught his attention; he held the binoculars and watched carefully.

'What have you spotted, Jack?' The group somehow sensed that he'd seen something that concerned him.

'There's a lad up there, and it looks like he's in a bit of trouble. I'll keep my eye on him.' Jack pointed out where the lad was on the edge. 'Andy and Paul, go on up and have a look, come back on the radio if it needs us to get involved.'

'What do you reckon, Den, you seem to be struggling?'

'I bloody am, and I'm nearly knackered. I think I'm gonna come off,' he said, almost accepting the inevitability of it.

'You've got nothing in place to stop you, Den,' Dave reiterated.

'Yeah, I'm aware of that fact,' he said, sounding exhausted.

'Look Den, I'm no bloody good to you here. Can you hang on a minute? I'll run round and drop a rope from the top, just hang on, alright.'

Den's mind began to drift like some kind of out of body experience. Tiredness percolated through his body, he had an overwhelming desire to close his eyes and go to sleep. His arms were on fire, his legs twitched uncontrollably. He could hear Dave scramble above him.

'Hang on Den, the rope will be with you in a few seconds.'

Den felt as though he was going to die. It was as though he was drifting along on a magic carpet, he could hear his mother talking to his dad, something about how Dennis wouldn't work at school. He heard the rubbing of the rope as it slid down the rock above him.

Jack peered at the climber, who had been static on the rock for several minutes. 'Andy, I think we're going to get a job here, start moving up and to your left. I can see him, I'll guide you in.'

The rope slid quickly down the face but Dennis seemed unaware of it. He heard Dave shout, 'Grab the rope Den, slip your hand through the loop, and I'll have you.' Den removed his hand from the flake. Instantly his balance faltered and gravity took over; silently, Den fell almost twenty feet onto the jagged rocks at the base of the climb.

'Andy, he's off. Get a shuffle on, just about at ten o'clock from where you are now, you should get there in two or three minutes,' Jack called over the radio.

Dennis lay among the rocks at the base of the climb. He was conscious but in a lot of pain, his right leg twisted at a strange angle and a deep gash on his leg.

'You were right, Dave,' he said, attempting a smile. 'It is impossible with beer in your brain.'

'Yeah, I told you so. You hang on here, I'll get some help, I'll be as quick as I can.' He gave Den his handkerchief, 'Here, hold this on your leg, it'll help stem the bleeding a bit.'

Dave began the descent to the road to try to get help, and within seconds he almost ran over Andy and Paul, who had been moving quickly upwards guided by Jack over the radio. Dave was overcome with relief. The thought of his friend lying injured and untreated had scared him, and now these two men offered some salvation.

Andy spotted Dave and could see the panic written across his face. 'Where is he?' Andy said, his voice firm and decisive.

'Thank God,' Dave replied. 'Follow me, he's just up here.' Dave turned and ran, followed by Andy and Paul.

The fall seemed to have brought Den to his senses. The realisation that he'd fallen because he'd been cocky and ignored his mate and his own better judgement made him feel like an idiot, and now he'd have to face the consequences. The pain in his leg was excruciating, and even more so when he plucked up the courage to look at his twisted leg. Den and the two rescue men got to him in quick time; Andy looked at Den's leg and got straight onto the radio.

'Hi Jack, Andy here. Are you receiving, over?'

Jack was still sat on the wall with the binoculars trained on the bracken-covered hillside when he heard the radio.

'Yeah, receiving you Andy, what's the situation?'

'Jack, we've got a young male, early twenties, with a broken right leg, looks like Tib and Fib. We're going to need all the rucksacks I guess, and the rest of the lads up here to get him down, over.'

'OK, Andy. The rest of the lads should be here anytime, will get them to your location ASAP, over.'

Andy looked down at Den and gave him a reassuring smile.

'I'm Andy, and my mate here is Paul. You'll be OK now, sunshine,' Andy said. 'Your leg doesn't look too clever but when we get the gear up here and the rest of the guys, we'll have you sorted out in a jiffy.'

'Does it look bad?' Den asked, the pain now racking his body, causing him to wince.

'It'll be fine, looks like a Tib and Fib. When we get the tackle up here we'll give you something for the pain, get you splinted up, and get you down the hill and off to the hospital. Don't worry, we've had loads of jobs like this, if we keep practising pretty soon we'll know what we're doing,' Andy joked.

Den tried to laugh but failed.

Over the next five minutes, more rescuers began to assemble around Den.

'Right my friend, we're going to give you some of this gas, it'll help with the pain whilst we splint you up and prepare you for the trip to the ambulance. You OK with that?'

'Yeah, do what you like; just get rid of the pain.'

Andy placed the soft plastic mask over Den's face, and pretty soon he'd relaxed enough for the team to get a box splint around his leg.

'How's that feeling now, Dennis?' Andy asked.

'Feels great, the gas is good, where can I get some.'

'OK lads, let's get him onto the stretcher and away.'

Within minutes, Den was strapped to the rigid stretcher.

'Are you OK there, Dennis?' Andy asked.

Den's voice was distorted by the plastic facepiece of the Entinox kit, but he asked, 'Can't I have a slightly more comfortable stretcher than this? It's killing me.'

Andy laughed. 'Tell you what, Dennis, it's better to have an uncomfortable half hour on this than the rest of your life in a wheelchair, especially if you've a spinal problem.'

'Yeah, you're dead right of course, that's me being a prat; do you reckon I'll be able to climb again?'

'Yeah, no problem, six months you'll be up there trying to kill yourself again I'm sure.'

The team had him down to the road and into the ambulance within half an hour. Jack thanked the team for a job well done.

'So, Andy, tell me what happened.'

'Well, it seems to me, he was trying something pretty hard, in fact, it looked to me to be bloody impossible. He'd got no protection, and he just fell off. Those rocks at the base of the climb are pretty unforgiving. He's got quite a bad break, it'll be a while before he's back on the rocks.'

The whole team were involved getting him down to the ambulance. It was hard, sweaty work carrying him over the rough terrain and required fairly regular changes in personnel to keep the stretcher moving and getting Dennis to safety.

'Well, that's it boys,' Jack said to the team as they massed around the parking area. 'A job well done, thanks a lot lads.' Jack looked around at the team of volunteers and realised what a lucky man he was to be associated with such a professional bunch of guys. 'OK, we'll get back and get the gear sorted.'

CHAPTER 11

Mick Young was in the kitchen. He'd filled the huge aluminium teapot, ready for the guys to get stuck into when they turned up after drill. He set about wading through a huge pile of white bread, scraping something vaguely resembling butter over each slice, and then producing a large mountain of grated cheese he began the process of getting their sandwiches sorted. Half topped with grated raw onions, the remainder with chopped beetroot.

'Come and get it,' he called over the station address system.

The watch congregated around the mess table and began getting stuck into their sandwiches. The alarm actuated. Jake ran to the watchroom and ripped off the turnout sheet. Mac took the sheet from Jake, and the crew set off.

'What we got, Mac?' Brian asked, as he struggled to get into his gear.

'AFA at the Brightside printing works.' Other appliances had also been mobilised to fulfil the predetermined attendance for a fire call to this building. Red Watch heard them all booking out as they drove to the job.

Pete pushed hard on the accelerator, and the appliance flew down the city road. They could hear other appliances heading to the call. Then the crew from Halifax Road station booked in attendance, and within a couple of minutes the stop message came over the radio and control returned all other appliances to their home stations.

Pete Jacks powered the machine up the city road. Mac had decided that they would get stuck into some fire safety files which were overdue. There were some shops and boarding houses on his list today, they were going to have a look at a two-storey office block.

Mac got Brian to take Jake into the building with the file and get him started on some of the less exciting aspects of the firefighters' job. Brian introduced himself and Jake to the office manager and then began the inspection, first checking that the scale drawing of the offices in the folder still matched the building and that all of the fire precautions required under the legislation were as they should be, then that the fire extinguishers were all in their right place, tested and in good condition.

They entered a corridor which gave access to the staircase.

'Now, Jake, what's the problem here do you reckon?' he asked.

'Well, this is the main escape route, so there shouldn't be anything stored in the corridor,' Jake said, feeling pleased with himself.

'Tell me why?'

Jake looked at Brian. 'We did this at training school, escape routes should be kept clear, nothing should be allowed to reduce the width of the corridor. Someone could trip over it, or maybe worst case someone could set fire to it.'

'OK, so what are we going to do about it?' Brian asked.

'Tell them to move it, get it cleared away, and then we should record it in the file.'

'Right, let's go and see the boss.'

Jake and Brian got back to the machine.

'How was it, Jake?' Mac asked.

'It was good, I enjoyed it,' Jake replied.

'Well, young man, when we get back to the station you can do the paperwork,' Jake grinned.

'Love to,' he said cheerfully.

CHAPTER 12

It was seven thirty in the evening. Frank Jenkins slammed the front door of his house and walked out in the fading light of the evening. It was a cool and damp evening; he stopped to light a cigarette, shielding the flame of his match from the breeze. He discarded the match on the floor and walked slowly down the deserted street toward his local pub.

The car pulled to a halt twenty yards from the front of the pub. The occupant sat watching. He turned on the radio and waited. An hour passed but the occupant was patient, he listened to the low tones on the radio, waiting for his target to appear.

Frank had got through several pints of beer. At ten o'clock he decided it was time to go home, he had an early start in the morning. Driving his truck long distances often required him to sleep out overnight. He felt slightly woozy. He turned and waved to his pals, who were still leaning up against the bar. He walked up the road towards his house, some two hundred yards away. The street was dark and unlit. He passed the gap between the pub and a concrete outbuilding; there was little thought in his head, he felt casual and relaxed.

His wife was home. She'd gone to bed already, feigning a headache, but the reality was that her husband scared her, especially after he'd had a drink or two. She buried her head in the pillow and hoped that he wouldn't be home for a while yet.

Jenkins stopped by the gap in the building to light another cigarette. He didn't manage it. Out of the darkness a large hand grabbed his neck and pulled him into the recess. He had little time to react. The hand slammed him hard against the concrete wall, his head slung back almost like whiplash, smashing it into the wall; he was stunned, unable to comprehend what was happening. He began to say something, but before any sound could exit his mouth he felt the impact of a bony knee come into forceful contact with his scrotum. His head shot forward as he unleashed a sickening groan, only to be stopped by a hard forehead impacting on the bridge of his nose. He was dazed and dizzy;

he had a faint recollection of the sound of his nasal gristle snapping, the hand pressed his neck hard against the wall to prevent him from falling. He tried to open his swollen eyes but at that moment he felt the force of the bony knuckles of the hand impact on the side of his jaw. He noticed the warm, salt taste of his own blood just before his thought processes ceased. The hand released him, and allowed the by now limp body of Frank Jenkins to unceremoniously hit the dirty, wet floor of the recess.

The owner of the hand stepped slowly over the inert body, climbed into his car, and drove into the darkness.

Mac lay back in bed. Val was sound asleep, as was often the case lately. He had many thoughts being processed in his mind which were stopping him dozing off. He slid silently out of bed, donned his dressing gown and padded quietly down the carpeted staircase. He switched on the kettle and made a cup of tea, and sat for a while absentmindedly in front of the television. Thoughts raced around his brain, some happy, some sad, many mixed feelings; remembering his dad, who he felt would have been proud of the way he'd conducted himself in the job. Some would say that Mac had many of the older traits in the running of his watch, maybe others would say that his methods were outdated and maybe it was time for him to go. In some ways, Mac agreed with that view. He viewed many of the modern methods as being too soft, too careful, all of these in his view diminishing the role of the firefighter. However, he would still find it hard to leave it all behind. Mac walked quietly into the downstairs toilet, ran a bowl of cold water and soaked his swollen right hand. It was sore, but he felt it had been worth it. He looked at the bruised knuckles and his mind drifted back to a time after he left school.

He was in his first job, helping out at a local garage. He was the garage gopher. One of the three mechanics, who was a few years older than Mac, had for some reason taken a dislike to him and at every opportunity made things difficult for him. Mac was aware of this but was trying to ignore it. He needed the job, the wages weren't great, but better than nothing, but he liked the boss; and the work to some extent, he enjoyed it even though his days were not always that productive. The garage owner, Tom, an old friend of his dad's, gave Mac the job almost as a favour.

It was the end of the week; payday, and Mac had a plan. Go to the pub, have a night out with his mates and probably a game of snooker, the regular Friday night routine.

Friday morning, it was raining. The low-lying rainclouds made Mac feel depressed. He walked the half mile to work; he was wet and not very happy. Edgar Turner the mechanic was also in a bad mood. During the course of the morning neither had managed to improve their demeanour. Mac was washing a car that had just been serviced, getting it ready to be picked up by its owner after lunch. Edgar walked past and behind Mac, and in what Mac saw as a deliberate act crashed into him, sending Mac sprawling across the wet bonnet of the car. Edgar gave out a short laugh. Mac stood up and looked hard at Edgar but said nothing. Edgar turned and leered.

'What are you looking at?' he snarled.

'You,' Mac replied, his jaw set rigid, his eyes just slits glaring at this man who needed a lesson.

'Want to do something about it mate? After clocking off we'll sort it out, if you're up to it.'

Mac felt the red mist rising but resisted the temptation. He would wait.

During the day, Mac was kept busy with jobs, the potential confrontation with Edgar stored in the back of his mind, but not forgotten. He cleaned cars, swept the floor, got tools for the mechanics, but all along he kept quiet. He would wait.

The day passed quickly. Tom paid all the staff for their week's work, and they then wandered off to the clock and a weekend without work.

Mac went to the clock; most of the staff had gone. Mac put his card in the slot and slammed down the iron lever, then placed it in the 'out' section. He looked and noticed that Edgar's card still sat in his slot; he was still in the garage. Mac waited.

Tom, the owner, saw Mac and asked, 'Aren't you going home tonight Malcolm?'

'Yes I'll be away soon, Tom. I'm waiting for somebody.'

Ten minutes passed and there was no sign of Edgar.

Mac left the clock and went to the back of the garage. He noticed the single door to the toilet was closed; he crouched and saw a pair of shoes beneath the door.

'Is that you in there, Edgar?' Mac called. There was no answer.

'Edgar, we have an appointment. Come out.'

'Why don't you piss off James, I can't be bothered with you.'

'That's not what you said this morning. Come on out, let's do it, or shall I come in for you?'

Mac waited.

The door opened slowly and Edgar, a look of mild terror distorting his face, emerged from the toilet.

'Well done Edgar, I was beginning to think that you'd chickened out.'

'Well, I haven't got time for this stuff; just remember, I'm senior to you.'

'Yeah, you've also got a bigger mouth than me. Come on, Edgar; if you don't come for me I'm coming for you, we're not leaving till it's sorted. This is what you wanted, so here I am, all yours.'

Edgar made a move to try to escape, walking quickly around Mac; but Mac was quick too, and grabbed the back of his coat and hauled him back, pushing his face into the whitewashed brick wall of the garage.

The impact of his face on the wall made Edgar's nose bleed, and he let out a boyish, frightened yelp.

Mac pushed his weight against Edgar's neck.

'Listen, Edgar, you might be older than me and senior to me, but I can beat you with one hand tied behind my back. Just one more time and you won't walk away with just a bleeding nose, have you got that?' Mac spat the words close up to his ears.

Edgar's eyes bulged with fright.

'Have you got it, Edgar?' he spat, pressing even harder on Edgar's neck.

'Yeah, I've got it.'

'Right, you remember that. Just one more time, one little excuse, and we'll really fall out.'

Mac released the pressure and Edgar sank like a frightened deer. He looked at the floor as he made his hasty retreat to the clock.

Mac was tense, and then he breathed out. Problem sorted, he said to himself.

As he walked out of the garage, old Tom came out of the office.

'I just saw and heard what you did, Malcolm,' he said sternly.

'I'm sorry, Tom; he's been trying to give me a hard time.'

'You know what, Malcolm? It was good to see. He's had it coming for a couple of years. You're just like your dad, you know,' Tom said, a smile splitting his grease-stained face.

'I think that's a compliment, is it Tom?'

'You can be sure of that, youngster; your dad would have loved to see you do that. He'd have called it poetic justice.' Tom turned to go back to the office; he stopped and turned his head. 'Make sure you wash that blood off the wall in the morning.'

'I will do, thanks boss. Goodnight, see you on Monday morning.'

Mac walked out of the garage into the rainy darkness. It had been a good day at work today after all.

'Are you alright?' It was Val, she had turned over in bed and realised that Mac wasn't there. She'd guessed he'd be downstairs.

'Yeah, I'm fine. Couldn't get off, so came down for a drink, but I think I'm probably ready to go back up now,' he said, making his way back up the stairs.

'What's up, are you worried about finishing work?'

'No, I don't think so. I just keep running things through my head and can't seem to switch my brain off.'

Mac lay awake for some time before sleep overtook him; it wasn't long before images slipped into his brain.

He was on the upper deck of the bus heading into town. Freddie sat alongside him; they both had lit cigarettes between their fingers.

'So Freddie, how's life in higher education treating you?' Mac asked.

Freddie looked at Mac and smiled. 'It's good, it's certainly stretching me, the people in my year are bright, and most of them are from other places. A lot seem to come from pretty rich families. There's one girl who's become a good friend, her dad's a doctor. There's a lot of posh people there,' he said, not displaying any sign of envy.

'I'm glad; you'll do OK, I just wish I had your brain,' Mac said wistfully.

Freddie put his arm over Mac's shoulder. 'You, Malc, have got something just as important. You've got charisma, people like you. Just like your dad, you're your father's son and no mistake.' On saying that, he tightened his grip around Mac's neck. 'Do ya give in?' he laughed.

The Lacarno was packed, filled to bursting with what seemed hundreds of excited teenagers, the boys preening and prancing trying to impress the girls who sat at the small circular tables filled with glasses of Babycham and rum and black. The music started a heavy, rhythmic throbbing sound that made verbal communication difficult. Mac stood with Freddie at the edge of the floor, smoking a Woodbine and gulping heavily on a pint of beer. Some of the boys had found girls to dance with and there were several of the girls who danced together. Freddie Cannon's voice ricocheted around the dance floor, the girls spinning furiously, the boys contorting their bodies provocatively. Most of the dancers knew the words of the song by heart and mouthed 'way down yonder in New Orleans'. Mac glanced casually across the dance floor. He saw her for the first time, turning gracefully to the rhythm of the music. His eye caught hers; she smiled briefly and continued dancing. After the music stopped she stood with her hand covering her mouth, as she glanced across at Mac and spoke secretively into her girlfriend's ear.

'What do you reckon, Freddie?' Mac asked. 'D'ya think I should?'

'How would I know? If you like the looks of her, go and ask her for a dance.'

'Yeah, you're right, I'll go now.'

Mac put his drink down on the small table close to where they stood, and walked as casually as he could muster towards the girl.

'Hello,' he said.

'Oh, hello,' she replied, turning to face him.

'I wondered if you fancied a dance.'

'OK.'

'Good,' he said, breathing a silent breath of relief.

They walked slowly towards the centre of the dance floor.

The music started.

'I'm a gonna make a furse, I'm a gonna raise a holla, I bin a workin' all summer just to try to make a dollar.'

This was one of Mac's favourite songs, he sang along.

'Sometimes I wonder what I'm a gonna do, but there ain't no cure for the summertime blues.'

The girl stopped and looked at Mac. 'You may be able to dance, mister, but singing isn't your thing.' She laughed.

Mac laughed back and shouted above the sound of the music, 'You're dead right, never could, probably never will be able to.'

They carried on; Mac stomping his feet, the girl spinning lightly, her dress rising almost umbrella-shaped. Then it was finished.

Mac stood and looked at the girl. 'I've not seen you around before,' he said.

'No, we've not lived here long. We've just moved over from Rotherham a couple of months ago. My dad got a new job at Steeloe's; so we just moved into our new house.'

'Where do you live, then?' Mac asked.

'We've got a house at Dore.'

'Oh, that's a posh area, it's nice over there.'

'Yes, but we're not posh,' she replied. 'My dad worked in the rolling mills and mum worked in the glass factory in Rotherham.' She paused. 'But you know, my dad is clever, a few months ago he got promoted and now he's a manager. He gets better wages, so we moved out of the council house in Rotherham and bought this one.'

The music had started again but neither seemed bothered about dancing.

'Can I get you a drink?' Mac asked.

'That would be nice,' she said, smiling, 'can I have a little glass of cider?'

'Course you can, shall we go over there away from this crowd? I'll introduce you to my good friend Freddie.'

'Just hang on,' she said. 'I'll get my friend Debbie; we came together, so I *don't want to abandon her.'*

Freddie was tall and slim, with slicked-back black hair cut neatly in the Tony Curtis style. Debbie looked at him wide-eyed and drooled.

'So, Freddie, do you come here often?' she said, staring brazenly at him.

Freddie immediately felt threatened. He could see the girl had designs on him and thought it could be a bit awkward if she got too pushy.

'No,' he replied. 'I'm just home from college, so I spend most of my time away,' he said, hoping that it would divert her attention away from him.

'Oh, what college is that then?' she asked, sidling up closer to him.

'You wouldn't know it,' he replied, his discomfort at her obvious intent on getting close making him begin to perspire heavily. 'I'm just killing time before I go to Oxford.'

'Oh, that's interesting. What are you going to study?'

'Physics.'

'Oh right, sounds interesting,' she said, beginning to look bemused and also starting to get the message that Freddie wasn't in the market for a girl in his life.

The conversation came to a sudden halt; they stood side by side sipping their drinks, Freddie relieved, the girl starting to look around for another potential partner.

'So what's your name?' Mac asked.

'Val.'

'Nice name.'

'Thanks.'

'And yours?'

'Malc, but call me Mac.'

'And what do you do, Mac?' she enquired.

'I work in a garage, doing odds and sods. I'm not bothering with getting a trade, when I'm eighteen I'm joining the fire brigade; what do you do?'

'I work in a chemist's shop.'

'Do you like it?'

'Yes.'

'Fancy another dance?'

'Yes.'

The night passed quickly. At eleven o'clock the last dance was being played. Freddie was standing talking to another young man, they stood and drank and looked each other up and down. Mac glanced across and wondered.

'Well Val, that was a nice surprise meeting you. I've had a good time, how about you?'

'Yes, it was nice meeting you too.'

'I don't suppose you'd like to meet up again, would you, sometime, to suit yourself?' Mac said, suddenly feeling self-conscious.

'Of course I would, it's been nice. Providing you promise not to sing.'

Mac laughed. *'I don't know where your friend Debbie is, she seems to have disappeared.'*

'I never worry about Debbie; she'll have found somebody with a car to run her home,' she said, smiling.

'How are you getting home?' Mac asked.

'I'll get the bus, it's not far.'

'I'll get the bus with you, if that's OK.'

'Course it is, where do you live?'

'Not far away, I'd like to see you get there, if that's OK.'

'Yes, OK, but I don't want you putting yourself out,' she said, a broad smile lighting her face. Her features were highlighted every few seconds by the light from the glitter ball illuminating the floor of the hall.

The bus stopped abruptly, causing the few passengers who were preparing to leave the bus to stagger awkwardly in the aisle.

They quickly hopped down onto the pavement and watched the bus draw noisily away from the kerb, and rev loudly as it prepared to negotiate the rising ground before it.

They walked slowly along the dimly lit pavement and soon turned into a narrow road, which forked away from the main road.

'Well, Mac, it's been nice meeting you, and I'll see you again soon. Give me a ring and we'll sort out a date, OK?'

'Yes, sure, that will be good, I'll ring you soon. Goodnight.'

'Goodnight, and thanks for the company.'

Mac stood and watched as she walked up the narrow road and disappeared through a garden gate. He turned and set off on the four-mile walk home, happy about the night. I like her a lot, he said to himself. The hour-long walk home was a pleasure for Mac, his mind drifting backwards and forwards. He thought about the girl, Val; Valerie. He liked her, he decided. I'll definitely try to meet her again. In the distance he could hear a bell. He turned his head to try to work out where it was coming from. He peered along the length of the road before him, maybe a mile distance, where he could see the faint glimmer of blue flashing lights. The lights got brighter and stronger and in a few seconds the red Dennis fire appliance roared past him. He thought for a second that the driver had waved at him. His dad was on duty tonight; maybe it was his dad who had somehow spotted him. He began the process of imagining where it was heading; maybe a fire in someone's bedroom, or maybe a car crash. Mac felt the hairs on his neck stand up. He knew that it was his destiny to become, just like his dad, a fireman.

The beep of the alarm woke Mac from his deep sleep; the disturbed night had left him feeling tired.

'You stay there, Mac, I'll go down and make us a cuppa,' Val said, slipping into her towelling dressing gown.

'Thanks love,' Mac replied, burying his head deep into the feather pillow.

He lifted his head, then leaned across and turned on the radio which sat on the pine bedside cabinet. Terry Wogan's smooth, gentle tones slid out of the radio. 'And now for something completely different,' the lilting Irish voice said, 'you will like this, I think that it's wonderful.' Mac slid up in bed, resting his head against the timber headboard. 'We now have the beautiful, if unusual voice of Nadka Karadjova, singing "A lambkin commences bleating", you'll love it I'm sure,' Wogan said, with more than a little touch of ironic humour colouring his usual smooth delivery.

Val walked carefully into the bedroom with a mug of tea in each hand.

'What's that racket?' she laughed. 'It sounds like the cat's died.'

'I'm not sure, Wogan's got some unusual ideas of what good music is,' Mac said. 'The other day he had some German guy singing something about "A lighthouse across the bay".'

'You didn't sleep well last night, is your head still full of retirement stuff?' Val said as she slid into bed alongside Mac.

'Yeah, I suppose so. In fact, when I did eventually get to sleep I dreamt about the night we first met.'

'I remember that,' Val said, laughing quietly. 'You had a bit more hair in those days.'

'True; but then, I was a sexy beast in those days, don't you think?' Mac said, looking out of the corner of his eyes at her.

'You were certainly something, I don't know about being a beast though.'

'I loved those days, me and Freddie, then meeting you and getting around doing stuff.'

'Yeah, poor Freddie, I miss him too,' Val said. 'He was the bit of sanity around us, you were the mad fool. I tagged along because I liked you; and Freddie, he was lovely, such a nice lad.'

'I still miss him a lot,' Mac said, suddenly remembering the trauma surrounding Freddie. 'You know, you expect everything to stay the same when you're young. Me and Freddie, we'd been like brothers for as long as I could remember, the thought of not having him around just never ever entered my head. When we lost him, it hurt so much. When I remember it now, it still hurts.'

Val slipped her arm through Mac's. Mac wiped his eyes on the sleeve of his pyjamas.

It was Jake's mum's shopping day. Jake normally disliked shopping, but the fact it helped mum out meant that he put up with it. She'd shop; he would sit in the cafe reading the paper and drinking coffee, timing it perfectly to meet her at the checkout to transfer the groceries into the bags.

Jake turned the latch on the timber front door of their house. He heard the phone ring.

'Shall I get it, mum?' he said.

'No, you get the car started; I'll get it, I'll only be a minute,' his mother replied.

She disappeared back into the house. Jake sat with the car engine running. He turned on the radio and half closed his eyes, and the face re-entered his mind.

'Jacob, it's for you, I'll wait in the car,' she said, her face beaming with pleasure.

'Hello,' Jake said casually, unaware of whom the caller was.

'Hello Jacob, it is me, Antonella. I just had to talk with you, as I am gone to my rehearsal soon. I have to speak to tell you that I'm thinking of you with all of my heart and I am very exciting to be seeing you very soon.'

'Me too, really looking forward to the weekend.'

'I will bring some nice dress with me, if we go out somewhere I want to look nice for you.'

Jake smiled, the vision of her face filling his brain. 'You will look nice in whatever you wear, I'm sure,' Jake said.

'I love your mum, Jacob, she is a very nice lady and I think she likes me.'

'She likes you very much and so do I, it will be a lovely time for us together,' Jake said enthusiastically.

'I think I have to go now Jacob, I have to catch the train for work. I will speak soon, lots of love.'

'Thanks for ringing; we're really looking forward to seeing you.'

'And me, bye bye.'

The phone clicked and she was gone. Jake's heart ached, but ached with happiness. He couldn't remember a time when he'd ever felt so lucky.

Roll on the weekend he said to himself, as he closed the front door and went to the car.

'Are we still in the National Trust?' Mac asked.

'We've been in the trust for the last seven years, it's about time we went somewhere with it,' Val said enthusiastically.

'How about a trip out to Hardwick Hall. Not been there for years, maybe we could have a stroll round the gardens.'

'Sounds good, it will be a nice change for us. It's a beautiful place.'

Mac indicated and drifted into the off slip from the M1. The roundabout was quiet; he headed left, then took the junction heading for Hardwick Hall, built by Bess of Hardwick 400 years ago with the proceeds of the fortune made from four lucrative marriages. As a result, she had become one of the richest people in England.

The hall stood proudly on the prow of the hill, adjacent to the Old Hall; Bess's birthplace. Her fourth marriage, to the Earl of Shrewsbury, had projected her into the upper echelons of the aristocracy and Hardwick was the building with which she displayed her now considerable power and influence. To emphasise this, along the skyline of the hall were her initials, E S, signifying Elizabeth Shrewsbury, carved in six-feet-high stone letters. 'Hardwick Hall, more glass than wall' is a common phrase used to describe the style of the building.

Mac pulled up in the car park close to the hall, and he and Val walked slowly towards the entrance.

'It's such a nice day; shall we wander round the garden for a while and get some sunshine?' Val said, slipping her arm through Mac's.

'Yes, that sounds good,' he said as they walked into the main entrance to the grounds, showing the attendant their membership card.

Mick Young and Paula Townsend sat in the lounge of the Prince of Wales pub, Mick's local. They hadn't seen each other for a few days. Her work at service headquarters being regular days and Mick's shift pattern being fluid meant that occasionally their days off didn't match.

'I've missed you,' Paula said as she sipped her glass of white wine.

'I've missed you as well, but what the heck, we're here now, so let's enjoy.'

The waiter came to their table.

'What can I get for you, sir?'

Mick perused the menu. 'What do you fancy, Paula?' he said, glancing at her.

'I'd like a steak please, medium to well.'

'And the same for me, please,' Mick said, looking up at the waiter. 'Two steaks, both medium to well done.'

'Thank you, sir, madam,' he said, writing their order down in his pad.

'I'm ready for this, I didn't get a breakfast this morning.'

'Me too,' Paula added, 'I need to build up your strength.'

'Yes, why is that then?' Mick retorted, a wide grin splitting his features.

'Because you, mister – well, let's say I have plans for you this afternoon,' she said, looking at him over the top of her broad-rimmed glasses.

Mick felt something begin to stir.

'I love a woman who has plans,' he said, leaning across the table and grasping her small hand.

After an hour of gentle strolling around the gardens of the hall, Mac and Val headed for the restaurant located within some of the hall's original kitchens. Many of the tables were of old timber with forms to sit on, and it retained some form of ancient style, with large copper pots hanging from nails in the walls. They sat for a while and sipped on cups of hot tea and ate a scone.

'I've enjoyed this afternoon. It's nice to get out together, coming here has been something different,' Val said, looking at Mac.

'Yes, it's been nice, we'll have to do it again sometime. Maybe next time give ourselves the time to look around the hall as well,' Mac replied, returning her gaze. 'I reckon when I've finished with the job, we'll be able to do more of this kind of thing,' Mac said. 'In some ways I'm looking forward to having a bit more spare time. Maybe we'll be able get out with the girls more.'

Den lay in his hospital bed, his brown hair strewn across the pillow. He was staring vacantly at the ceiling, the dull ache in his leg being much preferable to the crushing pain he felt on the crag as he waited for his rescuers to get him down to an ambulance. He was dreaming of the climb and where it all went wrong for him.

I should have listened to Dave, he was spot on. I won't do that again. No beer before the climb, and then I'll manage it easy, he said to himself unconvincingly. *Still, a couple of hours and Dave should be here visiting. He said he'd come, and mum also, she'll be nagging me to stop climbing, she never liked me doing it in the first place.* Soon the effects of the drugs on his body were taking place and Den fell asleep.

CHAPTER 13

The first night shift of Mac's final tour of duty

The night watch was about to commence, the day shift was in an erratic line in the engine house, waiting for the two watch commanders to appear. Rod Jackson, the leading fireman for the day shift, spoke to Brian.

'Is everything now sorted for Mac's retirement do?'

'Pretty much. There are going to be a lot of people there, the collection for Mac's leaving present was really good, so we've got him some nice things to leave with.'

'You know, Bry, I don't think there'll be another one like him. He's a one-off. I tried for years to get onto his watch, but nobody ever left the Reds.'

'Yes, I think you're right. He's a great boss, we're dreading him leaving. He's just got something about him that makes you want to come to work.'

Mac and his opposite number came into the appliance room together.

'Crews… crews 'shun,' Brian called out loudly, and both watches came to attention. 'White Watch fall out, Red Watch stand at ease.'

The day crew took a half turn to their right and walked away, off duty. Red Watch stood comfortably at ease.

'Red Watch stand easy,' Brian called. The crew relaxed.

Mac stepped forward. 'Well boys, we're getting there, the penultimate shift. Tonight we'll be doing things a bit different. No drills. Get into the recc room and we'll have a chat. Jake, after the routines, you make the tea.'

The watch sat relaxed in comfortable upholstered chairs. These had been acquired over a period of time, some brown leather, some red cloth, none matching, just a casual assortment of functional, comfortable seating. They sprawled relaxed, with their mugs of tea clasped in their hands.

Mac sat up straight. 'Dya know boys,' he said, 'for thirty years I've been coming to work, doing routines, going in the yard and running up and down ladders getting wet through so I thought tonight, sod it.' He twisted in his seat.

'Mick, put the wireless on, will you?'

Mick got up and walked across to the table where the wireless sat as it had sat for many years, its brown Bakelite casing regularly polished by the station cleaner.

'That wireless has been on this station ever since I first came here as a young fireman,' Mac said, a smile creasing his ruddy face. 'It still works, it works because it's been looked after and respected, and it's given probably thousands of hours of pleasure to hundreds of firemen who've been lucky enough to serve at Graveton.' Mac paused. 'It's a piece of brigade history, just like us, I am, and so are you, a part of this fire service's history.' Mac paused and looked at his crew. 'We'll say that's been a bloody good radio, it always works when we want it, it never lets us down and it's there when we need it. We are Red Watch, we're like that radio. We don't let people down and we do the business, when we're needed. We're reliable and trustworthy; we're brave when we have to be, frightened when we need to be. We're effective as a team, and all these things we are, because we care, we care about the job and we care about each other and we care about the legacy we leave behind when we're done.' Mac paused again, longer this time, collecting his thoughts.

'Well, after tomorrow I'll be done, and I have no regrets at all. I love the job and I hate to say this, but I love you lot. But don't tell the other watches, it'll ruin my persona. I'm proud and happy to have served with you all; you're a credit to the job.' Mac paused again.

'Taff, you are legend, a great watch man. My replacement will rely on you, the older hands, to help him sort himself out. Brian, whilst you're here you'll carry on doing the good job you always do, I'm sure. Pete; do you know, you've surprised me, you've gone far beyond what I expected, even given the hard time you've had these past weeks, these younger lads are going to have to depend on you. Mick, you're a really good guy to have on a watch, solid, reliable. I look forward to seeing you working to get promotion, because I feel that's where you should be. Jock; we've known each other a long time you are a stalwart of this watch, it wouldn't have been the same without you, and I would expect you to keep the rest of these reprobates in check.' Mac paused.

'Clive, I'll miss you. I've watched you come on in leaps and bounds over the while you've been in the job, keep it up. You're a married man now, who knows, you will have a family, think about that. Get on in the job, you've got it in you to go far.

'And finally Jake, our new boy. You've done well son, really earned your spurs, keep it up, the world's your oyster. Learn from this lot, they've got a lot to pass on.'

Jock spoke. 'You know, Mac, we'll miss you but at the same time we knew it was coming, when Ray left it reminded us that nothing is forever.'

Mac looked at his crew. 'That's it, end of speech. Now, who wants to see if they can beat me at a game of table tennis?' he said, jumping up from his seat. 'Any takers?'

Just then, car headlights swung across the station yard.

'Don't worry lads, it's OK. I told division we were having a night off tonight.'

'It's only me,' the light voice called, as the station commander walked through the recc room towards the far end where the watch was sitting.

Station Officer Cork was aware of what Mac had planned for the night. He was the designated duty officer, and was on his rounds of local stations.

'Just thought I'd pop in and see what you were getting up to,' he said, smiling. Mike Cork, or 'Bung' as he was known since being a young fireman, was a popular figure. He had an easy style with the men under his command, but was also known to have a searing temper when he got upset, if he felt any of his crews were giving less than their best.

'So what's on the agenda tonight, Mac?' he asked.

'Nothing much, boss, just relax, have a chat. Hopefully we'll have a quiet night.'

'Let's hope so,' he said, 'I'm not stopping, I've got to get across to Div HQ to see the DC, so let's hope for a quiet one. Goodnight, and I'll see you all in the morning.'

The Temple family were having a late evening meal. Both parents worked, and the children, nine-year-old Matthew and seven-year-old Helenor, having come home from school and being watched over by the mother's ageing father, now all sat around the dinner table of their neat but small terraced home, eating the Chinese takeaway that father had brought home with him.

Beep... Beep... Beep... Beep... Beep... Beep... Beep.

'What's that beeping noise?' the mother asked.

Father looked annoyed, 'I think it's the battery's running low in the smoke alarm.'

Beep... Beep ... Beep...

'Hang on a second, I'll sort it out,' the father said, getting up from the table. He climbed the stairs and flipped the cover of the alarm and removed the battery. 'That's sorted,' he said.

Red Watch sat, relaxed, watching TV. Taff opened the cupboard in which the boys kept a small stash of soft drinks and chocolate.

'I'll have a Pepsi and a Mars bar, Taff,' Brian said.

'I'll have an orange juice and a Kit Kat,' Pete said.

Taff looked round at them. 'Well, let's have your money then.'

'OK, scrooge,' Brian said, flipping a note in his direction.

The watch table tennis tournament was won easily by Pete, who hadn't told them that he'd played at county level several years ago, so his victory was almost inevitable. Jake had a good try, but Pete stepped up a gear and soon Jake was beaten.

'One thing we didn't tell you, Pete,' Brian said. 'The winner has to make the tea for the rest of the shift.'

'You should have mentioned it earlier, I could have thrown a couple of games,' he responded, with a huge grin. Pete was well settled on the watch now and the problems at home with the children were becoming easier to manage.

It was almost eleven o'clock and the Temple children were asleep in their beds. Colin and Pat Temple were on their way to bed. Don, the grandfather, told them he would lock up and switch everything off before he came up; he was going to have a last smoke before he turned in. He sat watching TV for a while next to the window, through which he watched the occasional passer-by or a car driving past the house. He was tired, in his early seventies; he hadn't the stamina of his youth. He dozed and drifted, his hand relaxing. The cigarette fell from between his fingers and dropped easily down the side of the cushion of the old leatherette armchair.

It was eleven twenty; only Mac, Jake and Pete were still up, sitting talking in the recc room. The rest of Red Watch had gone off to the dormitory and got their heads down.

'So what have you got arranged tomorrow, boys?' Mac asked.

Jake looked up. He was beginning to feel tired, but was reluctant to leave Mac and Pete. He still wanted to absorb as much of watch life as was possible; very aware that soon Mac would be gone, and other nights like this wouldn't be quite the same.

'I've got to take mum to Tesco's; with my friend coming up from London for the weekend, she wants to feed her up.'

Mac lifted his eyes. 'So are you going to bring her here on Saturday night, and let the boys get a look at this girl?'

'Of course I will; she's looking forward to meeting you all, although I've warned her that you're all a bit rough round the edges.'

'You cheeky little sod,' Mac laughed. 'What about you, Pete?'

'Not sure, I've got a load of jobs to do in the house. I love decorating,' Pete said, grimacing as he spoke.

'I'll give you a hand if you like,' Jake volunteered.

'That's nice of you Jake, but I guess you'll have more interesting things to do with your time.'

'No, really; I get bored if I haven't got anything to do.'

'Well, if you're sure, leave it till after the weekend and come round. It'll be nice to have a bit of company.'

Mac felt the hairs on his neck stand up. He knew what was coming, and was already standing when they heard the familiar clunk as the lights came on and the station alarm began to sound. Jake hit the pole and slid smoothly down to the muster bay in the appliance room. As he hit the mat at the bottom, Brian ran past, tightening the belt around his waist. He darted into the watchroom. Jake heard the message being ripped from the teleprinter.

'House fire, persons reported,' Mick called out to the crew as they jumped onto the appliance.

'37, Blenheim Road,' Brian called as he leapt onto the appliance.

Mick Young slammed the appliance into first gear and pressed hard on the accelerator. The machine lurched out of the bay, its wheels squealing as he pulled hard left on the steering wheel.

The cigarette smouldered in its hiding place. The leatherette covering of the chair soon broke down, exposing the foam which didn't ignite readily, but produced a highly toxic cocktail of chemicals. In its early stages of development the foam gave off an almost invisible vapour, invisible but deadly. Don was asleep. He inhaled the smoke and was soon overcome, never aware of his cigarette which was slowly but surely burning its way deep into the foam of the chair in which he sat.

The fire in the chair developed slowly. The room was sealed; the windows were closed and the door leading to the stairs was closed. The smoke was now being generated faster, and soon flames began to emerge from the chair; the smoke hit the ceiling but had nowhere to go. It began to descend around the now lifeless body of Don. The heat in the room increased, slowly at first; the glass on the window becoming discoloured. Minute rivulets of smoke squeezed their way through the small gaps around the door and soon flowed up the staircase, embracing the now useless, disabled smoke detector, then onto the landing where the remainder of the family slept in their rooms behind closed doors, unaware of the fire developing downstairs. The flames became more intense and the smoke thickened as yet more of the toxic foam burned. Soon, the oxygen in the room was depleted, the flames receded. The heat continued to rise, and in a very short time almost every combustible item within the room was decomposing and giving off a dangerous mixture of flammable gases.

The situation was critical. The fuel was ready to burn, there was ample heat in the confined space of the room to ignite the materials, but the fire lacked its third element: oxygen.

Donna Blake walked gingerly along the street. The hip operation she'd recently endured was now allowing her to walk, albeit with the aid of two walking sticks, but it still required her to exercise her willpower to get out and do it. This was her nightly ritual. Before going to bed she would walk the one hundred yards down the street, and then return to her house one hundred yards back, then she would have her glass of hot milk and get herself off to her bed.

She walked slowly past number 37. She knew the family; she had, before her operation, babysat for the children a couple of times, to allow the parents out for a night out, a rarity when you have young children. As she walked by, she looked casually at the house. She saw something flickering in the downstairs window, it caught her attention; she stared, wondering what it was that had caught her eye. Then she saw flames on the other side of the now darkly stained glass. She stopped and peered carefully at the darkened window. *Oh shit, there's a fire,* she thought.

'Help,' she called, as loud as she could. 'Please, help, someone. Fire!' she shouted as loud as she could. She looked around and shouted weakly again, but there was no response. She turned as quickly as she could, and moving faster than she thought possible struggled back to her house.

'*Emergency, which service do you require?*' the calm female voice on the other end of the telephone said.

'Fire brigade. Please hurry up, there's a family in there,' she shouted down the mouthpiece, barely able to contain the panic in her voice.

Mick picked his way expertly through the congested streets of the old part of the estate, the lights flashed their warning, other traffic pulling over and out of the way. It was almost as though they realised this was a very urgent call for assistance.

'Are you guys rigged and ready?' Mac called from the front seat of the machine.

Pete and Taff, their nerves tense, adrenaline pouring into their bodies, replied that they were set and ready to go.

'OK guys, get your tallies in the board now, let's be fast. I want water on it first thing, fast as you like. Jake, you get the hose reel off, OK?'

'Yes, Sub,' Jake replied. Every centimetre of his body was taut as he wondered what they were about to face. His heart quickened as they approached the incident.

The heat in the lounge of the house was at the point where everything in the room was turning to ash: carpets, curtains, wallpaper dried to a dust in the searing atmosphere. The plastic of the television had long since dissolved. Then the TV's tube exploded. The noise woke some of the neighbours, who initially peered inquisitively through the curtains of their bedrooms, but weren't able to see anything. The noise also jolted the family into consciousness.

Tony, the father, quickly jumped out of bed and opened the bedroom door. The faint smell of smoke hit his nostrils and instantly his eyes were flooded with tears.

'You two stay in your rooms,' he called down the landing to the children, 'and don't open the door,' he emphasised.

He descended the stairs quickly. He carefully turned the Bakelite knob of the door leading into the lounge. He pushed the door slowly.

Whoosh.

In the bedroom, Pat heard a muffled bang and thought she heard a cry from her husband; the children remained in their rooms, scared but unaware of what was happening.

As the door opened, the fire which had been starved of oxygen now had what it needed. The contents of the room, which had burned slowly for so long, had built up a substantial pressure; the sudden introduction of oxygen caused an instant ignition of everything combustible within the room, the pressure burst through the door, rapidly followed by a fast-moving tongue of flame. Tony was unable to move fast enough to duck out of its path, and was engulfed by the fire.

Pat Temple heard the roar and a cry from her husband, and a sense of panic shot through her body at the sudden realisation that something was very badly wrong. She quickly put on her dressing gown and opened the bedroom door.

Flames surged up the stairs and were beginning to engulf the landing. She felt the intense heat, but the mother's instinct took over her body. *I've got to get to the kids*, she thought.

'Stay where you are, kids, I'm coming to you,' she shouted above the roar of the flames. She crouched low on her hands and knees, attempting to get below the heat. It was dark, but the upper floor of the house was now illuminated by a dull, sinister orange hue as the flames took hold. She crawled as fast as she could. The heat soon ignited her hair and then her dressing gown began to shrivel and catch fire; she screamed. Unable to douse the flames, her final thought was of her two children, trapped behind the door. She rolled slowly on to her side and died four feet from her children's bedroom door.

The intensity of the fire soon burned away the ceiling of the lounge, plaster and debris quickly covering the burning body of Don. Seconds later, the ceiling collapsed into the lounge, followed by the smouldering contents of the bedroom above.

The children in the back bedroom, away from the worst effects of the fire, were paralysed with fear. Helenor cried uncontrollably as her brother tried his best to comfort her. The door of their bedroom was closed tight.

The window of the lounge disintegrated and flames issued horizontally into the small front garden. A neighbour, alerted by the cacophony of noise, left his house to investigate. Seeing the fire in the front of the house he went to the back, but couldn't break through the secured back door. He could see a ladder lying alongside the garden fence and decided that he'd try to do something to help. He placed the ladder against the window of the back bedroom then climbed upwards, but was soon driven down by the fierce heat. A small crowd of neighbours was gathering outside the house. The fire fizzed and banged, everyone now feared that the family was beyond saving.

Mick Young pulled hard right into the street, and the crew were instantly aware of the task they had before them. Mac picked up the radio handset.

'Control from Alpha 010, in attendance, make pumps three, informative to follow.'

Mick braked hard and slammed on the appliance handbrake, instantly pushing the lever in the cab to put the pump in gear, and then leapt to the ground. The crew moved fast; Pete and Taff were rigged in their breathing apparatus sets, and their tallies were in the board; quickly checked by Mick. Jake grabbed the hose reel and pulled it from the spinning cylinder on which it was coiled. Taff had the hose reel branch and ran to the front of the house, the hard, black hose trailing behind him.

Jake grabbed the hydrant gear from its locker, his brain now operating on autopilot, and ran the twenty yards down the street. He removed the cast iron hydrant's lid and screwed the standpipe onto the outlet from the water main. He located the key on the spigot and bar, and in seconds was turning the key, sending the water fast into the inlet of the pump.

'Water on the hydrant,' he shouted, but Mick was too busy to hear.

Seeing the water arrive at the pump inlet, Mick closed the tank valve, directing the high-pressure water from the hydrant directly into the pump.

Mac stood back for a second, looking and thinking. He took the arm of a young female neighbour. 'How many people in the house, love?' he asked. The woman was transfixed by the fire but did manage to pull herself together.

'I think there are four, but sometimes the granddad stays, so could be five.'

Mac looked around. 'Jake, you get a line of two lengths of 45-mill hose and a diffuser out, as quick as you like.'

Mick upped the pressure on the hose reel; the BA team were struggling to get close, but were hitting the fire hard.

Mac moved fast to the back of the house and immediately spotted a neighbour half collapsed, and leaning heavily against the brick outhouse wall. He saw the old wooden ladder pitched up to the back bedroom window.

Jake had run out the 45-millimetre hose and had given the diffuser to Taff, who was making determined efforts to have a significant impact on the flames, which were now pouring from the ground and first floor windows.

Mac guessed that the fire had not yet devastated the back of the house, so he reasoned that any survivors would be there, in the bedrooms at the back.

'Jake, take the branch and keep at it here,' Mac said, 'keep hitting it hard.'

He grabbed Pete's arm. 'Get the hose reel, Pete, and both of you come with me.'

The second appliance pulled up behind the Graveton appliance. The leading fireman in charge of the appliance found Mac.

'Right, LF, I want a ladder round the back, fast as you can and into the bedroom window. Then I want two BA teams, one in each loft space on each side of the house, to make a stop. Can I leave that with you?' Mac asked.

The young LF responded immediately, 'I'll do that Sub, no problem.'

'Good, let's get to it then,' he said.

The crew slammed the aluminium ladder into the bedroom window, smashing the glass. A ribbon of hot smoke poured from the bedroom window. Taff slung the hose reel over his shoulder and moved quickly up the ladder; as his head became level with the sill, he took the hose reel from his shoulder and shot a wide arc of high-pressure water spray through the broken glass.

'Anybody in there?' he shouted. His heart pumped wildly. He listened, and immediately heard a low whimpering sound. 'If you can hear me, crawl to the window,' Taff called out.

'I think my sister's dead,' the frightened voice said from within the darkened room.

Taff made a decision. He hung the hose reel over the horn of the ladder and in an instant stepped up two rounds and dove headlong into the room.

Pete was spurred into action. 'Foot the ladder,' he called to the young firefighter, who was standing close by. Pete darted up the ladder and peered into the room. He could make out the shape of Taff, who was scrambling round the room, the light from the torch which hung loosely from the metal 'D' ring on his BA harness swinging wildly, the torchlight swinging violently around the room. 'Have you got them Taff?' he called. He heard the muffled cry.

'Yep, I've found them, be there in a second.'

As he spoke, the fire broke through the bedroom door. Flames shot rapidly across the bedroom ceiling, the radiated heat instantly igniting the remnants of the curtains and bedding.

Mac jumped into the appliance and pressed the switch on the radio.

'Control from Alpha 010 informative message, over.'

'010 go ahead, over.'

'Informative message, from Sub Officer James at the same address, a two-storey terraced house approximately five metres by eight metres, ground and first floor well alight. One jet one hose reel two BA in use. Believe four occupant, search in progress.'

'Alpha 010, your informative message received, out.'

More fire appliances arrived at the incident, soon followed by ADO Paul Davis, who spoke briefly to Mac and took over control of the incident. Two more jets were got to work at the front of the house, each pouring large amounts of water into the spaces where the windows had once been. A BA team forced open the front door and began hitting the fire inside the hallway and made their way to the base of the staircase, swinging the jet of water from side to side, hitting the ceiling; then the hot smoke and steam, an almost animal-like response to the attack by the firefighters, soon engulfed them. They pushed on blind to their surroundings.

Taff heard the *whoosh* as the room began to burn. He could see the children lit up by the light from the fire, cowering by the side of the bed, which was now burning freely.

'Get the jet in over here, Pete.'

Pete noticed the desperation in Taff's voice. Almost instantly a torrent of water covered them all, cooling them and momentarily reducing the intensity of the fire. Taff put his arm around the barely conscious girl and crawled for the window. Pete stood tall on the ladder, calling to Taff to get her there and he would get her down to the ground.

A group of firefighters were now gathering at the back of the house and were positioned ready to receive the casualties. The ambulance had arrived and was set up and ready to deal with any injuries. Taff reached the window and stood up, quickly passing the girl to Pete on the ladder, her face blackened by the thick smoke. Pete descended fast and the girl was soon passed to the ambulance crew.

The fire was developing quickly and Taff moving as if on autopilot, quickly moved back across the room to collect the boy. There was a sudden crack and a deep rumble sounded. Taff stopped and looked up. Pete's heart sank as he saw the ceiling collapse, followed by the contents of the loft space, the metal water tank; heavy, filled with water, it crashed down around him and caused a partial collapse of the bedroom floor. The tank caught Taff a glancing blow on his helmet, making him stagger to one side. Momentarily he was stunned, but the seriousness of his position and the young boy who lay by his feet soon brought him back to the reality of their situation.

Visibility in the confined space was nil, and the boy had disappeared from view under a thick cloud of dust and smoke. Taff bent down and foraged amongst the debris. He found the boy's upper body, but quickly realised that his legs had been trapped by the heavy water tank. He tried to move the tank but it was too heavy. 'Get in here, Pete,' he shouted to his partner.

Pete had witnessed the collapse of the ceiling and was already climbing into the room through the window, realising the sudden escalation of danger to the boy and his partner. He was soon standing alongside Taff.

The smoke was thick and choking, the boy was struggling to breathe. 'Hold on, sunshine,' Pete called down to the boy. He quickly removed his BA set and placed the heavy rubber facemask over the boy's dust-covered face. The boy coughed. Pete tried desperately to hold his breath, but it was impossible. Taff spoke.

'Let's get this tank off his legs and have him out of here.'

Pete nodded, unable to speak. With a supreme effort they managed to lift the tank, Taff taking the weight whilst Pete dragged the boy away towards the window. Jake had been taken off the jet at the front of the house, so made his way to the rear of the house. He heard the collapse, then saw Pete climb into the window to help Taff.

Jake raced up the ladder and peered desperately into the smoke. The sounds of coughing and cracking glass surrounded him. His heart was pumping fast.

'Get him over here, Pete,' Jake shouted above the noise of the fire. Seconds later, Pete appeared with the boy, who had the mask pushed hard over his face. Pete was struggling to breathe and seemed almost at the point of collapse.

'Give him here, Pete,' Jake called as he saw him emerging from the smoke and dust. Pete passed the boy to Jake, who took his weight easily then moved fast down the ladder to the waiting ambulance crew, who pushed an oxygen mask over the boy's face and quickly moved him away to the ambulance.

The combined effect of the water being driven into the fire from both the inside and outside of the house soon began to overpower the fire. The BA team had forced their way up the staircase, killing the fire as they went. They stumbled across the badly burned body of the mother as she lay on the landing, half covered by burning timbers from the roof. A second BA team entered the house and made their way into the lounge, where the fire had started; they found the body of the father, lying across the bottom of the stairs covered by debris. They entered the lounge and saw that nothing was left, the ceiling had gone and the view above was of the underside of the tiled roof. Nothing remained but the scorched, blackened remnants of a chair and, amongst the metal springs, lay the remains of the grandfather.

The supervisory officer, now having all of the occupants located, concentrated his efforts into finally extinguishing the fire. The decision was made to leave all of the victims in situ as there was no great risk of their loss due to further collapse of the house. A fire investigation would follow to ascertain the cause of the fire.

Mac stood at the front of the house, the incident now illuminated by heavy-duty lights powered by the fire appliance engines. He thought of the number of times in his career that he had stood like this, looking at the scene of tragedy, it brought back many memories. The realisation that this could well be his last fire hit him. He remembered his first fire, and all of the details of the job, the crew that were there with him, the occupants of the house who had left for work only to be called back home to find that the strong wind that day had blown over a tree and gone through the roof of their house. He remembered his guv'nor, Tom Atkins, who had him climb the old Ajax ladder with a saw to start the process of removing the tree, and thought that wouldn't happen these days. He remembered the look on the faces of the family, grief, fear, and relief that they weren't in the house when the tree fell. He remembered the sense of satisfaction he got at the end of the job when back at the station the boss took him to one side and told him that he'd done a good job. Something he always remembered, praise when it's earned, a kick up the backside when it's needed. Something that he subsequently applied to the people he worked with as he got to a point of running a watch. He stood in an almost dream-like state, aware of everything around him but at the same time in a state of grace.

A large hand tapped him on the shoulder. 'A penny for them, Mac.' Mac half turned. It was his long-time friend and colleague, George Collier, the officer in charge of Red Watch at Central.

'Oh, hiya George, what are you doing here?'

George smiled at Mac; behind George was part of his crew. 'Well Mac, we were already out at a job when you picked this one up, so we thought as you were out, we would just pop across to see if you were managing all right without us.'

Mac looked at the crew and recognised them all. The sudden realisation that they were aware that he was leaving after the next shift and were probably taking this opportunity to see him at a fire for possibly the last time impacted on him, and he felt his heart swell with emotion. 'Nice of you, George. As you can see, the roof is off, but yep we managed to save a bit of it.' Mac could see Jake's friend Devo stood looking around in awe at the destruction.

'George, this may be a good intro to the bad side of the job for Devo. Shall we get him and young Jake in to have a look around?' Mac said.

'Good idea Mac; Devo, get round the back, pick up your pal Jake and get him back here sharpish.' Mark almost jumped and a rush of blood to his head made him feel light-headed, knowing what they were about to experience. Mark stumbled around the side of the terrace, the jumble of hose and broken tiles littering the darkened passageway. He emerged into the illuminated concrete yard. Jake was there damping down debris with a hose reel, Taff and Pete were about to return to entry control, their BA low-pressure warning whistles now beginning to operate.

'Hiya, Jake,' Mark called out.

Jake looked around. 'Oh, hiya Mark. What are you doing here?' he asked.

'We were out at a job when you got the call, so the guv'nor thought it would be a good idea to come round for a look on our way back to station.' He paused for breath. 'Mac wants us both round the front, he wants to take us through the job, show us what's happened. I have to say, I'm a bit nervous.'

They went into the wreck of the house, Mac in the lead followed by Jake, then Mark. The destruction shocked them. Every centimetre of plaster had come off the wall; there was the stench of death all around. Mac took them into the front room, realising that this would be tough for the young firefighters, but that it was part of the reality of the job. They needed to see this, understand that what they did was vital but dangerous work. 'Don't touch anything; the forensic people have to come in before we move the bodies.' They stood for a moment, unable to speak. Mac could sense the tension and stress they were feeling.

'This is the room where we think the fire started. Not sure as yet what the cause was, but you can tell from the way the fire burned it was a fire that began slow and cooked up for a long time.' They turned and left the room, the scent of burned flesh almost making them gag. 'We can see here easily how the fire travelled,' he said, as they walked carefully around the body of the father still almost invisible due to the volume of debris covering him. 'It seems, and it's only a theory at present, that this person opened the door on the fire and was caught by the blast,' Mac said, looking carefully at the boys. They returned his gaze, their faces betraying the sadness and horror at the situation they were now witnessing. Mac leaned over close to the top of the stairs. Amid the dust and ash he saw the remnant of the smoke detector.

'Look,' he said, 'smoke alarm, no sign of a battery there. It could have saved their lives.'

Before them lay the mother, the clothing burned from her distended body. 'We can only guess how the lady got here; maybe she was trying to get across to the children. Clearly she didn't make it.'

There was sadness in Mac's tone. He'd seen this too often in his thirty years in the service. The fire had roared up the staircase and incinerated everything combustible in its path. The doors to the bedrooms and bathroom had turned to ash, the ceilings and the roof above their heads had gone. Mac turned to look at these two young men, realising that this was a salutary lesson for them. It was hard but necessary for them to understand what they would have to face in the future.

'So boys, this is the reality of fire. Nothing gallant or romantic, just pain and loss and fear. All you can ever do is show it respect, never underestimate it or it may get you. Any questions?' The boys were silent. Jake felt the beginnings of a tear building up, he wiped the sleeve of his jacket across his face.

'No, Sub,' they said in unison.

It was two thirty in the morning. Antonella stirred in her bed; she rolled over onto her back, she could hear the sound of sirens in the distance and immediately her mind turned to Jake, her young man in Sheffield. She climbed slowly out of her bed and walked the few feet across the bedroom to the window. She pulled one curtain back a few inches, just sufficient to see the street below. The area was quiet but for the siren in the distance. The immediate area was illuminated by sodium street lights and as her eyes became accustomed to the light she thought she could see in the distance flashing blue lights, beyond that she could just see an orange glow in the sky; she wondered if it was a fire. She closed the curtain and walked back and sat comfortably on the side of her bed. The air had a chill, she shivered and quickly slipping into her dressing gown, then made her way slowly down the stairs into the small kitchen she shared with her friend Petra from Russia, a flautist in the orchestra. She warmed up some milk and made herself a cup of drinking chocolate, then returned to her bedroom. *I wish I could speak to Jacob*, she said to herself. She knew he was on duty tonight. Something in her made her pick up the telephone and dial the number of his fire station.

Mick Young pulled the appliance into the wash down behind the appliance room.

'OK guys, re-stow the hose, service the BA sets. Jake, you get the kettle on, still time for us all to get a couple of hours' kip before we finish the shift,' Mac said to the crew.

As Jake wandered through the appliance room he heard the phone ring. He walked casually into the watchroom and picked up the phone.

'Hello, Graveton, firefighter Higgins speaking.'

'Hello Jacob, is that you?'

'Hello Antonella, is that you?' he said, his voice betraying his surprise. 'What are you doing up at this time of night?'

'Yes, Jacob, I'm sorry that I'm telephoning you, but I woke up, I think I had a dream and I worried of you, are you very well?'

'Yes, I'm well; well I'm tired, we've just got back from a bad fire so my head is very sad at the moment,' he said, his mind still adjusting to the fact that she'd called him at such a strange hour.

Antonella felt guilty about her thoughtlessness in telephoning Jake, especially now, as she began to wake up to the reality of his life in the fire service.

'I'm sorry to having to phone you, at such a bad time for you Jacob,' she said, her voice reflecting the guilt she was feeling.

Jake quickly picked up her embarrassment. 'Look Antonella, it's OK, it's great to hear your voice, I was just a bit concerned that you were alright. So don't worry, you should go back to bed and get your sleep, or you'll be tired later.'

'Alright my Jacob, I will, but I am thinking about you and I am very exciting about coming to see you and your mother.'

'Me too, I think of you all the time. I have to go now, I have to make tea for Mac and the boys.'

'Alright Jacob, I go back to my bed now, I love you very much.'

'And I love you too,' Jake replied. Jake sat for a minute after the phone had clicked. It dawned on him that they had both, for the first time, openly and honestly expressed their love for each other. He sat and wondered and mused, feeling thankful that he'd found this girl.

'What's this then, Jake; was that call from who I think it was?'

Jake turned around in his seat. It was Mac, his face showed no emotion.

'So, Jake, you're in love.'

Jake looked at Mac, the man he hero-worshipped. Was he in trouble, or what? He couldn't read what Mac was thinking. 'I'm sorry about the call, Sub.

She woke up and felt she wanted to talk to me, I'll tell her not to call again.'

Mac smiled at the young man, his protégé, who Mac felt was born to be a firefighter.

'It's not a problem, Jake, just tell her the times when it's convenient to ring. I think none of us would have appreciated it had we all been asleep, so you have a word. But don't worry.'

The boys sat around the table, drinking their tea and eating from the box of digestive biscuits. Taff and Pete were in desperate need of a good wash, their faces blackened by the smoke and sweat.

'So, how are we all?' Mac asked. 'No problems or injuries to report?'

'I thought it was horrible. Just a few hours ago that family were alive and now… well, it's devastated them, just two youngsters left without mum or dad and granddad. I wish we could have done more to save them,' Jake said, his face displaying his torment.

'We did what we could,' Brian said. 'Good as we are, sometimes a job's beyond us when we get there. I reckon that all of the fatalities tonight happened before we got the call. What we did do, we did well. Taff and Pete got the kids, so that's a positive thing, but we all wish for a better result sometimes, it's natural.'

Jake looked around the table. They were all tired and all seemed, like him, to have suffered the effects of the trauma of the loss of the people at the fire.

'Yeah, I'm sure you're right, Bry. I suppose I'll get used to it.'

Taff piped up, 'I never got used to it, I just learned to live with it. I just somehow manage to shove it to the back of my mind.'

'Well I'm off to get some shut-eye, see you all later,' Mac said as he stood up from the table.

Mac climbed into bed, his single room being a privilege of the officer in charge; the rest of the watch all slept in their dormitory. Sleep soon overtook him, and within minutes, thoughts and memories from his past began to flood into his mind.

He'd just come home from his job in the garage when his dad came home from work, still wearing his undress uniform.

'Hello son, what sort of day have you had?' he said, wrapping his big arms around Mac's shoulders.

'It was OK, the usual stuff, cleaning and running around after the mechanics. They let me change the brake pads on a couple of cars, which was a nice change. Not long to go now though dad, I'll soon be in the brigade, I can't wait.'

'I've got something here for you, Malcolm,' his dad said. 'We had a job in Bakewell today; with all the floods, we've spent most of this tour of duty well off our own station ground. I got this for you,' he said handing Mac a piece of grime-covered paper. 'That poem,' he said, 'came from a pillar by the door of the Rutland hotel in Bakewell, and I reckon it is just what a fireman is, so you have it, from me.'

'Thanks, Dad,' Mac replied. He stood and read the poem; it struck a chord with him. Anything from Mac's dad instantly became a treasure. Mac, even at seventeen, still thought of his dad as a hero.

In a second, Mac was at Division Street fire station and had taken and passed the physical and written tests. He was a physical young man and the tests posed him no problem; the written, however, was more problematic. He struggled with the maths, but the kindly station officer who was watching over the candidates helped Mac with the answers, so Mac passed and was quickly processed. Within a week he was kitted out with his uniform, helmet, axe and belt and was sent to begin his career at Darnall fire station, where he was to spend two weeks before being sent to training school. Firefighting in the industrial section of Sheffield takes on a different style. Ninety per cent of fires at Darnall were in the steelworks: oil fires, slag spillages, salt bath incidents. Occasionally there would be a house fire, but they were a rarity. They always said Darnall firemen could be identified by the state of their boots, the nature of the jobs they got made getting a shine on their boots impossible. Often their uniforms were also covered in oil and grease.

Mac arrived early at the station and was welcomed by the sub officer in charge of the night shift, who told Mac that he was unfortunate to have to spend his first shift in the job with such a dodgy bunch of blokes as the ones on White Watch.

'Aren't you Dave James's boy?' he asked.

'Yeah, he's my dad.'

'Well, if you are half as good as him you'll do well, he's a really top man, I worked with him about five years ago at Rocko. When you see him, remember me to him.'

Mac looked at the sub officer; hearing this made him proud to be following in his dad's footsteps. 'Yeah, I'll tell him tonight,' he replied.

The men of Mac's new watch began to filter in to work, and soon they spoke to him and began to talk about how their watch operated and what they expected from him. He felt happy and comfortable, in the place he knew he was meant to be.

The lights in the station came on. Mac had trouble opening his eyes, he felt as though he'd been asleep for only five minutes. He glanced at the clock on the small table by his bed: it was a quarter to five, dawn was just breaking, he noticed, as he looked up at the small window of his room. He slid into his tracksuit bottoms and his slip-on shoes and jogged blearily into the appliance room. Pete had the sheet of paper from the teleprinter in his hand.

'What have we got?' Mac asked, as he climbed up into the cab.

'Lorry fire on the Parkway,' Pete called, as he struggled to put on his fire tunic.

Mick Young bombed up the dual carriageway; in the distance, a cloud of angry black smoke curled into the early morning sky. The traffic was light.

'Slip your sets on, lads. Jake, you get the hose reel off.'

Mick pulled the machine to a halt twenty yards back from the lorry, to give the crew some protection as they fought the fire. Jake pulled the hose reel from its drum, and in quick time. Taff and Pete had hit the flames being expelled from the engine compartment with a jet of high pressure water. The fire was quickly subdued with no injuries to the crew or the driver of the lorry. The police were on scene and quickly began the process of getting a breakdown vehicle to haul away the now dead truck, and getting the road cleared before the rush hour got fully underway.

'Right, Mick, get us back before they need us again,' Mac called across the cab above the roar of the diesel engine. Mick drove fast, and they were soon close to their home station when the radio crackled into life again.

'Alpha 010, over.'

'Alpha 010 go ahead, over,' Mac replied.

'Alpha 010 proceed to a shed fire at Mapleton Avenue Graveton, over.'

Mac sighed, still feeling tired after the early call.

'Alpha 010 your message received and proceeding, over.'

It suddenly registered that he wouldn't have to do this many more times, everything was closing in very quickly. He decided to concentrate hard to absorb every last grain of the remainder of his service, so now he had a new focus. Mick hit the horns as they approached a small tailback of vehicles at the roundabout, the sound resonating in Mac's head. He wondered if his dad had felt this, when his service was coming to its close. They turned into Mapleton Avenue and saw that there were several residents waiting anxiously in the street. Mac sensed something wasn't quite right; he jumped from the cab and spoke to the person who appeared to be the owner of the shed, which was burning furiously in the back garden of the house, its flames being driven sideways by a strong, gusty wind. Pete and Taff disappeared through a gap between the houses as Jake pulled hard on the reel to make it easier for the boys to drag the hose to the fire. There was a sudden dull thud and a bowl of blue flame erupted from what remained of the timber shed. Then another thud, followed by the same blue flame. They ducked low, unsure of exactly what was blowing. Mac followed them up the garden, 'Stay low boys, the owner reckons he's got a stock of the little camping gas cylinders in there. Just keep putting water in there and keep your heads down, I'll get a message off.'

'Control from Alpha 010, over. Garden shed well alight, hose reel and two BA in use, over.'

There followed a series of minor explosions, each explosion lighting up the early morning sky with the now familiar blue flame. Taff turned to Pete.

'All we need now, Pete, is for Georgie Fame to turn up and we could have some music.'

Pete looked into Taff's facemask.

'I don't quite get that one, Taff. Who's Georgie Fame?'

'Don't you know, boyo?' Taff said in his broadest Welsh accent 'You should get out more!' he laughed.

'Hurry up, will you, I gotta go,' Pete smirked. The fire was almost quelled so Taff turned and gave Pete a short burst of water into his facemask.

'That'll teach you to take the piss out of me, Pete. I'm Welsh you know, and we are a very sensitive nation.'

Just then, Mac came up behind them.

'How's it going, lads?' he asked.

'Almost done, Mac. Not had a bang in the last couple of minutes, think they've all gone up.'

The sun was now climbing higher into the sky; it looked like it was going to be another nice day.

'*Control from alpha 010, stop message. From Sub Officer James, stop, for the same address. Timber garden shed and contents severely damaged by fire, hose reel and two BA. 010, over.*'

'*Alpha 010 your stop message received, timed at 0735, out.*'

'OK boys, get it all back on the motor and let's get back for a nice cuppa.'

'Right Mick, let's see if we can get back this time, I'm parched,' Mac said.

Taff leaned forward in the cab. 'Turn the bloody radio off, then they can't get us.'

'That sounds like a good idea,' Mac laughed, 'but it'd be me that would have to explain the sudden loss of radio signal.'

'*Alpha 010 are you receiving, over.*'

'*Yes control loud and clear, over.*'

'*Alpha 010 proceed to the Northern General Hospital, automatic fire alarm actuating, over.*'

'*Thank you control, we are mobile to the Northern General Hospital,*' a sound of resignation registering in Mac's voice.

Mick pulled hard on the steering, making the tyres squeal in protest as they swerved around the roundabout. They thundered down the hill as the city below began to come alive; the traffic was now becoming busier, they heard other mobiles on the designated first attendance for the hospital booking mobile.

Mick juggled the machine expertly through the traffic crossing the Parkway roundabout at speed, the lights flashing and the wailers sounding; most of the traffic managing to clear a path for the appliance. They sped down toward the Wicker. As the nearest appliance to the incident booked in attendance, Mac relaxed. Usually these calls were false alarms, and after so many recently it was easy to become complacent. Mac looked across at Mick, who drove expertly, but like many drivers sometimes the supposed urgency of the call and the sound of the wailers got to the driver.

'OK Mick, let's steady it down a bit, we should get a message back soon.' Mick relaxed and took his foot off the pedal, just a shade, but still made fast progress.

'Control from Charlie 210, over.' Mac cocked his ear and listened.

'Control, alarm actuating, mechanical defect, other appliances not required, over.'

Mac breathed a sigh of relief, 'OK Mick, take me home. I need tea and toast.'

It was eight twenty when the Graveton appliance pulled up at the back of the station.

'OK lads, get it sorted. Jake, mess deck, tea and toast.'

The watch sat around the mess table, as the sun streamed in through the window.

'It looks like it's going to be another nice day,' Taff said, as he stuffed a large wedge of toast into his mouth.

'Dya know, Jake, I'm getting used to burned toast. I'm beginning to acquire a taste for it.'

A few of the day shift wandered into the mess room and sat at the table with Red Watch. They chatted about the night shift. The day watch leading fireman came in and sat next to Mac.

'How's it going, Mac? I reckon you must be looking forward to getting this all done with and having a rest?'

Mac smiled. It was a question he'd asked himself many times. There were days when it all seemed too much trouble, and other shifts where the old excitement still lingered. It was these days that made him sorry it was all coming to an end.

'You know, Alec, I've got mixed feelings about it; after thirty years you would think you'd get bored, but I never have. I get tired, I suppose age catches up with us all in the end, on the other hand I'm sure there's life after the job. I'm going to sign up with the rangers in the Peak Park, so a new interest and a lot of stuff to learn.'

'Well, you know this lot will miss you, don't you?' he said. 'From what I hear, your retirement do is going to be a pretty good one.'

Mac smiled at him.

'Nothing much to hand over. We've been in and out so the machines have been re-stowed and the BAs have been serviced, but we've not had chance to do any cleaning up, sorry about that.'

'No worries, we'll sort it out, Mac.'

After the change of watch, Mac stood in the locker room. The poem his dad had given him all those years ago had been photocopied and stuck on the inside of Mac's locker door. He looked at it and thoughts of his dad streamed back into his mind. His mind wandered to his early years, to a fire in the steelworks at Shepcote Lane.

He was at Darnall. His dad was on the same watch but at Division Street, so there was always the possibility that they would meet up at shouts in the city. The fire involved a large container of quenching oil, the flames shot thirty feet in the air on the inside of a huge corrugated foundry. When control got the call, three machines were mobilised, two from Darnall and a backup from Division Street. They set up ready to attack the fire and had only a short while to wait for the third machine to arrive. The heat being given off made all the crews crouch low. This was a familiar job for these firemen, this was their stock-in-trade; unique almost to these stations in the whole of the country. Mac's boss Station Officer Wally Walters had the equipment positioned and waited. They were happy and confident, it had been done a hundred times before, they all were aware of the potential dangers of dealing with large oil fires, but the dangers actually showing themselves was a rarity.

Mac was crouching low beside Danny Flanagan, a crusty old-timer who was rapidly heading for retirement, and wasn't about to do anything that would cause him to lose his pension. 'You stick with me, boy. And keep your bloody head down.'

Mac could feel the rumble of the oil as it heated and boiled, the dense smoke being driven into the roof of the foundry. The heat was something far beyond Mac's previous experience; he was now beginning to really understand what his dad had been experiencing all those years. The Division Street backup appliance arrived amid the loud ringing of bells and the roar of its diesel engine. Mac looked around. He saw the crew dismount, then his dad appeared from around the side of the machine, running with a foam branch tucked under his arm and a length of 70-millimetre hose trailing out behind him. Mac felt his chest swell with pride. This was his greatest ambition being fulfilled, he was going to fight this fire with his dad.

ADO Alan Coglan arrived at the job and assumed overall control, then on the signal from him three pumps and three large foam branches began delivering thousands of gallons of foam across the surface of the boiling oil. Initially there was little change in the fire's intensity, just the occasional eruption of oil as the water held within the foam boiled, expanded and threw out small pockets of burning oil. Mac was backing up his partner, supporting the heavy water-filled hose and ensuring that the tube which fed the concentrated foam into the water stream was maintained. He looked across at the other firefighters who were involved, straining to maintain the steady stream of foam. He caught his dad's eye; he looked across at him, smiled and winked. Mac lifted his head and grinned back. It was a moment that was burned forever in his memory.

Mac was jolted back to reality as the station telephone rang.

Alec said, 'I'd better go and get that, Mac. I'll see you in the morning.'

'Yeah, OK Alec, have a quiet night.'

'Chance would be a fine thing,' he said, as he jogged easily out of the locker room.

Mac climbed into his old Volvo and drove out of the station yard. He stopped at the road junction to wait for a gap in the traffic. Looking in his mirror, he could see the night crew moving around doing their routines, routines that would continue ad infinitum, long after he had left the scene. He could feel the sense of sadness entering his body; this was something that he would not be doing for very much longer. As he drove the now familiar route home he reflected on things. He remembered now the look of loss on his father's face when he retired from the job. Mac felt it hard to understand at the time, but now, for the first time, he was very aware of how he must have felt. The fire brigade had been his life, all of his friends; all of his, and his mother's social life had been centred around fire stations. His dad didn't have the luxury of going onto something else after he retired. He was worn out; all the years of eating smoke, the unsocial hours, working long, hard shifts for peanuts, had taken its toll. Things were very different now, Mac had a whole new life ahead of him; his health was good, and he had a purpose: more time with Val, doing their own things. Mac joining the rangers was something he was really looking forward to. He was also looking forward to having more time with his daughters; they were grown now, but still needed his time and expertise more often than Mac sometimes appreciated. So, despite the wave of sadness and trepidation he was feeling, it was somewhat tempered by his excitement for the future. In his mind, he had a plan for the immediate future. A holiday in Scotland, or more specifically Skye. They had been several times over the years but each time it had seemed to go too quick. This time they would have longer to tour and relax and take it all in.

CHAPTER 14

Mick Young got home and quickly changed into his casual clothes. He'd arranged to meet his girlfriend Paula in town, and the plan was to do a bit of shopping, have some lunch and just spend a bit of time together between his shifts.

His phone rang.

'Hello.'

'Hi Mick, it's me.'

'Hiya, I was just going to come over and get you.'

'Yeah, well that's OK but I don't fancy shopping. How about we go out somewhere, have a little walk, and maybe have a bite out in Derbyshire somewhere?'

Mick smiled to himself. He disliked shopping, and getting out into the countryside was a much better prospect.

'OK, get your walking shoes ready, I'll be there in ten minutes.'

Mick powered the car up from the prominent rock that everyone knew as the Toad's Mouth, the roof of his convertible down. Then he took the right-hand bend and the surprise view confronted them. The whole of the Hope Valley lay out before them, the sunshine creating shadows on the distant hillsides making for a spectacular sight.

'I never get tired of turning that corner,' Mick said, as he turned and smiled at Paula. As he drove downhill the views off to their left were spectacular, then he turned sharp right, up the narrow road which exposed the views of the rocky escarpment of Stanage Edge.

'I love it out here,' she said. 'I remember Mum and Dad bringing us on Sundays on the train; we had a picnic and did a bit of walking, it was lovely.'

'I reckoned on parking up at Burbage Bridge and just doing a short walk across the moor, and just lazing about for a bit,' Mick said, his hair being buffeted in the wind.

The car park at the end of the Burbage valley was half filled with a mixture of cars and vans, some from organisations which brought disadvantaged or disabled children out into the Peak to experience the outdoors. Mick pulled into one of the few remaining spaces.

'Well, here we are,' he said. 'I fancy having a stroll over there,' he said, pointing in the direction of the craggy escarpment. 'Do you see that big rock on the end? It's called the Cowper Stone. It should be nice to sit there in the sunshine for a while.' Mick threw the small day-sack over his shoulder, which contained a couple of cans of fruit juice, some biscuits and a blanket to sit on.

'Come on then, let's go,' he said, grabbing Paula's hand and walking quickly across the tarmac road. The prominent track trended gently upwards across a large area of gorse moorland. The walking was easy, Paula threaded her arm through Mick's and they chatted easily.

'What was it like in the army, Mick?' Paula asked.

Mick turned his head to look at her. 'What makes you so curious about that?' he replied.

She pulled her arm tight, drawing him closer to her.

'Well, young man, I've not known you very long and I only know you through the fire service, and want to know more about you.'

The wind blew lightly across the moor and caught her long, dark hair, blowing it across her face. Mick stopped and pulled the hair away and looked at her.

'There's not much to tell,' he said, putting his arm across her shoulder. 'I did my time, spent a while in Ireland, that was OK; I liked the people there, the good ones that is.' He paused for a long few seconds. 'But Croatia was different. I've never seen so much hatred among people. Some of the things they did to each other... well, you don't want to think about. It was horrible.' He paused again. 'In fact, I hate thinking about it. I reckon that's what made me decide to leave the army.'

This sudden outburst shocked Paula; the sudden change in Mick's demeanour, almost like a dark cloud had descended around him, had taken her by surprise.

'I'm sorry,' Mick said, 'let's just forget about it and think about today.'

They walked, the mood now sombre. She looked at Mick and could see that his mind was somewhere else; in another place and time. She felt a wall of guilt begin to blanket her. She pulled herself together.

'Come on you rough, tough firefighter, I'll race you to the gate up there,' she shouted as she sprinted away from him; her laugh artificial, but hoping it would snap Mick out of his present gloom.

Mick jumped. The sudden shout pulled him back from the dark place he had gone to in his mind; Paula was jogging tiredly up the track. He forced a smile and ran after her.

'Got you, you little minx,' he said, as he easily caught up with her. Putting his hands on her shoulder, she stopped and turned. She grabbed his face and pulled it firmly down to hers and she kissed him hard on the mouth.

Mick could feel the dampness of the perspiration on her face and the raggedness of her breathing. He pulled away and crouched, picking her up in one swoop.

'Right, young lady, I've got a special treat for you,' he said, laughing as he jogged easily with her in his arms.

They soon reached the end of the track, where it met with the base of the escarpment. Mick contoured to the right, heading for a huge gritstone boulder, scarred with horizontal fissures which had allowed ugly brown plants to grow from them.

'Here we are,' he said, placing her down gently on the ground. 'Let's have a little wander around and find a comfortable spot to have our lunch.'

They wandered around the back of the high block of grey stone, to be met by a further jumble of huge broken rocks, amongst which were small plateaus of smooth grass.

'This looks like a good place,' Paula said, sitting down on a slightly raised platform surrounded by smaller rocks. 'It's very private here,' she said, her face giving strong suggestions that the lunch could have more than one course.

Mick sat down beside her. 'I'm sorry about that earlier,' he said, as he began taking the food and drink from the small rucksack.

'No, I'm sorry for bringing it up. I hadn't realised how it had been for you.'

'Well, it's done now, forget it. Let's have lunch,' he said, forcing a smile onto his face.

Mac had changed into his gardening clothes, and with Val had decided to have a blitz; he was cutting the lawns whilst Val did the delicate tasks in the borders. The hover-mower buzzed and hummed as he walked back and forth, taking care to leave neat stripes on the grass. Mac was no gardener, but he did get immense pleasure from seeing it tidy and colourful, due largely of course to the efforts of Val, who would happily spend hours – as she would say – fiddling. Mac emptied the grass box for the third time and decided to make a cup of tea for them.

They sat on the old timber bench Mac had made from the recycled branches of a tree, and sipped at the drink. Mac dunked his digestive only to see it disappear into the hot tea.

'Oh bugger,' he said as he began fishing out the now soggy biscuit. 'Well lass, at last it's here,' he said, 'the last shift. It seems a long time since the first one.'

Val took his hand. 'It's been a good life, Mac; I wouldn't have changed a thing.' She squeezed his large, calloused hand. 'We've had the best life. We got the girls, they're all settled and happy, we've got our friends and now the commutation and the pension, what could be better?' She looked dreamily across the garden at the woodland which sat across the lane from their house.

Mac had a vision of his dad come into his mind.

He was just home from work. It had been busy at the station, they'd had about half a dozen calls, which had kept them on the go. Then the telephone call from Division Street, telling them that Mac's dad had left to go to the hospital.

'How's Mum?' he asked. He noticed that his dad looked tired and upset.

'She's in hospital, in the best place, she's very poorly son. I got the call at work this afternoon saying she'd collapsed in the yard while she was hanging the washing out, so I don't know. I got back from there an hour ago, she's still unconscious. We'll get on the bus later and go and see her, I've told Wendy; she's pretty upset.'

'I'll get changed, Dad, I'll go in and see her.'

Mac climbed the familiar steep, narrow staircase. He opened the door to his sister's bedroom. She was sitting on the edge of the bed looking blankly into space. Her eyes were red, she was trying hard to muffle the low sobs which emerged from her.

'Is mum going to die, Malcolm?' Wendy asked.

'I don't know. We'll go and see her soon, we'll know more then,' he said, trying to sound positive.

The old red bus chugged slowly up the steep, sloping roads which led to the hospital. Mac sat on a seat behind his dad and sister; he stared out of the front of the bus, noticing the steam being emitted from the bus's radiator, and wondering if it would reach the hospital before it gave up the ghost. He felt an overwhelming sense of sadness come over him and tears filled his eyes. Something inside him knew she wouldn't recover and things would never be the same again. His mother had been his comfort blanket for all his life. Just now it was beginning to dawn on him. He looked at the back of his father. For the first time in Mac's life, his dad, his hero, looked vulnerable. Mac stood up and rested his hand on his dad's broad shoulder.

'I hope she's going to be alright, Dad.'

'So do I, son,' he said, his voice for the first time uncertain and weak.

Visiting was finished; the nurse had come round and informed everyone that they should leave.

'You go home with Wendy, Malcolm; I'm going to stay a while with Mum. Look after her for me.'

Mac had an ache in his chest he couldn't shake off, his mind was filled with a whirlpool of emotions. He wanted to let it all out and just cry, to release the pressure filling his body. Mac's dad noticed his struggle.

'You need to be strong for both me and Wendy, Malcolm; always remember, your mum loves you both very much. I'll be home later.'

Mac had never heard his dad speak in such terms, and he realised now that this could be the end.

'Can I just say something to her, Dad?'

'Of course you can, son,' he replied.

Mac looked at his father, who appeared shattered, but seemed somehow to be holding himself together in an attempt to soften things for his children.

Mac stood by the side of his mother's bed. Her breathing was shallow, she was asleep, peaceful, it seemed. Mac wiped the tears from his eyes and leant over the bed; he stroked her hair and put his face up close to her ear.

'I love you, Mum,' he said, his voice wavering; then he kissed her cool, pale cheek. He imagined he saw her lips move, almost as though she was smiling. He stood and looked at her in an attempt to embed a vision of her in his mind. He realised then that he wouldn't see her alive again. 'OK Dad, we'll go now. We'll see you later.'

It was almost eleven o'clock; Mac had given Wendy her usual supper of Shredded Wheat and hot milk. He lay in bed; Wendy was asleep, worn out by the trauma and pain of the day. He couldn't sleep. He heard the door latch click downstairs. He jumped out of bed and went quickly down the stairs.

'How is she, Dad?' Mac asked, his voice unable to disguise the trepidation he was feeling.

'I'm sorry, Malcolm; Mum died about an hour ago.' He could tell by the look on his father's face that he was taking it hard. Mac had lost his mother, but he realised that his dad had lost the love of his life.

'Come here, son,' he said, motioning for Mac to come to him. They stood for several minutes just holding each other, Mac's sobs of grief seeming to reinforce his father's resolve to stay strong.

'Do you want another cup of tea?' Val said, her voice bringing Mac back to the present. 'Are you OK?' she said, seeming almost telepathically to realise that he had been daydreaming something which he'd found hard.

'Yeah, I'm fine, just mulling things over,' he said, but unable to rid his mind of the image of his father.

'Why don't we go down to the Bear for a bite of lunch, Mac?' Val suggested. She felt a bit weary after the effort she'd put into the garden.

'That, my girl, is a very good idea,' Mac said. 'Let's get a quick shower and get down there.'

The pub was pretty busy, atmospheric; a gentle rumble of mixed conversations filled the room, punctuated by the occasional burst of laughter. Almost all the tables in the lounge bar were in use. Val found a table as Mac sidled up to the bar.

'Hiya Glen, have you got something suitable on the menu for a couple of old codgers?' he said, his face stretched wide by the huge smile.

'I think I can fit you in,' he replied, 'what can I get you to drink, sir?'

'Just a little bit less of the sir, young man,' Mac said, licking his lips. 'I think that I will have a pint of mild and the good lady here will have a glass of white wine.'

Mac turned as he spoke, and noticed a movement across the room; a couple were just getting sorted out before sitting down on one of the richly upholstered red bench seats at the edge of the room. Mac focused on them; there was something familiar about the couple. His mind went back. It dawned on him and he felt a sense of pleasure. He'd seen the woman the other day when her kitchen had caught fire, the man who now sat next to her had a black bruise across the side of his face and a plaster across the bridge of his nose. They sat quietly for a few seconds, then the man made his way gingerly to the bar. Mac felt the soreness still in the knuckles of his right hand, and felt the conviction in his mind, that he had done the right thing by the woman and for Pete. He sat down next to Val.

Val said, 'It looks like he's been in the wars.'

Mac smiled inwardly. 'Yeah it does, doesn't it?'

Val spotted a subtle change in the look on Mac's face. 'How do you reckon he got that, then?'

'He probably banged his head on a door,' Mac said, a fragment of a smile forcing itself onto his lips.

Val had known Mac for a long time, she could read him like a book. She noticed now how he held his hand, and the look on his face, and came to a conclusion. She smiled to herself. 'I don't suppose that sore right hand of yours had anything to do with it did it, Malcolm?' she scolded.

'Why would I do anything like that? I'm an old man, retiring tomorrow you know,' he said, grasping her hand in his. 'What shall we have to eat?'

Paula poured the coffee from the flask into two plastic cups; the coffee was still hot and steamed freely in the cooler atmosphere.

'Have you planned your holiday yet?' Mick asked.

Paula turned her head and smiled, 'No, I was hoping you would invite me to go somewhere with you, where are you going?'

'It would be nice for us to go off together, but I've not got anything planned yet. Where do you fancy?' Mick asked.

'I don't know, you decide, I'm just a woman. Just make it somewhere nice.'

'OK, I'll keep you posted,' he said, giving her a smile. 'And by the way, I had noticed that you are a woman.' He laughed.

The sun was high and the breeze was gentle. They lay back, resting against the cool rock, the sun warming their bodies. Paula took Mick's hand in hers. 'I like you a lot, mister fireman,' she said, gently placing her hand on his thigh. Mick noticed immediately and felt the buzz of excitement flow through him.

'What have you got for the main course?' she said, her face now close to his.

He turned to her. 'OK, if I have to, what would you like?'

'Well I had a sample before, it was nice. I wouldn't mind a bit more of the same,' she said, as she began unbuttoning his shirt.

'Well go on then, you've talked me into it,' he said, as he began the slow process of loosening some of her clothing.

High above, drifting in the warm thermals, a buzzard surveyed the ground, searching for its next meal.

Maddie and Jim sat by the stream, where only a few months ago their burgeoning relationship had been so sorely tested. They sat on the grassy bank, dangling their feet in the brown tinted water. Henry, their newfound friend and pet, paddled stiffly in the water taking occasional gulps, quenching his thirst.

'It's been an interesting few months, Jim. Who would have thought we'd be here now on the cusp of our wedding? I just can't wait.'

Jim sat up straight. His life had been transformed; he was happy and relaxed, in the exact place he wanted to be. He was still almost overpowered by the feeling of awe that such good fortune had come his way. He knew he'd done nothing to deserve what he now had. One day he'd have to tell Maddie the full story, but that was for another day.

Jock had all but finished working on the extension to the house. It had helped that some of the lads from the watch had come along and given their time and energy to get the job going again, after it had stalled for a while. Fraser was doing well at the football club; it had somehow taken over their lives. They were happy, though. The father–son relationship had never been better, Jock's relationship with his wife was settled, and he'd had the chance to go back to being a doorman but had declined. He'd moved on from that, Fraser's career at United was now their first priority.

As he sat on a bag of cement in the garden his mind began to wander. Mac was finishing tonight. He'd been with him for years, he loved Mac and the boys, but he fretted, feeling that it was almost inevitable that things would change once Mac had gone. He found himself remembering his first shift with Mac. Of course, the crew had changed over the years, some of the old hands had passed away, the rest had retired, some moving away mainly to the coast – Bridlington or Filey being the preferred place to move to, it seemed. For a while, after each one retired, they would come back to the station and revisit their past, but their visits faltered after a while.

He'd been put as the middle man on the back seat of the machine; it wasn't long before the alarm sounded, and in what seemed like seconds they were out of the door and off up the road in a heartbeat. Jock's mind was racing, he wasn't sure what the call was they were attending. He felt his heart lurch as he saw the plume of black smoke drifting over the nearby rooftops, he remembered the excitement as the machine plunged back and forth, picking its way through the traffic.

Mac turned to him from his seat in the front. 'Jock, you get the hose reel off and put this one out, the lads will help.'

Jock remembered fondly how he raced round the appliance looking for the locker in which the hose reel was located. He slammed open the sliding aluminium locker door, grabbed the nozzle of the hose reel and ran almost blindly towards the fire. The bread van had smoke and flames issuing from the engine compartment. The driver, unfazed by it all, sat idly on a nearby garden wall, smoking his woodbine. Jock smiled to himself as he remembered the water hitting the fire and the large, stinking, dirty cloud of smoke and steam drifted on the breeze and completely engulfed the hapless driver, who very quickly relocated up wind on the fire. They were good days, Jock mused.

Jake and his mother were trawling through the suit shop. She'd decided that Mac's retirement function should be marked by her son with the purchase of a new suit, shirt and tie. Jake acquiesced, of course, and agreed that it would be a good thing to do to show respect for the man who had had so much influence on his life. Also, Antonella would be here – he wanted to look his best for her, too.

'I like this one, Jacob,' she said, running her fingers down the grey cloth. 'Why don't you try it on?' she said for about the tenth time.

Jake's patience was beginning to wane. He didn't like shopping but he rationalised that it was necessary, if only to make his mum happy, and to be fair she was pretty much always right. Jake went into the fitting room with a choice of three suits lying across his arm. He put on the grey suit first. It fitted perfectly. He drew back the curtain and his mother smiled.

'That looks very smart, son,' she said proudly. 'Have a look in the mirror.'

Jake smiled a smile of resignation. The suit she had bought him for his interview to join the brigade no longer fitted him. At eighteen and still growing, along with the physical nature of life in the brigade, he'd put on bulk, still very fit and strong but no longer slim, now more powerful. The jacket was too tight for comfort. Jake moved around. The suit felt comfortable; he looked in the full length mirror the shop had placed in a convenient position. To his surprise, it looked good.

He grinned. 'I like it, Mum; I think we'll have this one,' he said to the pale young shop assistant.

'Aren't you going to try the others on, Jacob?' his mother said.

'No. I like this one, any more will only confuse me.'

Ten minutes later, Jake and his mum walked arm in arm across the car park, Jake whistling happily. His mother looked up at her son. He'd changed. The last few months had caused a dramatic change in her son. He was no longer a boy; now a man, her son, and she was so proud of him.

Pete was in the kitchen of his house, peeling potatoes, getting ready for when the boys got in from school. There was a knock on the door.

'Hello, Brenda,' Pete said, 'come in, do you want a cup of tea?'

Brenda, his neighbour, had been a friend of Pete's wife for several years, and since Pete's wife's death she'd kept her eye on the boys until Pete got home from work, and latterly had had the boys stay at her house when Pete was on the night shift. Pete frequently offered to pay her for her trouble, but her answer was always a firm 'no thank you'.

They sat drinking tea in the conservatory at the back of the house. Pete had put the radio on and they talked in a neighbourly fashion about the boys and how they both missed Trudy.

Pete sat up in his padded cane seat. 'You know, Brenda, I'm very grateful for all the help you know.'

'Think nothing of it, Peter, you're a good friend, and I get lonely on my own sometimes. Having these times with you and helping with the boys is good company for me.'

'Well, just so long as you know I really appreciate the help,' he said. 'You know if there's anything you need, just give me a call.'

'I will,' she replied. 'In fact, I could do with you coming round sometime and having a look at the timer on my central heating. I tried to adjust it and now it's all over the place, I don't have a clue how to work it out.'

'I'll come round in the morning if you're going to be in. I'll pick the boys up from you; get an hour's shut-eye, then I'll be round and have a look at it.'

Brenda was a similar age to Pete; she was a larger than life character, a very determined woman with a strong mind of her own. She was a substantial woman with a significant head of bleached blond hair, very different from his late wife, who was tiny and very quiet.

'Well, Peter, I'll get off; I've got ironing piling up ,so I'd better get making some inroads into it.'

Pete opened the front door for her. 'Thanks for coming round, Brenda, I'll bring the boys round about half five if that's OK.'

'Yeah, that will be fine,' she said. Then, without warning, she leaned forward and kissed Pete on the cheek. 'Bye then, I'll see you later,' she said, with the slightest hint of a smile on her face.

Pete was slightly shocked. The feel of her lips on his cheek had affected him; he felt a mild buzz in his head. He could smell her perfume. He put his fingers where her lips had touched him and then saw the lipstick on his fingers. He put his fingers to his lips and tasted the taste he'd not experienced for a long time. He felt hot, and at the same time guilty, as if he was already being unfaithful to his wife.

Mac stood in the shower, allowing the hot water to pour over him; he rubbed soap into his hair and allowed his mind to drift.

He was standing outside the cinema, waiting to meet Val on their first date. He wasn't particularly interested in the film, but more in getting to know the girl he'd met only a week ago at the dance he'd gone to with Freddie. He'd made an effort; he'd shaved and slicked his hair back with a good scoop of Brylcreem. He felt groovy, the word of the day, the modern youth with his tight trousers and sleek jacket. He stood for about twenty minutes and was beginning to wonder if she was going to stand him up. He lit another cigarette. He'd not long since started smoking, much to his dad's annoyance, who would chastise him every day.

'It'll not do you any good, Malcolm, pack 'em in before you get addicted; you get enough smoke at work.'

Mac resisted, it was the thing to do; he would have been the odd one out on the watch if he'd stopped. It was the watch convention, after drill: have a fag, tea break, have a fag, come out of the fire, have a cough and then have a fag. Mac could see his dad's logic, but he was keen to fit in on the watch. He was just about to leave, thinking that Val had had second thoughts about the date; he stubbed out the cigarette on the floor and started to turn to leave when he heard her.

115

'I'm sorry I'm late,' she called, as she tried to run in her tight-fitting dress and high-heeled shoes, which clattered loudly on the pavement as she ran. 'The bus got a puncture so I had to wait for the next one, and I didn't think you'd wait too long.'

Mac breathed a sigh of relief. 'No, I thought you'd be here,' he said, taking care to hide the anxiety he'd felt.

'You look smart,' she said, running her gaze up and down over his body. Mac smiled.

'So do you,' he replied.

They watched the film in silence, neither taking in what was on the screen, it was more a case of mulling over in their heads what the reaction would be if one took hold of the other's hand. Val gave in, and putting her hand across she grasped Mac's hand tightly. Mac showed no reaction other than to smile to himself, feeling the warm sensation of her small, smooth hand encased in his large, calloused fingers.

The film was over; they trooped out of the cinema, neither able to recollect what the film had been about, but happy that they'd been together. Neither said the words, but they knew; words weren't needed. Mac had known the previous week that he really liked her. Val was less sure. She knew she liked him, he was a rough diamond but he seemed to have an ethic, a gentle strength; and respect, she liked that. The boys she had previously been out with had been blatantly after a bit more that a kiss, and often she found them to be childish and crude. Malcolm was none of these things. He was mature and thoughtful, the only thing she didn't like was his smoking habit.

'It's been nice tonight, Mac,' Val said, in a matter of fact way.

'Yeah, it's been nice; I didn't reckon much to the film, though.'

'Oh, I didn't think you were watching it.'

'No, you're right, I wasn't, but it was nice just being out with you.'

'Yes, it was nice,' Val said. It seemed that they both wanted to say something that was a commitment, but neither could say the words; hence there were a few awkward silences.

Mac eventually broke the silence. 'Would you like to meet up again sometime?' he said.

Val looked at him and smiled. 'That would be nice, how about the same time next week?'

'Where?' Mac said, his speedy reply giving away his enthusiasm for a further meeting.

'I don't know, shall we meet at the bus stop near my house, then ride out into Derbyshire?'

'Yes, that's a good idea; I've not been out there for ages.'

Mac was jolted back to reality when the water in the shower quite suddenly went cold.

Pete knocked on Brenda his neighbour's door. He could feel his heart thump inside his chest. The kiss earlier had somehow resurrected his thoughts about life after the death of his wife. His body hadn't reacted this way for a long time. Brenda opened the door.

'Hi Pete, have you brought those little tykes for me?'

Pete glanced at her and saw her in a way that he'd never noticed before. She was strikingly attractive; her long, dyed blond hair fell across her shoulders, her blouse was stretched tight, as was her dress, exposing her full figure to Pete, and Pete was now noticing. Before, these thoughts had not entered his head.

'Yes, they've had their tea; their pyjamas are in their bags so I think that's all. And thanks, Brenda, I really appreciate your help.'

Brenda noticed Pete's struggle, and how he looked at her. Where before she had just been a neighbour, now she felt that the kiss earlier had awakened something inside him.

'You get yourself off to work, and be careful.'

'I will, and thanks. See you in the morning, boys,' he said.

Brenda took Pete's hand, 'I'll see you tomorrow. Here, give me a kiss.'

Pete blushed, the blood pounded in his head. Brenda leaned against him and kissed him gently on the lips. 'Goodnight Peter, I'll see you tomorrow,' she smiled.

Mick and Paula lay quietly, the afterglow of their loving lasting as they stretched out on the soft grass sheltered by the mounds of splintered rocks.

'That was nice, fireman,' Paula said, rolling onto her side and planting a kiss on his damp forehead.

Mick rolled onto his side to face her, the muscles on his lean body shining with sweat in the late afternoon sunshine. 'I enjoyed it too, we should come here again,' he said, grinning widely at her. 'What time is it?' he asked.

Paula looked at her watch. 'It's nearly four o'clock,' she replied, a look of disappointment on her face. 'It's been a nice afternoon, thank you.'

'It's been a pleasure, but it's time we were moving,' he said, leaning forward and planting another kiss on her forehead.

The day shift at Graveton was mopping the appliance bay and leathering the machines down ready for the change of watch. It was twenty past five. They'd had a busy day, spending several hours washing and testing hoses, testing the rescue lines, and generally getting the station spotless in preparation for the weekend.

The alarm actuated. The young firefighter ran from the watchroom with the message from the printer in his hand.

'What have we got, Ali?' the officer in charge called, as they began getting rigged in their fire gear and climbing into the machine. The appliance room doors slammed open and the machine lurched out of the red doors. Several jackets and shoes were left randomly strewn across the appliance room floor, along with two mops and buckets.

'Control from alpha 010, we are mobile to City Road, over.'

'Alpha 010 received, out.'

Mac had showered and changed into his uniform. He was very conscious that this was the last time he would ever do this. He looked in the full-length mirror in the bedroom; he could clearly see that he'd aged. He looked at the clock on the bedside cabinet. He'd got plenty of time. He felt an almost overwhelming sense of sadness that the career he'd loved for most of his life was finally ending. He pulled open the wardrobe door and rummaged around until he finally found it. It had a stained, dark blue cover and the spine was split. But to Mac it was a most important piece of his life. He sat on the bed and began page by page to look through the old photo album.

Some of the old pictures were held in by triangular adhesive corner pieces; some now so old that their adhesion had failed and they were ready to fall off the page at the slightest disturbance. The first picture was of Mac as a baby; his round face split by a toothless grin, his legs kicking in the air. Mac turned the page. There was a picture of his mum and dad on the beach at Bridlington. Alongside it were pictures of his aunties and uncles, most of whom were long gone. He smiled; these were his days of innocence. There was a picture of Mac on his first little tricycle with his dad standing behind him. He smiled at the clothing his dad wore, a knitted sleeveless pullover, a shirt with no collar and wide-bottomed trousers with turn-ups. He turned the page again; a picture of Wendy, his sister as a baby in her pram. He turned the page again. He stopped and his heart swelled. It was a picture of his dad in his uniform, standing outside Division Street fire station with Mac as a baby in his arms; his dad looked so proud. He turned the page again. A picture taken in a photographer's studio of his mother, aged about eighteen; she was very pretty, Mac thought. He remembered saying goodbye to his mum on the night she died, and the feelings of that painful night re-emerged in him. As he turned the pages, memories of his life flashed into his head.

Then there was a picture of Mac with Wendy and Freddie aged about ten, scruffy with a mop of unruly hair, collars twisted around, dirt covering their faces. He smiled to himself and remembered Freddie, the boy he loved more than anyone outside of his family. There was a picture in colour of Mac, just home from work at the garage, still wearing his oil-stained overalls. He remembered his dad had just acquired a new camera. He turned more pages. There was a picture of the wider family, all gathered outside their house on his parents' twentieth wedding anniversary. Many of the faces, their names now lost to him. *I really ought to do a family tree*, he thought. Then there was a picture of his parents standing with Mac between them, Mac in his school

119

uniform, washed and shiny, with his life before him.

Val shouted up the stairs. 'Come on, Mac, your tea's ready.'

Mac put the photo album back in the place that he'd taken it from.

'I've just been looking through that album in the wardrobe.'

'Which one, there's a few in there?' she said, seeming to understand what Mac had been doing, and why.

'The old blue one. There's a lot of old family pictures in there. It just got me thinking, now I'm going to have a bit more time on my hands I might have a go at doing a family tree.'

Val looked up at him. 'What's brought this on? I've not noticed you being interested in that before.'

Mac screwed his face up as he looked at her. 'I think it must be what's happening now. It's made me feel a bit nostalgic, and looking through that old album... well, it just got me thinking. There are relatives there that I sort of recognise, but don't know who they are.' He paused for a second. 'It would be a shame if our girls forgot who their ancestors were, so I thought it would be an interesting thing to have a go at.'

Val grinned at him. 'Well, I'm sure it will be a good thing, but I'm not sure when you'll find the time, with the rangers and the regular calls for DIY help from the girls.'

They sat and ate the rest of their meal in silence.

Mac sat alone at the table. Val was in the kitchen, making a cup of tea. He could hear her singing; a song that he recognised from their early days together. His mind drifted back to those times.

He was there, sitting next to Freddie. It was midterm for Freddie. He was home from college, and they'd gone for a walk, setting off from Cavedale in Castleton and climbing high up the steep, stony track to reach the top of the dale and into the sunlight. They'd stopped for a breather halfway and had spectacular views across the valley. They talked about the origins of Pevrill Castle, which sat on top of the gorge where they rested, leaning back against the steep, grassy bank.

'So what's college like, Freddie?' Mac asked.

'It's OK. I like the study, and the teachers are fine, but some of the people there are...' he paused, 'well, let's just say my sexual orientation doesn't sit well with some of them.'

Mac was shocked. 'What, I thought that people these days were more understanding, especially students?' Mac said earnestly.

Freddie shrugged. Mac noticed the pain in Freddie's face.

'I'm really surprised, you get on with everybody. Sod 'em, Fred; don't let them get to you.'

'That's easier said than done,' Freddie said, wistfully, 'there's only a couple who are a problem, the rest are fine about it; but it does sometimes play on my mind. It makes it hard to concentrate on what I'm supposed to be doing.'

They carried on walking; it was warm. Mac stripped off his shirt to expose his hard, tanned body, now covered with copious amounts of chest hair.

'Phew, it's warm, Mac,' Freddie said and followed suit, pulling off his shirt. Mac noticed his body. It was slight and pale; it was obvious that Freddie wasn't the madly active type of man. They strode along the worn bridleway with the land to their left falling away dramatically into the Hope Valley. To their right was a series of dry-stone walled fields, and beyond the ground rose into a series of round-topped minor summits.

'It's time for a break I reckon, Freddie,' Mac said, as he slid the rucksack from his broad shoulders and placed it by the side of the track. 'What will you have?' Mac groped around in the old khaki, ex-army rucksack that he'd had for years. He pulled out a brown paper parcel. 'You've got a choice,' Mac smiled. 'Egg or, let's see... egg.'

Freddie laughed. The worries he'd had at college, now he was back with his pal, seemed to be distant memories.

'Spoiled for choice. Better have egg then, before you scoff them all.'

'You're right there. Mum said, "Freddie likes egg sandwiches so I'll do plenty".'

Mac came back to reality when Val gave him his mug of tea.

'Are you daydreaming again?' she asked.

Mac looked forlorn. 'Yeah, I just got that last walk I had with Freddie on my mind, the one we did up Cavedale. That was the last time I saw him alive.'

'I know; you've been beating yourself up about that for years. You weren't to know what was going to happen.'

'I know, but there were signs there that I saw but didn't recognise.'

'You know, Mac, that's life. You can't live your life analysing everything; sometimes things happen, they go wrong. Freddie would be devastated if he knew how this has affected you all these years.'

'I know. I'm sure if he'd realised the impact it had on everyone, he would have thought again, or got it out of his system. I just feel helpless.'

'He was your best friend, Mac, that makes it even worse for you.'

'Yes, you're right, I'll just have to adjust to it. It's been years now, it's time I put it to bed.' He got up from the table. 'Well, I'd better start moving or I'll be late for work.'

He opened the front door, and stood. It was almost as though he was realising that everything he did tonight was being done for the last time. Even Val had sensed it.

'Come here, you,' she said, holding out her arms. Mac walked over to her. 'Give me a cuddle,' she said. 'This won't happen again.' She kissed him. 'I'll see you in the morning, don't go doing anything daft!'

CHAPTER 15

Mac's final shift

Mac climbed into the Volvo and sat for a few seconds. He felt strange. He'd done this a thousand times, but this was the last time. It was significant, and he knew it. He fastened his seat belt, turned the key and started the engine. He waved to Val, as he always did, and drove slowly from his drive into the familiar road, the beginning of his last journey to work as a firefighter.

Red Watch began to filter into the station. Brian was first in; he went direct to the watchroom and looked at the log book and the strip of paper hanging from the printer. 'What have they got, Bry?'

It was Taff, who had got into the station a couple of minutes after Brian.

'It looks like they've got some person trapped down City Road; I'll get in touch with Control, to see if they need a relief at six.'

The drive back to town for Mick and Paula was light-hearted. The afternoon had gone well, better than expected, and the sun had shone. They'd found a quiet place and done what young people in love do. Paula teased Mick by running her hands along his thigh, and kissing his ear. The traffic was heavy as he descended towards the city, there were school children standing in groups trying to cross the road. Mick was distracted and laughing; he looked across at Paula and began scolding her for messing him about.

'You should consider yourself very fortunate. Most men would be delighted that a virile young woman wanted to tease them,' Paula laughed.

'Ha ha,' Mick retorted as he turned his head back to the driving. His heart surged as panic struck. Ten feet in front of his car, a young boy was running hard in front of him, attempting to cross the road. A look of terror distorted his young face. Mick hit the brakes hard and dragged the aged steering wheel violently to his right, in an attempt to avoid the young boy. The car slewed around, the wheels squealed and a cloud of smoke erupted from beneath the wheel arches. Mick closed his eyes and gripped the steering wheel. Paula screamed as her head was swung to her left, against the rotation of the car, her head hitting the door window which shattered. Mick struggled to hold the car, and then he felt the crack in his wrist as the small bones dislocated. In a second, the car came into contact with a large metal lamp post. The side of the Rover buckled and stopped dead. Mick's head was driven into the door post. The car slowly came to rest. The wrecked vehicle was strewn across the pavement, clouds of steam spewing from the wrecked front of the car. The young boy stood shocked on the side of the road, holding his hands tightly across his face.

The watchroom phone rang. Jake answered it.

'Yes, just to let you know that the day shift will be back within twenty minutes, so no relief required. I need to speak to the OIC, please.'

Mac took the phone from Jake. 'Yes control, what can I do for you?'

'Well Sub, to let you know that one of your crew has been injured in a road accident on City Road.'

Mac was shocked. 'Who is it?' Mac said, swinging his head around, looking at the men on the watch, trying to ascertain who was missing.

'I'm sorry Mac, it's Mick Young. He was in his car with a young woman when they left the road and it seems that they hit a lamp post. They're both being taken to the Northern General.'

'Do we know about their injuries?'

'No, sorry Mac. We've just had the stop from the day shift, they'll be leaving the job any time now.'

'OK control, thank you.'

The watch had sensed there was something wrong, and had gathered in the watchroom.

'What's up Mac?'

Mac sat in the black watchroom chair.

'It seems this job they're out on is involving Mick and one other. Control didn't know the extent of their injuries, and they've both been taken to the

Northern General. Anyway, the day watch will be back in a few minutes, we'll get more information then.'

The Graveton appliance pulled in to the back of the station, and its crew disgorged, all looking pale and worried. Mac and his crew were there waiting to meet them, keen to find out what the situation was with Mick and his passenger.

'Hi, Dave,' Mac said as he met the officer in charge of the day shift. 'Tell us, how is he?'

Dave looked at them, obviously very well aware of the concerns they had about their colleague.

'We had to cut the pair of them out. I think Mick's got a broken collarbone and wrist, and some cuts and bruises. His girlfriend, Paula, you know the lass from Headquarters, not too sure. She was in and out of consciousness, she had a pretty bad head wound and a broken leg. I reckon they'll both be OK, but Paula's the worse of the two.'

'Thanks Dave, I'll speak to the DC about getting across to see them.'

Janet sat at the kitchen table. Duncan, her husband, had come home from his trip to London a couple of hours ago, and broke the news that he thought they should move south. This had come as a complete surprise to her. This hadn't been discussed at all, not at any time had there been any indication that he needed or wanted to move.

'Come on, Jan, it's not the end of the world. I've taken the business as far as I can here, we need to go south to develop and expand.'

Janet was silent, unable to think of the words she so needed to say.

'Well, what do you think?' Duncan said, realising that the prospect of moving had come as a shock to Janet.

'What do I think?' she said. 'You obviously don't care what I think. How long have you been planning this?'

'What do you mean, I don't care? We've been married all these years, of course I care.'

'Well, clearly you don't care enough to consult with me, or ask me what I think. Why on earth would I want to move?'

Justin stood up from the table. 'Well, just think about it. We'll talk about it tomorrow when you've calmed down a bit.'

Janet's heart beat loudly in her ears; she could feel the blood rushing to her face. She felt the anger rising in her. 'You think I should think about it, do you?'

'Yes.'

'Right; I've thought about it. I am not moving anywhere.'

'We need to move for the business to grow.'

'You may need to, I don't.'

'What are you saying?' he replied, now beginning to realise that Janet was going to fight him.

'Work it out,' she spat.

'Are you saying you won't move?'

'You're not completely stupid then?'

'I don't know why you're getting so upset; I want to do it for us.'

'Oh, thank you,' she retorted sarcastically. 'When you want to do things for us, that requires me to move house; up sticks and move 150 miles from where I live. You might consider how I feel about it before you start booking the removal van.'

'I've not booked a removal van.'

'Good, because I'm not moving, you move if you like.'

'Maybe I will.'

Janet was furious. She rarely got angry, but the fact that he'd assumed this was what they would do had really angered her.

'I'm not interested in your maybes. I'll get your bag and help you pack.'

Duncan was knocked on his heels. In all their years together, he'd never seen her react this way. He'd expected a bit of resistance, but what was happening now was way beyond anything he'd planned.

'Come on, Janet, it's not that bad. It'll be an adventure.'

'I've got nothing left to say to you. If you want to go, then go, but you'll be going on your own.'

Duncan too was becoming frustrated and angry, at his plans being usurped.

'I will go, and maybe I won't be on my own, you selfish cow,' he spat.

Janet reacted to the insult; she picked up a plate from the kitchen table and threw it. It narrowly missed him, bouncing off the door frame where he stood and shattering on the tiled floor. Her face was scarlet with rage, all thought of any reconciliation now gone.

'I assume from that statement that there's someone else around, then,' she snarled.

'So what if there is? You don't care.'

'Dead right, mate, I don't, so whoever he or she is, have fun. Just know it's going to cost you.'

Duncan was stunned at the turn of events; he had badly underestimated Janet's ability to resist him. Throughout their marriage, he was always the decision maker. Janet had drifted along by his side, undemanding, loyal and supportive. Now he had got a tiger by the tail and he was shocked.

Janet stood up. 'I'm going out, you just do what you like.' She snatched her jacket from the coat hook and marched determinedly out of the door, slamming it hard behind her.

The phone in the watchroom rang. Jake answered. 'Hello, Graveton, Firefighter Higgins speaking.'

'DC here. Let me speak to Sub Officer James, please.'

'Just a second, Sir, I'll get him for you.' Jake spoke into the PA. 'Sub. Officer telephone call for you.'

Mac trotted across the appliance room, where he'd been in discussion with Brian about training. Jake looked at Mac and mouthed silently to him, 'It's the DC.'

'Hello Sir.'

'Yes Mac, DC here, what are you doing about Mick Young?'

'I was going to call you, boss, we only found out a few minutes ago. We were hoping that we could fix it for us to get over to see him with the machine.'

'You should, I'll contact control and arrange a standby machine to cover. It's only right you go. Also, Mac, the girl in the car is Paula Townsend from

HQ. Mick will be at the Northern General, but I'm told that Paula, who has an head injury, will go into the ITU at the Hallamshire Hospital.'

Taff pulled the machine into a vacant ambulance slot, close by the casualty entrance at the Northern General hospital.

'OK Taff, if we get anything give us a shout on the radio. We won't be very long.'

The hospital corridors were busy. Mac and the crew walked quickly to the A & E department, where they spoke to the doctor in charge. They were soon standing in a curtained-off area, where Mick was in the final process of his treatment. His left arm was being supported by a triangular bandage and the small cuts on his forehead has been cleaned and dressed.

'So what have you been up to, Mick?' Mac asked.

Mick looked at his friends from the watch and hung his head. 'It was my fault, I got distracted and almost ran over a young lad who ran across the road. I had to swerve to avoid him.'

'Well, from what I've been told you're going to survive, but the collarbone will take about six weeks or so, so you'll be off the run for a while.'

'They've taken Paula to the Hallamshire. She's had a bang on the head and got a broken leg, I think.'

'Yeah, we were told that. The DC was going to get hold of her parents.'

'They'll blame me, I think,' Mick said, his face contorted in pain and misery.

'Don't you worry about that now, Mick. How are you getting home?'

'I was going to get a taxi.'

'Mac, we've got a shout.' Taff's voice came across on the radio.

'We've got to go, Mick; we'll be in touch soon, we'll see you.'

'What have we got?' Mac called across to Taff as he climbed into the machine.

'We've got a bedroom fire, Omdurman Street.'

Janet drove for a long time, her headlights bouncing back from the heavily foliaged roadside. She had no plan, just turned spontaneously heading nowhere in particular. Eventually she found herself in a small village, its market square deserted except for a few cars parked on the cobbled area in front of the small row of shops. She braked hard and turned, pulling up close by the other cars. She sat and reflected on the argument she had just had with Duncan. Somehow this had been a catalyst. She had had moments of doubt, small questions which had entered her head and then been instantly dismissed. She sat on a wooden bench, lost in her thoughts. The fish and chip shop on the corner of the square was still lit up, the woman owner was about to begin the process of cleaning up and closing. *I'll just have a fag first*, she said to herself. She stepped out of the door, clicked the lighter and lit the cigarette. She looked across the square and noticed a woman sitting on the bench looking troubled.

'Are you alright, mi duck?' she called out in her broad Derbyshire brogue.

Janet heard the call and sat up from her slumped position. She looked across at the woman standing in the door of the chip shop.

'Yeah, I'm alright, thank you.'

'Do you fancy a bag of chips?' the woman replied, intuitively knowing that Janet had a problem.

Janet's head was filled with a concoction of thoughts. A few hours ago everything was as it had always been: normal. The expectation, albeit unthought, was that she would spend the rest of her life with her husband. Now that had changed, his determination to move had triggered something in her that had lain dormant in her for years.

'That would be nice,' Janet replied.

'Come and sit here in the shop, mi duck. Do ya want a nice cuppa tea to go with it?'

'Yes please, that would be nice.'

Janet walked slowly across the cobbled square. The woman said, 'Come on inside love and sit down, I'll get you that cup of tea.'

The chip shop had a series of Formica tables and metal-framed chairs; the tables were laid with a neat tablecloth and salt, pepper and vinegar. The smell of the chips made Janet feel hungry.

The woman brought Janet a small mug of tea and a plate of chips. 'Get these down you, luvvie, you'll soon feel better.'

'Thank you, you're very kind,' Janet replied.

'Actually, I'm not. Most of the locals think I'm a hard case. It suits me, because I don't get groups of youths loitering around, I just give them a verbal thick ear if they get too lippy.'

Janet sighed and sipped her tea between mouthfuls of well-salted chips.

'The chips are nice, I feel a lot better now, thank you.'

'I'm glad,' she said. 'So what's the problem with your man then?' she said, smiling gently. 'Let's call it Dot's law.' She paused. 'I can see it from a mile away. Women like us give out a light that only we can see, it comes from bitter experience. I'm on my third marriage and this one's not looking too clever at the moment, either,' she said, a knowing smirk on her face.

Janet gulped down the last remnant of tea from the mug. 'Thank you, errr Dot? I'm grateful for this; it was just what I needed.'

The woman stood up and put her hand lightly on Janet's shoulder. 'Don't take any rubbish from him, luvvie. Be your own woman and sod him.'

'I've just one question,' Janet said.

'Yes.'

'Where am I? I just drove, so I haven't a clue where I am?'

'This is Longnor, near Buxton.'

'Oh, I've not been since I was a kid,' she said, a smile creeping on to her lips.

'Well dear, next time you're here, come and see me again, maybe have another bag of chips.'

'I'll do that; thank you for those words of wisdom, I'm very grateful.'

Janet climbed back into her car. She was now more certain than before of what she would do. She pushed on the accelerator and drove, heading she knew not where.

Mac hit the button to sound the wailers, Taff stepped heavily on the throttle and the machine powered through the city centre, heading for the fire.

The Western Estate comprises a series of terraced houses, each row having a tarmac yard at the rear. The light was beginning to fade in the eastern sky as Taff sped onto the estate; he wove expertly along the narrow terraces, occasionally brought almost to a standstill by cars parked on both sides of the narrow roads. Mac sounded the wailers sporadically as they approached the fire. They could smell the smoke, a thick cloud of dense black smoke filled the street. Jake looked intently into the smoke-choked street, and suddenly his mind went back a couple of months, to the night where he'd risked it all and almost lost everything.

'Right, listen,' Mac called to his crew. 'Jock and Jake, get in there, round the back. Pete, you get a hose reel out for them. We know the layout, hit it hard and fast.'

Taff screeched to a halt just past the house, leaving the pump bay of the machine adjacent to the passageway giving access to the back of the houses. He slammed the pump into gear and pulled open the tank valve, allowing the water from the tank into the pump. Pete sprinted up the passage, dragging the hose reel behind him. Jock and Jake started up their BA sets, checked their gauges and slid their completed tallies into the control board. Mac checked them and sent them on their way into the house.

'*Control from Alpha 010, in attendance Omdurman Street and informative message, over.*'

'*Go ahead, over,*' came the instant response from control.

'*Two-storey terraced house, first floor well alight, hose reel and two BA in use, over.*'

'*Your informative message received, out.*'

One minute later, a second machine booked in attendance.

'*Alpha 020 in attendance, over.*'

'*Zero two zero, received.*'

The officer in charge of the Billing machine came across to Mac. 'What do you need?' Sub Officer Henry said.

Mac had recently had cause to have strong words with Henry. It was something that neither one had forgotten, but for Mac this was now and it was business, so it was put to one side.

'Right, Sub. Get your guys; I want a ladder up to the front bedroom window, and a jet in there to back up my BA team, OK?'

Mac grabbed a neighbour, who was casually standing watching the action.

'Do you know if there's anyone in there?' Mac asked, peering into the face of the middle-aged man, who seemed to be a bit the worse for wear with booze.

The neighbour leered at Mac. 'They're away on holiday in Spain. They think they're better than anyone else around here, a right couple of cocky snobs.'

Mac hadn't the time to spend with him. 'Thanks,' he said, as he darted away to organise the firefighting. The Billing crew were sliding the nine-metre ladder from the roof of the appliance, and getting hose laid out along the roadway. Taff was setting into the hydrant, having charged the hose reel with water ready for the BA team. By now, flames had begun to erupt through the roof slates above the window of the front bedroom, blasting heat out into the roadway.

Jock sent Jake back to the machine to get a crowbar to spring the back door.

'Are you ready, Jake?' Jock asked, turning to his young partner.

Jake grinned. 'Yep,' he replied

'OK.' Jock slammed the crowbar into the door frame. 'Right, Jake, lean on that. I've got the hose reel ready.'

Jake pressed his weight hard against the crowbar and it easily prised open the door. A blast of furnace-like air funnelled out into the yard and disappeared over their heads as they ducked low. Then there came the dense cloud of angry smoke-filled fumes, and the sound of crackling, burning timbers.

'OK Jake, let's go,' Jock called back.

They crouched low, protected from the worst of the heat by their heavy fire gear and flash hoods. They felt the draught of cool air being drawn into the fire around their legs. The visibility in the kitchen was OK, the smoke was moving in a thick layer across the ceiling, Jock opened the nozzle of the hose reel to send out a wide spray and swirled the fog-like water around the room. The fine mist of water rapidly absorbed the heat; instantly they were enveloped in a cloud of steam, but there was a noticeable fall in the temperature of the room. They moved forward, fast and low. Jock took off a glove and felt the door which opened up onto the staircase. It was hot; they could see the paint of the door blistering and knew they had a hard few minutes to face. Jock knelt low and carefully opened the door. They saw that the whole of the staircase was involved in a severe fire. Jake gulped hard and steeled himself.

Jock turned to Jake, his face taut and red with effort. 'Right, young Jake, time to move. Keep low.'

Jock pulled the lever of the hose reel branch and delivered a wide arc of high-pressure water into the flames. They climbed the stairs fast, Jock driving the flames ahead of them, beating a pathway to the first floor of the house.

The Billing crew had pitched a ladder against the windowsill and were preparing to deliver water in through the window. The firefighter on the top of the ladder had locked his leg through the rounds and fed the hose over his shoulder, and was delivering water into the flames. Jock and Jake got to the head of the stairs, turned and crawled fast into the heat of the upper floor of the house. The ceiling had collapsed and the contents of the roof space were sporadically plunging into the bedrooms, along with electric cables which hung menacingly across their path. Then there were streams of water beginning to pour out of the loft as the pipework began to fail. Jake and Jock were both being drenched in a concoction of water and plaster dust. The fire was rapidly being quelled, the jet coming in from the front window allied to the water being delivered by Jock and Jake soon made the environment more comfortable. In fifteen minutes the fire was finished. There were just a few pockets of smouldering embers in the hidden places in the roof space, which were quickly dealt with.

'Control from Alpha zero one zero, over.'

'Alpha zero one zero go ahead, over.'

'Control from Alpha zero one zero, stop message. From Sub Officer James at 17 Omdurman Street. A two-storey mid-terraced house, slate roof approximately five metres by ten metres. One hundred per cent of the first floor and ten per cent of roof destroyed by fire. Ground floor damaged by smoke, heat and water. Two jets and two BA in use. Alpha zero one zero, over.'

'Alpha zero one zero your stop message received, control out.'

Mac told the Billing crew to return to their station, thanking them for their work. The Billing officer in charge walked over to Mac.

'Well, Mac, I guess this will be the last time we meet up on the fireground. I just wanted to say to you that there are no hard feelings. You've been a credit to the job, and despite everything I'll be sorry to see you leave.'

Mac was taken aback. Henry was someone he had never got on with, but he decided that maybe now was the time to let bygones be bygones.

'Well, thank you for that, I'm sure I'll miss the job.' Mac leaned forward and offered his gloved hand, which Henry promptly took.

'Good luck, Mac,' he said, glad that at last they were able to put the previous animosity behind them.

Red Watch spent another twenty minutes damping down and attempting to work out what the cause of the fire had been. They knew it started upstairs, but here was so much damage that to be certain was almost impossible.

'What are you going to put as a cause on the fire report?' Brian asked Mac.

'Not too sure. It's only a supposed cause, it could have been electrical. There was a lot of wiring in the back bedroom: TV, computer, music centre.'

'Yeah, guess you're right there, not really much else to start a fire.'

'Tell you what, Brian,' Mac said, 'you get the details and you can help me do the report later.'

'Alpha 010, mobile to home station, over.'

'Alpha 010, message received, out.'

Mac sat in the front of the machine. He could hear the chattering of his crew and the rumble of the diesel engine, but somehow he felt far removed from this place. He became aware that if they got no more calls during the shift, that was the last fire he would ever go to. Mac strained his ears to listen to the chatter in the back of the machine as Brian, Jock and Jake talked about the fire, his head a mixture of nostalgia and pride.

'So, what did you reckon to that, Jake?' Brian asked.

Jake's voice sounded very young to Mac, but he knew this young man was a good man. He hadn't been wrong that day on the moors, when he had made an instant evaluation of him.

'I loved it, Bry, but then I love all of it. Even making the tea and you lot taking the piss out of me.'

'OK lads, let's get the motor re-stowed and inside for a nice cup of tea.'

As Mac climbed out of the machine he spotted a couple of cars parked in the yard. *I know those cars*, Mac thought. He walked into the back of the appliance room.

Leaning against the white tiled wall were two figures, smiling broadly.

'Well, you two are a sight for sore eyes,' Mac laughed and walked across to them, grabbing their hands.

'We thought we ought to pop in to see you, Saturday night could be a bit busy. How are you feeling, Mac?'

'Better for seeing you, Ray. How long have you been back? How was the camper van?'

Ray had been Mac's leading fireman, but he'd had to retire early because of a heart condition.

'We had a good time, we saw most of France and part of Germany, but it's nice to be back home.'

'So what brings you here?' Mac asked his old friend.

'Well, I was missing home, and strangely missing you and the job, so I thought I'd call in for a chat, get the latest scandal.'

'Well a lot's happened; in fact, we were at the hospital when we got the call to this last fire. Mick Young and his girlfriend were hurt in a road accident tonight. He's at the Northern General, broken collarbone and some cuts and bruises, so he's going to be off for a while. How are you fixed if we get short? We've got a new lad on the watch. Jake Higgins got "best recruit of the year" at training school.'

'Well, we're looking forward to Saturday night. I guess it will be pretty crowded, from what I hear,' Ray said. 'It'll be nice to meet up with the boys and have a chat.'

'And Tony, it's nice to see you back here again, have you missed us?' Mac said, shaking the hand of Tony, who had been on Mac's watch but had transferred out, getting promoted at Divisional HQ. 'The lads will be pleased to see you; they've been at the mercy of Brian since you left. And you probably know he's applied for a job in Training School, so he'll soon be moving on. Nothing stays the same for long. So, I think that now would be a good time to have a chat with the lads, don't you?'

Twenty minutes later, the watch were all crowded around Ray and Tony on the mess deck, having re-stowed the machine and recharged the BA cylinders. They all sat round the white Formica dining tables, resting their elbows and chins supported in their cupped hands.

'Well lads, maybe it's the right time to clear things up,' Mac said, looking at Ray and Tony. Tony looked at Mac sheepishly.

'I want you to meet your new Sub Officer. As from next tour, Tony, or should I say, Sub Officer Ellis will be your boss.'

There was an audible gasp, and then it was quiet for a few seconds.

Tony spoke. 'Well t-t-thanks for that f-fabulous wel-welcome, you b-b-bastards.'

'Na, it's not that, Tone,' Jock spoke up. 'It's great, but it's a surprise. We thought you were going the boring route to the top, yi knae, kissing the DC's arse, yi knae, or in FP sitting on yi backside and talking posh.'

'C-c-come on Jock, m-m-me talk p-posh? I have trouble j-j-just talking.'

'True,' Jock said. 'No, Tone, don't take it the wrang way, it's gunni be good tae have yi back.'

Mac sat back in his seat observing his watch. He knew that things would be OK after he left, his crew were the best. Now Tony was coming back he was sure that he was leaving it in good hands. They saw the headlights of a car swing across the window of the recc room. I wonder who that could be, Mac thought. In a couple of minutes, they heard footsteps coming down the corridor and the door swung open. It was the divisional commander.

'OK lads, relax,' John Blain said. 'I thought I'd just pop in for a chat and see how things are, and to see the Sub of course. Have you got any tea made?'

Jake got up out of his seat. 'I'll make some tea, sir; do you all want one?'

There was a unanimous 'yes' from the watch. John Blain sat with Red Watch, talking about the job and families and football. He now felt that he was an integral part of his division and the brigade.

'Right lads, I have to go,' he said, getting up from his seat. 'It's been good seeing you all again. Mac and Tony, can we have a chat in the office?'

They all settled down in Mac's office.

'Well, Mac, the final shift. How does it feel?'

Mac still had a general feeling that it wasn't really happening.

'Well, boss, the only way I can describe it is that it's a bit like an out of body experience. Because I know it's the last one I'm noticing every detail, in a way that I've never done before, almost as if I need to store it away for the future to look back on. It's weird.'

'And what about you, Tony, what reaction did you get from the boys?'

'Pretty much what I expected, s-surprise, a lot of p-piss-taking but generally they seem glad to have me back.'

John said to Tony, 'You got the job because you were the best candidate, it was nothing to do with the fact that this was your old watch. But mark my words, Mac has left a big pair of boots to fill, so give it your best shot. I'm sure you'll be fine.'

Tony felt a bit embarrassed by the DC's comments. 'I'll give it all I've got; I'm looking forward to the challenge.'

Mac looked at the DC and then at Tony. 'Let me just give you a bit of advice, Tony. Don't try too hard, but be consistent, be fair and honest, they'll respect you for that.'

'Wise words, Mac,' John said. 'You did really well at division, Tony, so no self-doubts, you're capable of doing the job well.'

The watch sat in the recc room, chatting to Ray; not having seen him much since his retirement, there was a lot to catch up on.

'So, Ray, how was the holiday? You seemed to be away for months?'

Mac sat back and relaxed. His last shift was underway and he felt somewhat detached from reality. He had spent hundreds of nights over the years, and had never considered how it would be on his last shift. He closed his eyes and almost instantly he was in his bedroom at home.

His mother and father were downstairs. Mac had been at work; he'd had a busy day, he was weary, the fire had been particularly hot and energy-sapping. He was reading when he heard a knock on the door downstairs. He heard his dad answer the door, then a woman's voice, but he couldn't hear the detail of the conversation. He heard the word 'Freddie' and then the tortured cry of a female voice. Mac stood up and a tremor came across his body, almost as though he knew it was bad news and it involved his friend Freddie. He made his way quickly down the narrow staircase. In the kitchen, his parents were comforting Freddie's mother.

'What's wrong, Dad?' Mac shouted, already certain that he knew the answer.

'Sit down, son,' his dad told him, 'just sit there a minute.'

Freddie's mother was almost in a state of collapse, and was sobbing uncontrollably.

'You go up to your room, Malcolm; I'll be up in a minute,' his dad ordered. Mac felt a wall of dread approaching. He didn't know the detail, but he knew it was bad.

'Up you go, son, now. I'll see you in a minute.'

Mac slowly made his way back to his bedroom with a heavy heart. He knew it was Freddie, he felt it almost impossible to control the desire to cry. The conversation he'd had with his friend not long ago had said a lot to Mac, but he'd not fully absorbed the possible consequences of the situation Freddie had spoken about. After a few minutes he heard the back door close and footsteps making their way from the house. He waited. He heard the stair creak as his parents came to talk to him about the conversation they'd just had with Freddie's mother. The door opened slowly. His dad came in, his face betraying his feelings. He sat on the bed alongside Malcolm.

'I've got some bad news, Malc.'

'It's Freddie, I know. What's happened?' Mac said, a heavy weight seemed to be crushing his chest.

Mac's dad put his arm around Mac's shoulder, aware that the message he was about to deliver would devastate him.

'Freddie's died, Malcolm.'

Although in a way Mac knew and had expected the bad news, his dad's

138

words hit him like a dagger in the heart. A massive feeling of grief swelled up in his chest and despite his efforts to stop himself loud sobs exploded from his body.

Mac's dad pulled him tight to him and held Mac's face into his chest.

'I'm sorry, Malcolm, there's nothing I can say. We loved Freddie like a son but you two together were special.' Mac's dad wiped a tear away from his own face, clearly he was also very upset.

'When can I see him, Dad?' Mac managed to say, before another burst of emotion poured out of him.

'I don't know, son. I've spoken to his mother, and they're obviously devastated, so we didn't get to ask about the details.'

Mac's dad stood up. 'Right, son, I'll leave you alone. Your mum is upset as well, so I'll go to her now, and I am really sorry, Malcolm.'

'Thanks, Dad,' Malcolm said, managing to pull himself together.

Mac slept fitfully, images of the past sliding through his mind. The long, hot summer days spent with his friend, playing in the woods, making bows and arrows, chopping saplings down for the bonfire, knowing they'd be in trouble with the police if caught, attempting to mask the fact they'd just been felled by rubbing dirt onto the fresh cut timber. The messing about at school and being told off by the teachers, Freddie allowing Mac to copy his work. And Freddie's turmoil as he told Mac the secret that he was homosexual and Mac's surprising response. Nothing could alter their friendship. Not even lengthy separation, whilst Freddie was away doing his degree. When he came home they quickly fell back into their well-practised routines.

He dreamt about his last time with Freddie, the walk up Cavedale where Freddie had confided in him that he was being victimised by a few people at the college. In his dream, Mac felt a rage flowing through him, and he vowed that the people who had caused Freddie this pain, sufficient for him to end his life, would pay a price – and he would be the one to make sure it happened.

Mac was startled; he sat upright. Had he been asleep, or just lost in his imaginings? The station was quiet except for the occasion distant voice. Probably one of the lads mopping the appliance bay, he assumed. Mac felt calm. He understood the nature of these thoughts which kept finding their way into his head. He laid his head back against the back of his chair and soon began to drift.

It was his second date with Val. They'd gone to the pictures and shared a bag of sweets and a tub of ice cream. The film was of no consequence. Mac was nervous, Val was reticent, neither confident enough to make any move that may offend the other. The film was coming to an end and Mac, unusually, was not sure of himself. The film ended, and as they stood up to leave their seats Val stumbled. Mac caught her hand, preventing her from falling. Once the move was made, their hands remained clasped together. They walked out of the cinema into the cool night air, both feeling happy to be together. This seemed to be perfect, the most perfect thing, and the most natural thing. It seemed to be obvious that they should be together. They stood by the bus stop and talked about their daily lives, all the time getting to know each other better. The bus came and they climbed on board, the ten-minute journey flew by. Mac walked Val to her gate and then set off on the long walk home, all of his money spent. He visualised her face as he walked, the way she stood the way she spoke, how she looked at him and smiled the smile that told Mac that she liked him the way he liked her.

The station alarm sounded and Mac leapt up from his seat, and trotted easily down the stairs into the appliance room. The engine was running, diesel fumes were gathering in the bay as the doors swung open and locked back with a loud clunk.

'Where are we going, boys?' Mac asked, as he kicked off his shoes.

'Someone stuck in a lift in Sunnyside Old People's Home.'

Taff drove fast but safely. After a couple of minutes the machine pulled into the yard at the front of the home, the lights from the home delivering a warm glow into the evening's gloom.

'Jake, you get the lift keys. Taff, stay on the radio. OK, let's get in there.'

The carer in charge, a black nurse from Nigeria, met them as they entered the lobby.

'Thank you for coming so quickly,' she said, in her broad African brogue.

The crew knew the layout of the home and the whereabouts of the lift motor from previous visits they had made. Mac inserted the key into the slot in the lift door. The door slid open; he could see that the lift was stuck between floors, trapping two elderly ladies who appeared to be enjoying the attention of the crew.

'OK ladies, are you both OK? We'll have you out of there in two minutes,' Mac called up. 'Brian and Jake, you go to the basement. I'll tell you when to operate the valve.'

They made their way to the basement; it was a small room, kept very tidy. The only thing in the room was the lift motor. Brian asked Jake if he'd ever dealt with a hydraulic lift before. Jake shook his head. Brian gave him a brief description of the mechanism and what they would have to do when Mac called down to them.

'Right, Jake, when we get the call we open this valve. It lets pressure out of the pipe and the lift car comes down under its own weight, simple as that.' Brian showed him the valve. 'So when Mac calls, you open the valve slowly. Mac will tell us when to close it when the lift car is lined up with the floor upstairs.'

'OK Brian, open the valve,' Mac's voice echoed round the small room.

'Will do, doing it now.'

They could hear the sound of the hydraulic oil being forced back through the valve, telling them that the car was descending.

'OK, close the valve,' Mac ordered.

Jake closed the valve; they heard the gentle clunk from above as the lift car stopped.

'Right Jake, that's it. Let's go and say hello to the ladies.'

The two old ladies beamed at Mac as the lift gently came to a halt.

'I think, Iris, that we'll have to fix it to get stuck in the lift more often, and get these good-looking blokes up to rescue us,' she retorted, as Mac helped them out into the foyer.

'Now, ladies, are you unscathed?' he said, his face covered in a big friendly smile.

'We certainly are, young man, it was very exciting.'

'I'm glad you enjoyed it,' Mac laughed.

Mac climbed on board. Taff had the engine running.

'OK guys, let's get back.'

Taff accelerated away, leaving a cloud of diesel fumes hanging in the still evening air.

The sun had set behind the western London skyline; Antonella sat quietly, peering out of the window of her first-floor apartment. The lights of the city flickered as the starlings swirled and danced their magic patterns in the sky, opting for a roost for the night close by. She sat half awake. The work schedule for the week had been tough, and she was shattered. She sat back in her armchair and tilted her head back. Tiredness overcame her and she was soon in a deep sleep.

She was walking up Oxford Street, window shopping, when suddenly she felt a tug on her arm as a young man tried to drag her handbag from her shoulder. She instinctively resisted; he shouted something at her and pushed her hard, she fell to the pavement. The man persisted and dragged the bag from her hand. She was shocked, it had all happened so fast. She saw the attacker run away, so she shouted after him. Then there was a scuffle and she could see her assailant on the floor. A powerful young man knelt over the robber and held him by the throat on the floor, she saw him struggle and then saw the young man hit her attacker, and the mugger collapsed unconscious.

She spoke to her saviour. He was young, powerful and, she thought, the most handsome man she had ever seen. She spoke at length to his mother.

Then she was on the stage, playing her violin. Jake and his mother were in the audience, she saw them and smiled. Later they met in a public house, and later that evening she walked along the river hand in hand with Jake and they kissed; her heart was filled with passion and she knew instantly that she had met the person who she would be with forever.

Her bag was packed, she was on the train heading for Sheffield to meet Jake and his mother, she was so excited.

The phone rang and Antonella was jolted back to consciousness.

'Oh yes, is that Miss Garardi?' a female voice asked.

'Yes, I am that person,' Antonella replied.

'Oh, good. I'm Danni Cartwright and I write for the *London Girls* magazine.

'Yes.'

'Well, I understand that you were recently attacked in London, we hoped that we could speak to you about it and maybe do an item in the magazine about it. How you feel now, that sort of thing?'

'Oh, I'm not sure.'

'Well, we feel it would be useful. There are quite a few incidents like this every week in the capital, and we think your experience would be helpful in preventing other ladies suffering the same attacks.'

'Can I have think of it? I go away this weekend for two or three days, can you ring me again after I think about it?'

'Well yes, that should be OK, but we do want to do the item quite soon,'

'OK, contacts me middle of next week please, in evening, and I will talk to you.'

'That will be fine, thank you,' the reporter agreed.

Antonella hung up the phone. She trembled. The dream and then the phone call; it was all back firmly engrained in her mind again.

Jim laid back full-length on the sofa, his head resting on a cushion with his feet on the other arm, in his hand a can of beer. The TV was on. Henry had settled in with Jim very well. He also lay on the sofa, with his head resting comfortably on Jim's shoulder.

'Well, Henry, shall we go for a little walk then?'

Henry's eyes widened. He shook his head, appearing not too keen. He was comfortable. He'd had his dinner, which comprised half of Jim's chicken breast, a banana and half a Mars bar; he was content. The idea of walking on his painful legs was not something he was in a hurry to do. He turned his head towards Jim and wiped his large, pink tongue across Jim's face.

'I'll take that as a "no" then, shall I Henry?' Jim said, as he stroked the area between Henry's eyes.

Maddie was on the night shift and she was tired. She loved her work but sometimes it was tough, she always had a list of duties to perform, often with little sign of appreciation; but not always, some of the patients in her care were, as she described them, 'sweeties'. She was always sorry to see them go home, having spent a lot of time caring for them and listening to their worries and hopes for the future. Sometimes one of her sweeties would die and for a while she would feel the pain like any other human being. She was looking forward to a couple of days' rest, a chance to recharge her batteries. She'd be meeting Jim and they would probably have a walk and take Henry with them.

It was nine o'clock, and Maddie was on her break. She walked slowly along the highly polished corridor heading for the canteen, a welcome rest for twenty minutes or so.

The corridor was quiet, her footsteps echoing as she walked. She turned left into the corridor which would lead her to the canteen. Before her on the floor lay slumped a young man, who seemingly had slipped on his crutches. She walked quickly to him and knelt by his side. She was pleased to see that he was conscious. He wore the regulation hospital red-striped pyjamas, his face was contorted with pain; he had long, brown hair and was pale and gaunt.

'What are you doing here?' she asked.

'Not very much,' he replied, trying hard to smile through the pain.

'Well, I can see that,' Maddie said. 'Here, let me help you get up.'

'Thanks,' he said, looking closely into Maddie's eyes. 'Tell me I'm not dreaming. You're Florence Nightingale, aren't you?'

'I'm afraid that I'm not, I'm just a nurse, and I think I'll get you back to bed.'

'That's the best offer I've had all day,' he said as he winced.

'You hang on here. I'll go and get a wheelchair and get you back to your room,' she said, leaning him back against the white painted wall which was adorned with local landscape paintings.

One minute later she was back, and quickly helped him into the chair.

'Right, young man, let's get you sorted. What on earth were you doing out of bed?'

144

'I got bored; I've nothing to read, everyone else was asleep, so I thought I'd get a cup of tea from the canteen.'

'How did you break your leg?' Maddie asked.

'Fell off a rock, being a daft prat.'

'Oh yes, where was that then?'

'You probably don't know it. I was climbing on Stanage, trying a new route, but I'd had a lot of beer the night before and hence the broken leg.'

'What do you mean I won't know it? Me and my boyfriend walk out there nearly every week, I know Stanage pretty well.'

'I know that you're very pretty, in fact you are beautiful.'

'Cheeky man, I'm almost a married woman. And I know you rock climbers. We were on Higgar Tor a while back and watched some of your gang falling off a big overhanging rock.'

'That could have been me. I was there a few weeks ago with some of my mates, we were trying a climb called The Rasp, and it's a very tough climb.'

In that instant, the awful memory of the problem she'd had with Jim that day came back to her.

'Are you alright?' the young guy asked. 'You look as if you've seen a ghost.'

'Yes, I'm OK, just feeling a bit tired.'

'Well, I'm Dennis, and I thank you for rescuing me. I hope that we meet again,' he said, as she pushed his wheelchair into the ward and helped him back into his bed.

'It was nice to meet you too, but you do what the nurses tell you, they have a difficult enough job without you causing them even more problems.'

'Thank you, nurse Madeline, I will do as you tell me.'

'Good, the staff will appreciate that. Goodnight, Dennis.'

Maddie turned and walked out of the ward, and spoke to the nurse who by now had returned to her station, telling her that one of her patients had been returned.

The night seemed to be passing too quickly for Mac. The boys, now back from the shout, were getting the supper ready. His mind was swirling with a myriad of thoughts. He was on his last shift, and tomorrow it would all be over.

Mac's mind flickered from one thought to another, almost as if he was flicking through the pages of a photograph album.

He was standing by the gate of Val's house; they had just been on their third date. It was dark, Mac remembered Val telling him that she wanted to keep seeing him and he was remembering how he felt about the prospect of a permanent girlfriend. He pictured Val putting her hand on his shoulder and kissing him, taking his breath away, and telling her that he wanted to keep going out with her.

Just then his thoughts changed course, and he was on the fireground.

He had just emerged from the front door of a house which had been very badly damaged by fire. As he walked out he heard a crack, almost like a rifle shot, followed by a shout from somewhere, then the crushing pain as the gable end of the wall collapsed on top of him. He felt the pains in his left leg and immediately realised it was broken. Then his mates were around him, lifting timbers and bricks from his bruised body. Then there was old George the ambulance man, who told him not to worry. 'It'll be fine, young man,' he said. 'I'm here now to sort you out, so don't worry.' Those words stayed with Mac for the rest of his life. Somehow George had done something magical, and it took away the worry and stress of his situation. They had been friends ever since, albeit there was always a lot of banter between the two of them.

He was in the Northern General Hospital with his sister, standing by his father's bed. He hadn't regained consciousness for a couple of days and they were worried about him. There was the constant hiss of the respirator as his lungs were filled with oxygen, and then the crackle of mucus on his father's chest. The doctor had told them that he would not last too long now. There was a steady stream of old firemen who over the years had worked with his dad. He remembered the things they said about him.

'He was a really good fireman, one of the best.'

'You could always rely on him when the going was tough.'

'He was a hard man, but honest as the day was long.'

'The best firefighter I ever worked with.'

All of this served to reinforce Mac's opinion and respect for his dad, and made Mac want to emulate him the best he could.

He was standing by the exit from the college where Freddie had been so mercilessly victimised. Over the past few weeks he'd asked around and found out who the culprits were. Mac stood and waited, he knew who he was looking for.

It was five thirty in the evening. Two youthful-looking boys walked casually out from the building, Mac peered at them, making sure he had the right people. He followed them about twenty yards behind; the track went beneath a low railway arch. Mac closed in and jogged past them, then stopped dead and turned to face them.

They stopped; looking surprised, they asked what he wanted.

'Let me ask you something,' Mac replied. 'No, let me tell you something.' Mac paused, looking into the young, startled faces of the boys. 'You remember a young man called Freddie Towner?'

'Yes,' they replied, a look of confusion spreading across their immature faces.

'Good. I'm glad you remember him, because I was his best friend.' Mac paused again and glared into the now shocked faces of his targets. 'I want you to understand what you did,' Mac said, his words fired into the faces of the boys. 'Freddie and me were born within a week of each other, he lived next door but one to me, we were friends from being in the infant school. We were inseparable through all our school days. Freddie was a nice lad, gentle, kind, he cared about people, he wouldn't hurt a fly.' Mac paused again. 'Because of that he got bullied. He wasn't the type to be aggressive or fight back, so that was my job. I looked after my friend Freddie.'

The boys' demeanours began to change; they noticed the subtle change in Mac, how he looked at them, the tone of his voice and the words he was saying. It began to dawn on them that they could be in big trouble.

'We had decided that when I got married he would be my best man, if I had kids he would be their godfather – that was the type of friendship we had. We were blood brothers.' Mac punched the brickwork close to where the boys

147

stood. This brought about the realisation in them that this man meant to exact some form of retribution, and their terror grew.

'Now, of course I always looked after Freddie, he was my friend and soul mate. Unfortunately, when he came here to this college, I was out of the loop. He was exposed and of course, as always, there are cowards. Yes, that's the word – cowards who decided that Freddie would be their victim, they would hound him until he felt that life was too hard to bear and so he killed himself.' Mac's fury was beginning to rise to the surface, his eyes were wide and spittle began to spray from between his lips as he spoke. 'Now, this is where you are going to help me. You do want to help me, don't you?'

Mac spat out the words as he went up close to the boys and glared into their terrified faces.

'Of course, yes of course we do,' one of the boys said, his voice shaking and his face contorted almost to the point of him bursting into tears.

'That's good; I thought I might have to force you to help me. So, tell me in your own words why; why you thought in your miserable little minds that it was alright to victimise and humiliate my friend? And I have to say, it had better be good.'

The boys stood unable to speak, their fear palpable.

'So come on then, you pair of—' Mac paused again. 'I'm sorry boys; I thought you said you were going to help me, so come on, let's have it. You must know in those feeble, demented, pea-sized brains of yours why you decided to victimise my friend to death.'

Mac's words now had a venom in them that hit the boys like a hammer. The younger of the two lost his bladder control and started to sob.

'Oh, I'm sorry, have I upset you? My friend Freddie, well, he would say to me "stop this", he would probably put his arm round your shoulder and tell you it was OK. Unfortunately for you, I'm not Freddie, and I'm telling you that it ain't alright.' Mac glared at the boys. 'So come on, tell me; why? I want to know, and so do his mum and dad. I don't suppose you even thought about it.'

The older of the two spoke at last. 'It was just a bit of fun, we never thought that it would get to this, we didn't hate him or anything. We're really sorry.'

148

'Well, I suppose if you're really sorry that makes it alright. Freddie's in his grave, his mum, dad and family are all heartbroken, I'm annoyed, and you're sorry. Do you think that puts it right?'

'No. Not really.'

'Well, just have a little think and then tell me how you can put it right.'

'I don't know,' he replied, his face anxious and staring vacantly into space.

'No, I don't suppose you do. I don't either. Freddie is dead, he will always be dead, even after you get married, do your jobs, have your own children – he will be dead, and you will always know he's dead because you killed him. So I've decided that you deserve to live, and I also know how you will.' Mac almost shouted the last word. 'You will try to put it as right as it can be.'

'Just tell us and we'll do it,' the boys said, beginning now to feel that maybe they could get out of this unscathed.

'Right,' Mac said. 'This is what you will do.'

'Supper's ready, come and get it,' the voice came loud over the station tannoy system. Mac sat up in his chair, brushed his hair back with his hands and made his way slowly down the stairs. The watch was getting ready, sitting in their usual places around the table, with the accompaniment of scraping chairs and a good deal of laughter. Brian came out of the kitchen, accompanied by Taff. They carried a tray each, stacked with two large pots of what was reckoned to be shepherd's pie. Jake jogged out to the kitchen and brought out a bottle of wine. Brian put the tray on the table and tapped a spoon on Jock's head.

'Can I have some quiet, please,' he said, a seriousness shrouding his face. 'Mac, we hope you don't mind, but as this is your last night with us as our gaffer we thought a little private party just for us would be good. Jake's mum fortunately has cooked the dinner for us, and we clubbed together to get a bottle of wine.'

'Yes, you tight git,' Jock said, 'we thought you meant you would get the bottle, not ask us all to help pay for it. And you say I'm tight. You should get a grease nipple fitted to your arse, to stop it squeaking,' Jock laughed.

Mac felt a warm glow cover his body, 'Right then, before we start I should say something.'

'Not too much, Mac, the pie will go cold.'

'No, I'll be quick,' he said, grinning at his lads. 'This is great, and unexpected. Just let me say that I appreciate every one of you, I'll miss this, the life in the job and you lot, but next tour nothing will change. Tony will be the boss, look after him. Keep being the best you can, make me and yourselves proud. That's it, I've got to save something for the do on Saturday.'

The cacophony of noise resumed, the clatter of plates and cutlery and the usual mockery of each other which typified life on Red Watch. In ten minutes the food had gone, along with the contents of the bottle of cheap red wine. The watch was in good heart.

Mac stood up and started walking, and then there was the familiar clunk as the station alarm actuated again. They all raced down the short corridor which led them to the appliance room. The machine pulled out onto the station forecourt, and they waited until the doors were closed before they left. The siren blared in the last remnants of daylight as the dull orange glow of light finally disappeared from view.

Mac turned, 'Get your sets on and started up boys, let's get at it.'

Jim stood by the entrance to his small apartment block, gazing absent-mindedly into the distance. Henry, Jim's pet Labrador, walked slowly around the bushes sniffing out anything interesting. In the distance he heard the faint wailing of an emergency vehicle, unsure as to its origin; maybe an ambulance or fire engine, he thought. Quite without any forethought, that night came back to his mind: the fear it engendered when the roof of the factory collapsed, almost killing some of the crew who were there fighting the fire that he had started. For months he'd been racked by guilt, soon after he met Maddie, the love of his life. Maddie had confided in him all her darkest secrets, probably expecting that Jim would reciprocate, but something inside him prevented him telling her about the fire. He felt the guilt wash over him again.

Maddie had been his saviour. He always felt that he was lucky that she wanted to be with him, he was fearful that given the right excuse she would change her mind. Maybe now would be the right time to unload all of this to her. She deserved to know the worst of him, before they were married. He thought he'd sleep on it and decide the next day.

Mac sat almost in a dream, as the machine flew at speed along the by-pass to yet another house fire. He'd lost count of the jobs he'd been to in kitchens, bedrooms, et cetera. Some still lingered in his memory; usually the hard ones, where people had lost their lives, or the funny ones. They stuck because they always became the subject of mess room chat. Mac remembered the one some years before, when they arrived at the address to find the occupant of the house running up and down the street in long, flowing women's clothes. Half of his wig had been scorched and he'd lost one of his high heels. The fire was only small, a chip pan on fire, but the sight of the transvestite lingered on the watch for a long time.

They turned into the estate. Mac gave the siren a blip, to let the homeowners know that they were close.

They were met with a small crowd of neighbours milling around on the pavement outside the terraced cottage, which was shrouded in smoke; a dull glow shone weakly out through the cloud of noxious fumes which was beginning to engulf the bystanders.

'Control from alpha 010, in attendance, over.'

'Right, hose reel off, let's go lads,' Mac called as he jumped down from his seat. He heard the clatter of doors slamming and metal lockers being slammed open.

Mac grabbed the arm of a middle-aged man who appeared to be the owner of the house.

'Is this your house?' he asked.

The man looked confused. 'Yes, it's my place,' he replied.

'Tell me,' Mac said firmly, 'what have we got in there?' Mac could smell burning flesh and his heart jumped. 'Is there anybody in there?' he said.

'No, it looked like it was going to rain so we decided to have the barbecue indoors. It flared up and it's set fire to the kitchen.'

'Right, so that's what I can smell is it, meat on the barbecue?'

'Yes.'

'OK, thanks,' Mac said.

Mac darted around the back of the cottage and called to Jock. Jake was the nearest to Mac, so came back the few feet.

'What is it, Sub?'

'Tell Jock it's a barbecue gone wrong, so hit it and then have a quick check around for spread. OK?'

'Yes, Sub,' Jake responded, and disappeared back into the smoke.

'Control from Alpha 010, over.'

'010 go ahead, over.'

'010 informative message; from Sub Officer James at same address, small fire in ground floor of terraced house. One hose reel and two BAs in use, over.'

'010, your messaged received, out.'

Jock and Jake found their way around the small terraced house. They extinguished the barbecue and damped down the damage to the worktops and kitchen units, and then they went up the stairs and opened the windows to ventilate the property. This small fire had caused a lot of smoke damage, and they figured it would be a substantial insurance claim.

Within the hour they had cleaned up the mess from the water and done what they could to reduce the impact of the fire.

'Control from Alpha 010, from Sub Officer James, stop message, stop for the same address. Small fire in kitchen of private dwelling, twenty-five per cent of ground floor severely damaged by smoke and heat ten per cent of first floor damaged by smoke. One hose reel and two BA. Crews involved in salvage work delayed approximately ten minutes, over.'

'Alpha 010 your message received. Control out.'

Mick Young sat quietly in his first-floor flat. He'd just come home from visiting his girlfriend in the hospital. The accident had traumatised him more than he had expected. His mother had taken him to the hospital. His injuries, the broken collarbone and dislocated wrist bones, were very painful and there was no possibility of him being able to drive for some time to come. He ran and re-ran the accident through his head many times, and on each occasion he came to the same conclusion: it was his fault. He had almost killed, or at least severely injured, a young boy because of his lack of attention and he felt a terrible guilt. His girlfriend was lying in hospital with a nasty head injury because of his failing; he was being overcome by guilt.

He switched on the TV and almost vacantly sat watching, not seeing what the programme was. There was a knock on the door. He jumped as the sound registered in his confused brain. He turned the handle and was surprised to see most of Red Watch standing on his doorstep.

'Just thought we'd pop in to see you, Mick. We were passing on our way back from a job. How are things?' Mac said, speaking for the watch.

Red Watch funnelled into Mick's small lounge and spread themselves around the chairs.

'You look shocking, Mick,' Jock said.

'Thanks Jock, you don't look too good yourself,' Mick replied.

Mac spoke up. 'How's Paula doing, have you heard?'

'Yeah, I've just got back, my mum took me over there and dropped me back.' He paused and wiped his hands across his face. 'She's a bit poorly. She had a nasty crack on her head and she could end up having a scar on her face, but the doctor said that she should make a full recovery.'

'Well that's good news, Mick. I'm sure it will all be OK in the end.'

'I feel so bad. It was my fault, I took my eye off the road for a couple of seconds and next thing there's this kid running across the front of me. I could have killed him.'

Mac stood up and knelt down in front of Mick. 'But you didn't kill him, Mick, you just gave him a nasty shock, and you can be sure that he'll think twice about running across a busy road again.' Mac stood up. 'Anyway, we can't hang about; we're still available, so we'd better get back to the station,' Mac said, as the watch stood up and began to shuffle awkwardly out of the lounge.

'We'll see you soon, Mick, take it easy.'

'You'll see me on Saturday night; I'll fix it to get a taxi to bring me in to your do.'

153

'You'll not,' said Clive, 'I'll pick you up and drop you back, no worries. I'll see you and sort out a time, alright?'

'Yeah. Thanks Clive,' Mick said, as he got stiffly up from his chair.

Dennis lay quietly in his hospital bed. He was happy; he was going home the following day, back to his stuff and his own empty fridge. He'd get Dave to get out and do some shopping to stock him up. He was glad, but he would miss the nurses, he had lived a rough and ready life. His time had been his own, didn't care too much about anyone, and to his knowledge no one cared much for him, except his good mate Dave, his friend and climbing partner.

He'd taken a fancy, however, to one nurse in particular. She was small with dark hair; he liked her a lot. Unusually for him, when he looked at this girl he felt a reaction, his heart beat a little faster and he found he looked out for her passing the ward. She'd helped him when he fell in the corridor and he'd checked her name on her badge. Madeline somebody or other. He knew he liked her and mused about the chances of getting to know her better; even though she'd discouraged him by telling him that she was engaged to be married.

Maddie was on her final night shift before she was due for a few days off. She needed the rest, and she needed to spend time with Jim and Henry the dog. She walked along the corridor and the incident where she had helped the young climber back to his bed came into her mind. She thought little of it, other than he had made a rather clumsy pass at her. She felt, despite herself, a bit flattered by his attention. He was a nice looking guy, even if he had some rough edges, and she dismissed it immediately. Jim was her man, she didn't need anyone. She knew he was as devoted to her as she was to him, so this feeling she got was strange. She passed the end of the ward and peered in. She saw him lying there, his hair strewn wildly across his pillow. She walked in without thought and stood by his bed. He turned to face her, his heart raced.

'Hello Madeline, it's nice to see you.'

'Hello,' Maddie found herself saying, her heart fluttered.

'How are you?' he asked.

'I'm tired, ready for rest,' she replied. 'How's the leg?'

'Go home tomorrow,' he said, looking down at his hands.

'That's good, isn't it? Get back to normal, do your physio and then get on with your life, back to work for you then.'

'No, not for me, haven't got a job.'

'Oh, sorry, I just assumed you had.'

'No.'

'How long have you been out of work?' Maddie asked.

'I've never worked.'

'Never worked? Why?'

'I never wanted a job, if I'm being honest.'

'Well, honesty is a good thing, but how do you live?'

'Benefits.'

'Benefits, so you don't work at all?'

'No.'

'You sound as though you're proud of that?'

'No, it's just the way it is.'

'So you're not worried about not working?'

'No, I never really needed to.'

Suddenly Maddie felt her heckles start to rise.

'Benefits. Do you know, that really disappoints me. Do you know where your benefit money comes from?' she said, her face becoming flushed. 'It comes from me. I work here all night, pay my taxes, and the likes of you sit on your backside and reap the reward for being idle.'

Dennis had never had anyone berate him like that before; benefits had become his accepted way of life.

'You should be ashamed of yourself, you really disappoint me.'

'I guess you're right,' he said, feeling his face begin to turn red.

Maddie scowled at him. 'So I've worked hard tonight, and thirty per cent of what I've earned will go to keep you scrounging from us.'

Dennis was speechless. He suddenly felt very guilty.

'Let me just tell you something, matey,' Maddie said, now feeling incensed at his attitude. 'My boyfriend Jim, he's always worked, he's hardly missed a day since he left school. Menial jobs mostly, but he had enough self-respect to want to do it; he could have been like you, but chose not to be and I respect him for that. As for you, well, respect? No chance. How could anyone respect you with that attitude? I'll say goodbye, I hope your leg gets better.' Maddie turned and stomped away, heading back to her work station.

Maddie sat at her station and slowly began to calm down; she turned what had just happened over in her mind and began to feel guilty about the feeling the man had engendered in her, before she got so angry with him. She thought about Jim, her man, the man who worked hard who loved her and would do anything for her. Then she thought of the other young man, who she had fleetingly taken a liking too. How could I be so stupid? she thought. Jim is my man, can't wait to see him tomorrow.

Janet drove slowly up the narrow road. She saw the light was on in the farmhouse, and he would be in there, probably sitting there listening to the radio with his dog sat by his feet. She pulled the car to a halt just short of the farm gate, and switched off the engine and turned off the lights. She began to mull over the conversation she'd had with her husband, and began to feel that her life had been a sham. Janet knew that she could not go back to that; she now began to feel that he had other plans, beyond the proposed move to London.

Don Maddern stirred. It had been yet another hard day, and he had dozed for a while. He shook himself and spotted his dog standing by the door wagging its tail, indicating it wanted to go outside. Don stood stiffly and walked across the room, and pushed down the latch of the timber back door. He felt the coolness of the draught as the door opened. He looked out: the sky was clear, and there were stars hanging bright in the dark sky. The dog stood by his side and whined.

'What's up, lass?' he said.

The dog walked toward the gate and barked. He looked down the lane and noticed the car parked about twenty-five yards away. The car looked familiar.

Janet heard the dog bark and suddenly was startled. She had sat for twenty minutes or so, her mind a thousand miles away. She sat there with no consciousness of why she was there, it had just happened. She saw the dark shape walking down towards her and felt a sharp feeling of fright. What have I done? she thought.

The shape came quickly up to the side of the car and his face appeared at the window.

'Hello again,' he said. 'I thought someone was staking me out,' he said, his voice now sounding lighter.

Janet wound the window down. 'I'm sorry,' she said. 'I'm not quite sure how I got here, I just came, I don't know why.'

'Are you alright, you look a bit stressed?'

'Yes, well, actually, no I'm not, but I'll go. I'm sorry that I disturbed you.'

'Don't worry about that,' he said. 'It was the dog, he wanted to come out and cock his leg, otherwise I wouldn't have known you were here. Are you sure you're alright?'

'Yes, I'll be fine,' Janet assured him.

Don could see that she continued to be tense. 'Look,' he said, 'you look really stressed, I'd worry about you driving in your present state. Why don't you come in, and I'll make you a cup of tea.'

Taff pulled the machine under the wash down at the back of the appliance room.

'OK lads, get the machine washed off and the sets serviced, then in for a cup of tea.'

Mac sat in his office and set about doing the fire report. He'd taken all the details down from the occupier of the house. He smiled to himself. It was the first time he'd been to a fire inside a house caused by a barbecue getting out of control. He always had some sympathy, though, because he knew that the victims now had a lot of hassle if they were insured, getting it all sorted out and the house put back into a fit state to live in. The uninsured ones he knew faced an even tougher task. Brian brought him a cup of tea.

'Well, Mac, I wonder if that's the last job.'

'Yeah, I wondered these last few weeks. I've thought about that quite a bit, how it would all finish.'

'Well, I'll get down and make sure the boys have got it all sorted, are you coming back down?'

'Yeah, I reckon so. What time is it?'

Brian looked at his watch.

'It's half eleven.'

'Yeah, I'll come down in a while, as it's the last one.'

Mac sipped his tea and his mind was filled by a parade of images: snapshots of his life in the job, fires he'd been to, people he'd worked for and who had worked for him, tragedies that had affected him. Suddenly the significance of the moment hit him hard in the stomach, he felt slightly nauseous. He stood up and opened the office window, which looked out onto the main road down into the city. He breathed the cool air and thoughts flooded into his mind.

Early in his career at Darnall, the lads on the watch were crazy; he followed them around the station as they set up pranks against other men on the watch, and also the public. He remembered the lads one freezing night; they put a wallet on the pavement, attached to fishing line. It was closing time at the pub up the road from the station. It wasn't long before the first old man appeared, clearly the worse for wear; he spotted the wallet, looked furtively around and bent to pick it up. The lads hid behind the appliance room door as the drunk bent to grab the wallet. They reeled it in foot by foot, the drunk in his confused state didn't realise what was happening and persisted in trying to grab the wallet all the way to the front door of the station. They had miscalculated. The wallet wedged under the door. The drunk persisted and got his fingers around the wallet and snatched, the line snapped and he walked off in a sort of zig-zag making his way home, proud that he had had such good fortune. Curly Thompson was not so pleased, and chased after the man and managed to recover the wallet after a long discussion with the drunk, and a small reward of one pound for his trouble.

Mac was roused by a knock on the door; it was Jake.

'Come in, Jake, sit down. What can I do for you?' Mac asked.

Jake sat opposite Mac and looked at the man who he saw as his role model.

'I just wanted to have a minute to talk to you, before the end of the shift. I'm going to be really sorry to see you leave. If it hadn't been for you, I wouldn't have joined the job, and I wanted you to know how grateful I am that we met.'

Mac was touched; he looked at Jake and smiled.

'Do you know what, Jake? You were destined to be a firefighter. If it hadn't been then, it would have happened at some other time. Meeting you was a good thing for Val and me, and you also helped to save that old man's life, don't ever forget that.'

'I know, I just feel so lucky, to have found this job. I love it and the lads are great.'

'You'll do well in this job, Jake, just concentrate on doing the job well and who knows where you'll get to,' Mac said, smiling at his young protégé. 'Tell me, how are things with this young lady we have all heard about?'

Jake ran his hands over his head, brushing his close-cropped hair.

'She's great, she's coming up on the train on Friday night; she'll stay at our house, Mum's got it all sorted out. I'll be bringing her with me to your party. She's looking forward to it very much.'

'Well, I have to say, we're all very keen to meet her. She sounds very nice.'

Jake felt breathless. 'She is, Mac. I would never have believed it, it's strange isn't it, how life changes things? A few months ago I was shovelling cement and hauling bricks, and now I'm here, with you and the lads, and I've got a girlfriend.'

'Yes, you never know what life's got in store for you. It is strange,' Mac agreed. 'When I met Val, all those years ago, things were very different. I knew straight away I liked her, but I was shy. Believe it or not, Jake, it was ages before I even held Val's hand, or got up the courage to give her a kiss. It's all very different now.'

'Yes, you're right there,' Jake agreed. 'I managed to kiss Antonella on our first time out together, she knocked me out; I can't stop thinking about her.' Jake sat back in his chair. 'How does it feel to know that this is your last shift?'

Mac looked around the room. It was quiet, just the distant sound of the TV playing and the low murmur of the occasional car as it drove past the station. He stood up and walked across to the window, which gave a glimpse of the city centre a couple of miles away down the road.

'Just look at that, Jake,' Mac said, 'isn't it just the most fantastic view. Not beautiful in the sense of landscape, you know, not like the hills up the road in the Peaks. But the lights and the shapes of the roads defined by the street lights, it's almost like a modern painting.'

Jake looked at the view. He'd never thought of the city in those terms, but now he could see it. 'Yeah, you're right, it is beautiful.'

'The other beauty is that when I look down there I can see my history, my life.' Mac paused for a moment, as if he was reliving something from his past. Jake looked at him, the man who he admired, the man who had changed his life. He was acutely aware that this was a time and a place he would always remember.

Mac spoke again.

'These are the places I used to go, the places that shaped me when I was a boy, the places my mum and dad would take me and my sister, places where I got into scrapes as a youngster, where I did my courting, the place where I went to my first fire with my dad. He was at Division Street, and I was a rookie at Darnall. So I feel comfortable with all that, it gives me a sense of security. I look at the city and I think, yes, that's me, and it's mine.'

They stood a while, just quietly looking at the city, seeing the lights of distant cars slowly weaving their way across the illuminated map which lay down below them.

'You know, Mac, I don't think I'll ever look at the city in the same way again.'

'That's good, Jake, there's a lot to see. Get to know it well, you've got thirty years or more to live and work in it.' Mac turned to Jake. 'Well, young man, I reckon it's my time to get some shut-eye, so subject to the city behaving itself, I'll see you in the morning. Goodnight.'

'Goodnight, Sub,' Jake said automatically.

Mac turned and looked at Jake, winked and walked out of the room.

Jake stood for some time peering vacantly out of the window, looking at it now with a different eye, seeing how the hills of the city were brought to life with the lights from houses and offices defining their location. He looked and tried to mentally navigate himself through the city.

CHAPTER 16

Friday morning

Janet heard the solid click of the grandfather clock and then the dull chime as it began to strike six times. She roused herself and for a long minute struggled to work out where she was. Had the happenings of the previous night really happened, or where they just figments of her imagination? She managed to clear her head. The room was unfamiliar, she realised, as she remembered that she must still be at the farmhouse. The single bed she lay in was cosy and warm; she stretched her arms and yawned aloud. There was a tap on the door.

'Hello,' Janet said warily.

'Hi, it's me. Do you want a cup of tea in bed, or will you come down for it?'

Janet suddenly began to feel uncomfortable. She was in a strange bed, in a strange house, with a man who she had only met twice.

'Err, yes, I'll come down, thank you.'

'OK, the kettle's on.'

She had slept fully dressed. Exhausted by the stress of the previous night, she'd slumped into the bed offered by the farmer and was almost instantly asleep. She peered through the curtains into the early morning light. The window faced directly up to the grey rocks of Froggatt Edge. The Peaks were deadly quiet at this time of the day.

Janet walked slowly down the creaky wooden staircase, clicked the latch on the door which separated the staircase from the kitchen, and felt the warm blast of air hit her face. The farmer had the kettle boiling on the Aga. Don turned to face her and smiled.

'Good morning, did you sleep alright?'

'Yes, thank you, I slept like a log,' she said sheepishly. 'I'm sorry I put you to all of this trouble.'

'It was no trouble, I was glad to help.'

'Yes, I'm very grateful, that's twice in one day,' she said. 'I don't know how I can repay you.'

The farmer smiled and said nothing.

Janet sat at the large pine kitchen table, resting her elbows, her hands cupping the large mug of tea.

'So, what are you going to do today?' the farmer asked.

'I'm not sure. I have to go home, I don't want to, but I have to.'

'Will you be alright?'

'Yes, I'll be fine. I just need to get my head straight, everything happened so fast last night, I didn't get much chance to think I just reacted instinctively.'

The farmer stood up; his dog, which had lain by his feet, moved and yawned. He knew it was time for breakfast and wanted to be on hand if his master decided to be generous today.

'I'm doing some bacon and eggs, do you fancy some?' he said.

'I'm starving,' she said, 'that would be great, thank you.'

The feeling of warmth and comfort surrounded Janet; accompanied by the smell of bacon on the cooker, she was relaxed almost to the point of falling asleep again.

The farmer looked at her. 'What happened last night is none of my business but remember, if you need a bolthole, well – you know where I am.'

'Thank you, that means a lot. I may take you up on that. So tell me, Don, how come you live here alone?'

He stood by the cooker and scratched his head. 'Well,' he said, looking at her, 'my parents were married for over sixty years and they loved each other to the day they died. Mum always said, "You'll find the right girl and you'll know that she's the one, don't get married for the sake of it, it's not worth it".'

'Wise words,' Janet replied.

'Yes, I think so. I've tried, but never come across the person who I think is the right one, until—' He paused and looked a bit embarrassed. 'Ah well, she'll come along eventually, I reckon.'

Mac dreamed, a muddled dream, *he was playing marbles with Freddie, then he was in the kitchen at home with his mum and dad, he was stood naked at the sink in the kitchen illuminated by a gas mantle, with his arms covered in the strong red Lifebuoy soap, his dad rocked backwards and forwards in his chair, it was all in very sharp focus, Mac could smell the strong aroma of his dad's pipe tobacco, he remembered the feel of his mother's arms around him and his dad calling him sonny Jim. Then he was dancing at the Locarno with Val, he was wearing his new blue brothel creeper shoes and drainpipe trousers. Freddie stealing the show in his immaculate Italian-style suit and Tony Curtis quiff held down by a handful of Brylcreem, he remembered how they laughed and under the influence of a bit too much beer would stagger arm in arm out into the street. Then he was in a fire in his BA set hearing the sharp influx of air into his mask and the equally noisy exhalation of his hot breath, he remembered lying on the timber floor of the shop, having been instructed by his guv'nor to stick there, stop the fire coming through and past him and Bonzo Brown his nutcase of a friend, overweight and full of fun but too brave for his own good at times. Mac could feel the heat rising around them as the fire got closer, their pulses raced, they had to hold it no matter what.*

They were being roasted; they could hear the sound of the fire close by, but being encased in heavy fire gear, and with their artificial atmosphere keeping them alive, they were at times separate from the fire, an almost dreamlike feeling. They saw the lath and plaster wall which separated them from the fire begin to turn brown, then black, the sparks and flame as the fire penetrated the wall. Mac remembered the feeling of something akin to fear, but it wasn't fear, it was almost a dreaded excitement. This was it crunch time: fight it or roast.

It felt like being in an oven. He could smell the rubber of his facemask as the heat began to degrade it. The fire had penetrated their space, they lay low. 'Right, Bonzo, shit or bust.' Mac pulled the lever on the branch and the silver rapier-like stream of water hit the fire. Mac felt relief; the waiting was over, now they could get their teeth into the job. A cloud of dense smoke fell around them, their visibility now zero as they powered the jet at the fire. He turned the nozzle and formed a cone-like spray, pushing the smoke away from them and giving them a sight of the fire. The heat was building and conditions were becoming unbearable. Bonzo slapped Mac's shoulder.

'I think we're gonna lose it, let's get our arses out while we still can.'

'No Bonz, let's just give it a while longer. I'll give us a spray.' Mac turned the spray and doused them both. The water almost instantly evaporated and they watched as their jackets poured out clouds of steam. 'I think if we're not positive, Bonz, we're gonna lose it,' Mac shouted above the noise of the fire. 'Let's go for it.' Mac crawled closer to the fire and pulled the lever, and smashed the fire. He waved the jet of water almost as though he were wrestling with it. He heard a rumble and then the floor of the adjacent room collapsed.

'I think it may now be time for us to take our leave,' Mac called and turned to Bonzo, 'come on, let's get out of here.' They heard the distant sound of blasts on whistles, the sound you don't want to hear when you're inside a job. The watchers outside of the fire had decided it was time to evacuate.

Mac remembered the speed of movement, having abandoned the branch. The razor-sharp thought process, his mind computing every hurdle, counting the seconds, knowing it was desperate. He could hear the whistles clearer now, he could hear shouts of encouragement. Then the exit appeared before them, Bonzo in front, Mac following him up. Then daylight, fresh air, then the rumble as the roof of the building folded inwards, seconds after they stepped out to safety.

Mac tossed and turned as the images sped through his mind. He became vaguely aware of daylight beginning to percolate through the quarter-light of his room, and so began to consciously rouse himself, for the last time in this room.

Janet ate the breakfast that Don had cooked; the bacon was crisp, just as she liked it.

'That was lovely, Don, thank you. I should go; I've got a lot to think about today.'

'Of course. It's been a pleasure, a nice change for me to have a bit of company. I hope that everything works out for you,' he said, smiling at her. 'And if you need an ear to bend, then you know where I am.'

'Thank you, I appreciate that. Hopefully everything will settle down soon.'

Janet climbed into her car, somehow feeling reluctant to go. Something had radically changed in her life, she didn't know what but she would try to get things sorted out and play it by ear.

She drove slowly down the narrow track, emerging onto the main road. Traffic was light, it was still early. She pulled up to a halt in a muddy recess by the side of the road and began to think about her situation in the cold light of day.

Meeting Don, and the kindness he had demonstrated, had affected her. Somehow using her husband as a yardstick had brought unfavourable comparisons into her thinking, which she felt would have some influence on the decisions she would make.

Did she want to move house to the south? *No.*

Did she respect Duncan after last night? *No.*

Did she understand what he said correctly, that he may not go alone, and if that were the case, is there someone else in his life? If so, what does she think about that? *Really don't care that much*, she said to herself.

She ran rivers of thought through her mind, asking herself questions and coming up with the same convincing answers, which were telling her to let it go. She couldn't bring any positives to mind, nothing that said stay, make it work.

Do I love him? She thought for a minute… *No.*

Do I want to go home and see him? *No.*

Janet made a decision, put the car into gear and drove.

Antonella stirred; months of responding to the alarm at the side of her bed had imprinted the time 6.45 a.m. in her muscle memory. It was 6.40, and it wasn't time for her to get up yet, she could lie in for a while. She turned over and switched off the alarm. Today there was no work, today she was going to catch a train and travel to Sheffield and see the man whose image dominated her thoughts. Barely an hour passed when she didn't think of him, even in the middle of rehearsals she would somehow drift away in her mind and the image of his face would be there in her mind's eye. She loved the way he looked and smiled and the sound of his voice with the quirky northern accent. She lay for a while, and her mind meandered around what the weekend at Jake's mother's house would bring. She felt aroused at the thought of what could conceivably happen; she was prepared, but would just go with the flow. She never for a second expected Jake to be pushy about the really personal things in their relationship.

Antonella climbed slowly out of bed and went to the bathroom; she turned on the hot water and ran a bath. She was soon dozing in the warmth of the soapy water.

She was at the concert, playing her violin; she peered down into the auditorium and looked through half-open eyes. There was Jake and his mother. Jake's mother seemed to be moved by the music, she wiped her eyes with her handkerchief; Jake sat quietly, listening intently at the music but his eyes fixed firmly on her.

She smiled to herself. She knew that her man, Jake, felt the same way she did. She was so happy, and she would see him later today.

Mac slung his towel over his shoulder and stepped into the shower room. He was alone, the rest of the watch was still sleeping. He allowed the stream of hot water to cover his body. He poured shampoo over his head and rubbed it vigorously, watching as the foam slid down his body and gathered around the drain. He heard the clunk as the alarm prepared to sound. Mac looked at the clock on the shower room wall: six thirty-five a.m. He threw his T-shirt on and slipped into his tracksuit bottoms, and jogged up to the appliance room. The watch was gathering, slipping into their fire gear. Jake trotted out of the watchroom.

'What we got, Jake?' Mac asked, aware that this almost certainly would be his final shout.

'Three pump make up in town, a row of derelict houses well alight.'

Taff pulled the machine onto the station forecourt.

'OK Taff, let's get to it.'

It was almost as though every man on the machine knew it. Mac's last shout. Taff flew down the parkway, they could see the thin pall of smoke in the distance.

'Don't put your sets on yet, let's see what it is first,' Mac instructed.

The crew were sat quiet in the back, still in the process of waking up properly.

They pulled into the area of old streets, where over the past months dozens of houses had been demolished, and all that remained were the roads with pavements but no buildings. Then there was a cluster of houses, probably the last of this old community, built a hundred years ago to house the families who relied on employment from the steel industry. Maggie put paid to that, and then the steady decline. As the industry shrank, so did the population.

Two appliances were already in attendance, pouring water on to the fire.

George Collier walked up to the Graveton machine as it pulled to a halt close by.

'Hi Mac, can you get your guys to sort out the water? There's a couple of hydrants close by,' he said, pointing them out.

'No problem, George, we'll be happy to oblige. OK lads, let's get those hydrants in.'

Jake helped Taff set into one. He carried the aluminium standpipe key and bar. He quickly flipped up the iron lid set into the pavement, Taff then screwed on the hydrant gear whilst Jake ran the hose back to the pump inlet of the machine. Brian and Pete did the same with the other hydrant. Then they connected the Graveton pump to the central pumps, and gave them both a good supply of water to fight the fire.

Mac stood a while and watched. Jake trotted across in front of him.

'Come here a minute, Jake,' Mac called to him.

Jake stopped, turned and walked across to Mac. 'Yes, Sub.'

'This, Jake, is the sort of fire we often get, and as you can see there's no great rush. These jobs can be dangerous, there's nothing to be gained by chancing anything, the houses are going to be demolished soon, so we stand outside and pour on water, no risk-taking. Unless, of course, we get info that there are people inside, tramps, druggies, et cetera. Then it's a different ball game. Just thought I'd tell you that, in case you were wondering why everyone seemed a bit casual.'

'Thanks Sub, I was thinking that, but it's still exciting and makes you want to get stuck in.'

'Yes, but we have to be safe. There's nothing to be gained, the houses are coming down soon, and there are cases where firefighters have died putting these fires out, so be safe.'

'I will, Sub,' Jake said as he looked at Mac, who he thought seemed sad.

The high volume of water that had been poured onto the fire soon began to douse the flames; it was now just a matter of time before the fire would be completely extinguished. Mac looked on like a distant spectator, sure that this would be his last taste of the fireground.

George Collier appeared in front of him.

'Well, Mac, I reckon that's got it, we don't need to keep you any longer. Get off back to station, and I'll see you on Saturday night.' George leant forward and hugged Mac, realising that this was the end of a great career. 'It's often said, Mac, when we talk about a firefighters, that he was a good fireman – that, for us, is the ultimate accolade. But with you this is the absolute truth, the job will miss you and I'll miss you.'

'Thanks, George. I'll miss it all, but I'll see you on Saturday night.' Mac turned and took a last look at the smoking ruin. 'Right lads, knock off and make up, let's get back to station.'

Mac couldn't remember the journey back to Graveton. His mind drifted elsewhere.

He was sat on the bridge with Val. The day was hot, the next half mile was steep. They walked slowly up the rutted track to be surprised by a dog barking over a dry-stone wall, and the old lady came and offered them tea. Mac remembered how he instantly liked her. They talked and sat in her garden, drank tea, and then Mac mowed her lawn and promised they would go back; which they did. Then he and Val walked over the Chrome Hill ridge in the sunshine and Mac remembered the feeling of remoteness and space, and thanked God that he had his health and his wife and children. He felt no sadness now, this was the natural end to one page of the book of his life, a new page would open soon.

Taff drove into the Graveton drill yard. It was 0848 hours, and Mac came back to the present.

'Control from Alpha 010, over.'

'Alpha 010 go ahead, over.'

'Control from alpha 010, for the very last time, from Sub Officer James, Alpha 010 home station and closing down.'

'Alpha 010, it's been good working with you Mac, good luck, control out.'

There was silence in the appliance. The crew had heard Mac's last message and understood the significance of it. The day crew also understood, and crowded out of the rear of the station as Mac climbed down from the machine for the last time. There was a spontaneous outburst of applause from everyone on the station.

Mac shook the hands of all the crew, and issued his penultimate order.

'Right, Red Watch, get changed sharpish. Don't want you missing my last parade.'

Mac stood alongside Paul Adams, the Sub Officer in charge of the day shift. He called crews to attention.

He turned to Mac. 'Sub Officer James, will you fall your watch out.'

Mac shook his hand. 'Thank you, Sub,' Mac said, and pulled himself up to attention. 'Red Watch, on the order, fall out. You will take a half turn to the right and fall out. Red Watch, fall out. Duty crew, stand at ease.'

Janet had driven slowly, giving her the time to analyse the situation she now found herself in. She surprised herself; there were few regrets, no feelings of sadness, just a desire to sort things out, bring it to a close. She approached the long drive to her house. The wrought-iron gates were closed. She pressed the fob and they swung slowly open. The light was on in the dim lounge, she could see as she approached. There were no nerves, just a cold determination, no retreat, get it sorted out.

She placed the key in the door lock. The door would not open so she rattled the door, she guessed that he'd put the bolt across. She walked slowly around the house, peering through the windows, hoping to see him. Then she saw him slouched in an armchair. She tapped on the window; he gave no response. She tapped again, this time louder; still no response. She gazed intently at him. He made no move, she could just make out the slight movements as he breathed.

She shouted. 'Duncan, open the door we need to talk.' There was no response. She tapped the window again. 'Duncan,' she shouted at the top of her voice, 'open the bloody door or I'll smash a window.' He half turned his head and mouthed an obscenity. She noticed an empty spirit bottle on the table beside him.

'This is the last time, Duncan. If you don't open up, I will smash a window.'

He ignored her again. Janet could feel the anger growing inside her. She walked around the back of the house and pushed down the handle of the French window which led into the large conservatory. It opened; she walked slowly through and into the lounge where Duncan was sat, head bowed. A glass tumbler lay on the carpet near his feet, his eyes were closed and he made no move to acknowledge her presence in the room. She sat on a dining chair opposite him and looked, barely able to look at him with any sense of regret that she was about to leave him. He was a shadow of the man she had married. Before this, he'd been funny, lively and loving. These past few years he'd been introverted, sometimes secretive. She'd always put that down to his work. But after the previous night's confrontation she'd begun to wonder about his lengthy stays in London. Now, instead of love, affection and caring, these facets of her view of him had turned to distrust, anger, resentment and an abject dislike of him and his type – men who play fast and loose with their relationships. She momentarily began to compare him with Don, the man who had stepped in to help her. In a millisecond she decided that there was no adequate comparison: one was a real man, and Duncan was not.

She stood and put her hand on his shoulder, and shook it. There was no response, his brain dulled by an excess of alcohol. She went to the kitchen and wrote him a short note.

Duncan, ring me on my mobile when you've sobered up. Janet.

She undid the bolt on the door, walked out, got into her car and drove out of the yard. Her mind was now fixed on what the outcome should be.

CHAPTER 17

Mac folded his bedding, labelled it and placed it in the watchroom. He took all of his belongings, pens, photos and books from his office, put them in a box and carried them to his car, then systematically emptied his locker. He stood for a minute just looking around, his emotions a mixture of relief, pleasure and sadness, that at last it had come to an end. His mind drifted to the times when some of his colleagues from the past had retired, and one or two who had died in service so never got to this stage of retirement. It was quiet except for the sounds of the day crew doing the routines; routines that Mac had done a thousand times and knew by heart, as does every firefighter. For the first time in a long time, he took in a deep breath and sucked in the air of the station, smelled the diesel and petrol fumes that were part of the station's environment. He heard the driver sound the horn and give a blip on the wailers, and the heavy clunk of the roller lockers slamming shut, all familiar sounds that had been embedded in his DNA that he would no longer hear or feel. It was a strange place to be, no longer a firefighter, now just Mr Malcolm James, ex-firefighter, a civilian with the rest of his life to live. He smiled to himself, turned, and walked out of the station to drive home.

Mac opened the boot of the Volvo and placed the contents of his locker inside. The boys had disappeared; he wondered, half expected that they would be there to see him off. He felt a slight nag of disappointment as he climbed into the car.

It was nine thirty and the day was young. Mac steered the car through the familiar streets, seeming to see everything now with a different pair of eyes, the eyes of a civilian. His street was quiet as he pulled into the drive. Val stood by the window and waved at him as he climbed out of the car; he smiled and returned her wave. He slammed the door shut and suddenly felt weary. It had been a busy tour, and it seemed the adrenaline had finally disappeared from his system.

Val met him at the door, and said, 'We've got mice in the lounge, you know what I'm like, they terrify me. Can you see to them?'

Mac smiled. He was tired, but he'd sort it out and then relax. He walked into the lounge; it was full of bodies, the whole of Red Watch, including Mick Young with his arm and wrist strapped up. Tony was there in uniform with his sub officer's rank markings adorning his jacket. Ray Swift sat on the sofa, almost buried by Jock and Taff. Brian sat in a chair, Pete and Jake sat side by side on the floor.

'So what's going on here, then?' Mac said above the noise, a huge grin splitting his craggy face.

Brian stood up and put his arm round Mac. 'This, Mister James, is your pre-leaving-party party, and it is our job today to get you thoroughly pissed; excuse my French, Val,' he said, grinning widely.

The door to the kitchen swung open and Mac's girls came out, carrying large trays of sandwiches, sausage rolls and pork pies. Then Pete Brogan strolled into the room with several bottles of champagne. There was a loud cheer as the corks flew. Mac was soon overpowered and had several glasses of drink placed in front of him.

Tony stood up and called for quiet. He leaned against the settee. 'Sssh-sshut up, you lot. I'm g-g-g-going t-to make a sp-sp-speech.'

There was laughter.

'Well come on then, Tone, we haven't got all day,' Taff called out.

The noise reduced and Tony began to speak.

'Mac, M-M-Mac, we know that on Saturday night it will be b-b-b-busy and we thought w-we wanted to d-d-do something personal; very selfish we know, but—'

Mac interrupted him. 'I've got the message, Tony, thanks. It's good of you all to think of me like this, so yes, let's celebrate. However, it's a bit early for me to take in too much alcohol, have to think of my liver at my age.'

Jake sat with his friends on the floor of Mac's lounge; there was a lot of noise and chatter about Mac, and the things that they had experienced together.

'And Mac, I have to say that when you let me be in charge of the cow in the crap – excuse my French, Val – I now reckon it was your way of avoiding falling in and ensuring the rest of us did. Even the d-divisional commander got covered in the s-stuff.'

Mac laughed along with the rest of the boys. 'At last, Tony, you've sussed me out. That is what you call experience.'

Tony laughed along with them. 'Yes, b-b-but now I'm in ch-charge I reckon that I'll be delegating some of th-th-that to the ones who give me grief. So be warned, you m-motley crew, that Tone is on the throne and I'll be watching you.'

Brian turned to Jock. 'Do you know what, Jock? I'm really frightened now, are you?'

Jock grimaced at Tony. 'Aye, I heard him, and I'm terrified.'

Ian Blain was off-duty, he'd been invited to the get-together at Mac's house and gladly accepted. He'd be out of uniform and relaxed.

After a few drinks, which included three glasses of champagne, Brian was feeling happy and relaxed. He put his arm across Ian Blain's shoulders.

'So boss, how do you like Sheffield?'

Ian let a broad smile break out across his face. 'Well, Brian, I like it very much, but I'm not sure I like you putting your arm round me. People may get the wrong idea. Bearing in mind you want to go into training, people may think you got promoted on something other than your own merit.'

Brian gave a slightly intoxicated grin. 'Sorry boss, no offence meant.'

'No offence taken, Brian,' Ian said jovially. 'I think I have to go soon, the good lady is taking me shopping, wants to get me a new tie for tomorrow. I told her to pick me up at eleven, what time is it now?'

'It's ten to eleven, boss,' Taff said.

'Right then, I'll get ready to go.' He stood up. 'Mac, it's been a pleasure, we are both looking forward to tomorrow night.' Mac stood up and shook Ian's hand.

'No, the pleasure is ours. It will be nice to see everybody tomorrow.'

Antonella stood quietly in front of the mirror. She had on her favourite outfit: a mid-length, figure-hugging black dress, a white lace blouse, and around her neck was a long gold chain with a gold cross. Over this she wore a scarlet jacket with a large floral brooch. Her hair was a lustrous black and was cut to just below shoulder level. She looked from her window and saw that the taxi she'd ordered was sitting waiting by the entrance to her apartment block.

'Where do you want to go, love?' the taxi driver asked as she settled in the back seat of the cab.

'St Pancras station, please,' she said, smiling at the driver whose face she could see looking admiringly at her in his mirror.

The taxi made its way along the Euston Road. Antonella could see the impressive huge Victorian building, which looked less like a railway station than anywhere she had ever been; but it was beautiful, its decorative red brickwork shining brightly in the dull grey surroundings. He stopped by the front entrance. Antonella got out and handed him the money for her fare.

'Where are you heading today, my love?' the driver asked with a smile.

Antonella returned his friendly smile. 'I'm going to Sheffield, seeing my boyfriend for the weekend. He is a firefighter and we have been apart for many weeks.'

'Well, your boyfriend is a very lucky man; I hope you have a lovely time.'

'Thank you very much, I'm sure it will have a nice time together.'

This was her first time in this railway station, and she was awestruck at its beauty. The platform had an arched roof and gave the impression of a building built on a grand scale. She made her way to platform two. Soon her train arrived. Her excitement was building, she was going to a part of the country which was new to her, and she wondered if it would be like London.

The party in Mac's lounge broke up at around one thirty and the watch slowly began to leave, Mac giving each of his boys a handshake and a hug as they left. He began to feel the emotion of the day. He'd expected it, and had planned in his mind for the day. He'd relax for the remainder of the day, then have an early night to help recover from his last busy shift, and be fresh for Saturday, the day of his leaving do at the fire station.

The train pulled out of St Pancras station. Antonella had a seat to herself. She would spend a while reading her book, a book that she'd read several times before but never tired of going through again: *Pride and Prejudice*. She read the words and Jane Austen's words filtered into her mind visions of England, an England that she knew little of, but was keen to experience.

She had heard of places such as Chatsworth House in Derbyshire, she'd seen the pictures on the Internet. She was keen, if it was possible, to visit the house during this visit. She made a mental note to speak to Jacob about it.

The green countryside flashed by. Antonella looked out of the carriage window at the trees, almost blurring as the train powered north. She looked at her watch. It was four thirty, she'd be seeing Jacob in about thirty minutes. Her heart began to pound. She noticed the landscape beginning to change on the horizon; she could make out hills, which she guessed were the hills of Derbyshire. Jake had talked about them many times, and had promised her that they would go out into the Peak District and he would show her some of his favourite places.

Jake had driven home and spent a quiet couple of hours with his mum. They'd talked at length about what they would do whilst Antonella was with them. He'd helped his mum sort out the spare room, they'd made up the bed, Jake had run the vacuum cleaner round and washed the windows. On the dressing table were a couple of framed pictures; one was of Jake in his school uniform, with his brown leather satchel hanging from his shoulder. The other was a picture of his mum and dad taken about a year before his dad died. On the wall was a picture, a landscape, a print of a John Constable painting which Jake knew to be 'The Cornfield'. As a child he'd somehow seen the picture and really liked it and had pestered his mum, who in the end gave in and managed to acquire a print of the picture. It had hung there for maybe ten years. Jake always looked hard at it whenever he went into the room, there was something about the depth of the picture, and how the landscape seemed to go on forever beyond the trees. He liked the way the boy lay drinking from the pool, and the dog mustered the sheep. It was an idealistic view of an England that had long passed, but it connected with Jake's emotions.

Mac was in the conservatory; Val had done them a plate of corned beef sandwiches and a cup of tea. Mac had read the paper and commented to Val that there were now almost a million people out of work.

'Well Mac, you've done your bit. You've just created one job, now you've retired.'

Mac smiled at Val's amusing take on a bad situation. 'Yes, you're right. I'm glad in a way that I'm out of the job market.'

The train entered an area of large, dark buildings, not the ideal introduction to any town. It began to slow down. Antonella stood by the window. Looking out, she could see the station getting closer, and her heart began to beat loudly in her chest.

Jake had arrived early at the railway station and was waiting nervously. He looked at the large clock which hung high above the platform, and noted that the train should arrive within the next five minutes. His nerves began to jangle. It seemed so long since he'd seen her, they'd talked almost every night on the phone, but today she was coming to see him. He felt hot, edgy and excited. He looked up at the clock, his pulse pounded in his head; the train was due now.

He listened hard and could just hear the sound of a train approaching. He stood back from the edge of the platform, took some deep breaths and peered nervously up the line.

Antonella took her case down from the overhead rack and stood by the door as the train rumbled slowly into the station. She looked forward, hoping to get an early glimpse of Jake. He was there; she could see him standing on the platform waiting, looking as handsome as she had pictured him all the time since their last meeting. She trembled with anticipation and a little trepidation; she hoped fervently that everything would be as she had imagined it would be in her mind's eye. The carriage moved slowly, passing Jake. As it passed him he saw her, as she saw him. Their eyes met. Jake's face split into a wide smile, Antonella's eyes filled with tears of happiness. The carriage pulled to a halt, and Jake jogged the twenty yards to meet her as she dismounted carefully from the train.

She threw her arms around him. Jake pulled her to him, engulfing her body with his powerful arms. They held each other for a long time, Jake eventually relaxing his grip.

'Oh, my Jacob, it is so the best thing to seeing you again,' Antonella said, her voice filled with emotion.

Jake looked intently at her, noticing the tear which ran down her cheek. He brushed it away gently with is large hand. He put his hand under her chin and kissed her. His heart thudded in his chest and he felt almost unable to breath. He pulled away, held her shoulders with his hands, stood back and gazed at her, shaking his head almost in disbelief.

'You look absolutely beautiful, Nella,' he said, almost in a whisper.

'Thank you, my Jacob, I think you are the most handsome man I have known.'

'Come on, let me get you to the car and home. Mum's dying to see you again,' he said.

Jake drove through the city. It was dusk and the streetlights illuminated the roads. Antonella sat beside Jake as he drove carefully; he changed gear as he drove up the steep roads out of town, towards his home.

'Shall I show you where I work? It's on the route home,' Jake said.

She half turned towards Jake and rested her head on his shoulder.

'I'd love to see it, I have heard of your speaking about it so many times. I am so happy to be with you again Jacob, it has been so long time, I have missed you every day.'

Jake was so happy he thought his chest would burst. He was so lucky, the girl who had dominated his thoughts for so long was at last here, and resting her head on his shoulder.

'I've missed you too, all my friends at work are looking forward to meeting you tomorrow night, and mum of course can't wait to see you.'

The day was fading fast, and as Jake crested the hill leading to his village it was getting dark.

'Can we stop somewhere, Jacob, before we go to your house? I would like to hold you, just to having a little time with us together, do you mind?'

Jake's felt the pulse of blood racing through his head. He pulled the car into the car park at the rear of the village hall. He turned out the lights and switched off the engine.

Antonella turned to face Jake; she put her hand against his cheek and stroked his lips with her fingers.

'I love you so much, Jacob, I cannot breathe very well, and I feel that I am so lucky to have met you and your mama.'

Jake said nothing. He placed his hand over hers, leaned forward and kissed her gently. Her lips were soft and moist. They held each other for several minutes, hardly speaking. Jake spoke first.

'I think we should go home now, mum will wonder where we have got to.'

Antonella smiled a guilty smile.

'I think so too. I loved your kissing, you are a real man, Jacob, I am so lucky.'

'I'm the lucky one, my friends at the fire station will be amazed when they meet you. They are all looking forward to tomorrow night and meeting you.'

They drove through Graveton; Jake pointed out the fire station and slowed down as they drove past.

'Can I see it?' she asked.

'Well, it looks as though the watch are in the yard training, so I'll drive close so you can see what we do.'

Jake drove slowly up the drive, which gave a view of the drill yard, and stopped. The crew was running out hose and pitching a ladder to the tower, water was being splashed around and there was a lot of noise.

'What are they doing?' Antonella asked.

'This is an exercise. It's as if there is a fire in a high building, so the firefighters are putting a ladder up to allow the men to get in to fight the fire, and maybe rescue someone.'

They watched as two men ran up the ladder, and minutes later a firefighter climbed onto the ladder with a large dummy across his back and carried it down to the ground.

'Do you have to do this, Jacob?' Antonella asked.

178

'Yes, we do this or something similar every day we are at work. It's just practice, for the time when you have to do it for real.'

Antonella looked at Jake, Jake smiled at her.

'I love it,' he said enthusiastically.

'It all seems very dangerous, Jacob.'

'No, it's quite safe; we practise a lot, so that when the time comes at a real emergency we are prepared.'

'I see,' she said, not entirely convinced. 'I think that I would be very scared for me to do that.'

Jake looked at her. 'I think what you do is fantastic. To sit on a stage and play the way you have to do would terrify me.'

'You are right of course, Jacob, I suppose that it is what we are good at and have practised for many years. But being a firefighter still looks dangerous, I think.'

They sat in the darkness of the car and talked quietly, Jake explaining and answering her questions, both becoming unaware of their surroundings.

There was a light tap on the windscreen. It was the officer in charge, who had noticed them sitting, watching the drill.

'Well hello, Jake, and who is this young lady may I ask?'

Jake wound down the window. 'Hello Sub, this is my girlfriend. I've just picked her up from the station, she's come up from London for the weekend. I'll be bringing her to Sub James's retirement function tomorrow.'

Very soon the whole of Green Watch was congregated around Jake's car.

'Come on, Jake, are you going to introduce us?' they said.

'Did you hear them, Antonella? They want to meet you.'

'I would love to meet them, Jacob,' and she turned to get out of the car. Before she could, a hand came down and the door was swiftly opened and offered her assistance to get out.

Antonella stepped out of the car and was instantly surrounded by the young men of the watch.

'So you're the reason that Jake has been wandering around in a dream, are you?' one of the crew said.

Antonella smiled. She looked spectacular, and it was obvious that the boys had taken a fancy to her. Jake looked on, smiling, proud that the love of his life had opened herself up so easily to the guys on the station.

'Right guys, we've got to go, my mum's waiting, the dinner will be ready. We'll see you all tomorrow night,' he called above the clamour of the crew.

Jake steered the car into the village. It was dark, but Antonella was captivated by the small houses and the tree-lined streets.

'I love your village, Jacob, it is very cute.'

Jake turned into his street with its rows of neat terraced houses; he pulled to a stop outside the house.

'Well, here we are. This is where mum and I live,' he said.

'Oh, it is lovely Jacob; it is much bigger than my house in Italy.'

'Well, let's get in. Mum will be excited to see you.'

'Oh young lady, you look so beautiful, come here and let me look at you,' Jake's mother said as they walked into the small entrance hall.

'Oh, Mrs Higgins, I am so excited to be seeing you once again, and you also look very beautiful.'

Jake's mother wrapped her arms around Antonella. 'It is so lovely to have you come and stay with us. Come on in, I'll make us all a nice cup of tea.'

'Thank you, I am very thirsty from being on the train for a long time, and kissing your Jacob makes me thirsty also,' she said, giving Jake's mum a shy smile.

Jake's mum's face was split by a huge smile, she struggled to control the need to laugh. She looked at Jake approvingly.

'Jacob, at last you have demonstrated that you have the same taste in ladies as your father. He would be very proud,' she said, with a stifled chuckle in her voice.

Mac sat in the lounge with his feet on a stool. He'd read the paper, and was drinking a cup of coffee when he heard the front door of the house open, and voices speaking in low tones. He strained to hear them, wondering who it could be. The door of the lounge swung open, it was his daughters, his girls.

'Hiya Dad, we thought we ought to pop in and see how you were coping.'

'So far, so good,' Mac smiled. 'Do you want a cup of tea?'

'Yes, Mum asked us, she's doing it now.'

'So girls, what do you reckon to your dad being a pensioner, then?'

The girls looked at each other; Lucy spoke.

'Well Dad, all we've ever known is you working, so now you've retired it will give you and mum time to do other things. And time to do things for us,' she said with a laugh.

'Oh great, so that's going to be my life now, is it? Putting up shelves for the pair of you and tiling your bathroom?'

'Well, now you mention it, Dad…'

CHAPTER 18

Friday night

'That meal was very nice, Mrs Higgins,' Antonella said, as she wiped the side of her mouth with a napkin.

'You are very welcome, Antonella. It is such a relief to have you come to visit us, Jacob has been like a lost soul, he's missed you so much.'

'And I also have been missing Jacob,' she said, looking at Jake, who was looking slightly embarrassed by his mother's description of him. 'Do you know, I love your son very much, Mrs Higgins. We have been talking every day on the telephone, I think that we are meant always we will be together.' She grasped Jake's large hand and squeezed it; Jake could feel the electricity between them.

'I think you are Jacob's first real girlfriend, he has not bothered with girls very much; I think that he spends too much of his time looking after me. I hope that will change now he has you to care for.'

'I am very sure that we will be always in love,' she said, squeezing Jake's hand again.

Brian sat in the comfortable armchair opposite Jane. Jill was in her room, playing with her dolls. Brian looked at Jane and felt a rush of affection for her that he'd not known for a long time. It pleased him, he was happy. He was back with Jane and his little girl was happy about their relationship being reincarnated.

'Jane, can I ask you something?' he said.

There was something in the intensity of his words that startled Jane; she looked up at him from her magazine.

'These last few months have been the happiest I can remember. What do you think about the possibility of us getting married? I'd like it, and I know Jill would, she said as much to me last night.'

Jane put the magazine down on the seat next to her. She looked serious.

'I know these past months have been good – Jill's happy, I'm happy – but I'm just a bit concerned that, happy as we are, you hear about couples being fine and then getting married and somehow it all goes wrong. That's the last thing I would want to happen to us,' she said.

'That's fine, I get that. I just didn't want you thinking that I was scared of commitment. Let's give it some thought, and know I would be really happy to get married, but just as long as we're all together, that's what really matters.'

Maddie's phone rang.

'Hello, Jim.'

'Hiya. I'm just setting off, I'll be with you in twenty minutes,' she heard Jim say.

'OK, see you then,' she replied.

Maddie was sat on the edge of her bed, drying her hair. Tonight was a special night, it was their eight month anniversary, and Jim was taking her out to a pub for a celebration meal.

Jim slipped on his jacket and looked in the mirror. His reflection told him just how far he had come as a person since he met Maddie. Now he was smart and confident, not so skinny, he'd long since given up smoking, he had a job he was enjoying, albeit he was still in training to be a plumber; and he had Maddie, the girl who, despite his lack of everything, had taken to him and dragged him gratefully into a new life.

He got into his car and momentarily thought of the difference to the old banger he used to drive, when he could get it to start. He realised how fortunate he was. Twenty minutes later he was parked outside Maddie's home. He knocked on her door; her dad opened it and smiled.

'Come on in, James, she's almost ready. How are things on your course, James?' Maddie's dad asked.

Jim sat back in the soft leather armchair.

'It's really good. There's a lot to learn, a lot of technical stuff I have to memorise, but I like it a lot,' he said, his chest filled with pride. He remembered the first visit to Maddie's house when he was still a security guard, and remembered how inadequate he felt. Meeting Maddie had changed all of that. He was also grateful that her parents seemed to like him, and gave him some respect.

'And how is Henry doing?' Maddie's dad asked.

Jim smiled, as he remembered how they had come to get Henry and the hours of pleasure he had had looking after him.

'Henry is great. He eats like a horse and I think that he actually thinks that he's in charge of me, but he's great.'

Jim sensed Maddie coming into the room. He turned and saw her, dressed in her best clothes, a bright red dress with black patent high-heeled shoes and a black jacket.

'You look fantastic,' he said with a gasp.

'Well, thank you sir, you look half decent yourself,' she replied.

'So where are you both going tonight, James?' Maddie's mother asked.

'I've booked us a table at a place up the Ecclesall Road, The Prince of Wales. I've heard that it's nice.'

'It is nice, we've been there a couple of times. It's a bit pricey, though.'

'Yes, well, it's one of our special occasions, so it will be nice.'

'Oh yes, what is the occasion?' Maddie's mother asked.

Jim looked at Maddie and blushed.

Maddie stepped in and answered. 'It's our anniversary, eight months to the day since we met in Edale.'

She laughed. 'Ah well, I hope you have a lovely evening, drive carefully.'

Despite having visited the house several times over the past months, and having discussed with them the subject of his forthcoming wedding to their daughter, Jim still felt a bit tense in their company, although now he'd become more confident around people.

Night had fallen, it was dark outside. Antonella was feeling tired. She stifled a yawn. Jake looked at her as he sat next to her, holding her small hand.

'Are you OK? I guess you're tired after your early start this morning.'

'Yes, I'm feeling tired, the long journey. And also I have had a very busy week with practice and the concerts.'

Jake's mum stood up and took the hint.

'Look, you two, I'm tired so I'll get myself off to bed. Will you make sure Antonella is alright, and make sure you lock up before you come up to bed?'

'OK Mum, I'll do that, you sleep well.'

'Goodnight, Mrs Higgins,' Antonella said, standing up and kissing her on the cheek.

'Now Antonella, just one thing. From now onward call me Alice. That's my name, and I would prefer it,' Jake's mum said with a soft smile on her face.

'Oh, thank you Mrs— sorry, Alice. Goodnight, and love to you for making me welcome.'

The evening wore on. Jake and Antonella sat together on the sofa, each with a glass of wine.

'Jacob, I'm so happy to be with you, your mama is wonderful; you are very lucky man.'

'I know, she's a great mum. She looked after me since Dad died, we're very close. I got worried about her, that's why I brought her to London, where we first met. Someone I know asked how I would feel if I lost her, and it upset me a bit, it made me think. I realised how important it was to spend more time with her.'

'So I have to be thankful to the person who said that, or we would never have met.'

'I think we were meant to be with each other, no matter what,' Jake said, putting his arm across her shoulders and looking into her eyes.

Jake could feel his emotions rising, and he knew he would have to control his urge to push for more than a kiss. Antonella returned his gaze and leaned her head against his shoulder.

'You know I love you very much Jacob, don't you?'

'Of course, I feel the same,' he replied pulling her closer to him.

'It would be very easy for me to be making love with you tonight Jacob, but we must wait. It would be disrespectful to your mama, she trusted us alone.'

Jake's heart was pounding. Her words seemed to reinforce his desires, but he understood, and agreed with her.

'We have lots of times in the future, Antonella. I just want you to enjoy your weekend with us; nothing will spoil that for us.'

She turned her face to him and kissed him, her lips soft and warm. Jake's head was swimming, he felt unable to breathe.

'I am feeling very tired now, I will go to my bed, Jacob. Is that alright?'

'Sure, I'll come up as well. Tomorrow will be a busy day.'

'Goodnight my beautiful Jacob, I want to see you in the morning.'

Antonella stood alone in the small room; it was furnished with basic but good furniture. There was a single bed with a green duvet cover, a small pine bedside table on which was a wooden table lamp. There was a small chest of drawers with some photographs, black and white and clearly from some years ago, sitting on top. She looked carefully at them. One was of old people that she supposed were some of Jacob's elderly relatives, then a more recent picture of a couple: a man and woman and a young boy, held firmly in the big man's arms. She looked carefully and guessed the boy was Jacob, and the adults she thought were his parents. Fixed to the wall was a dark wooden plaque, with a chromium-plated axe fixed to it and a silver tablet with an inscription written on it. Antonella read it carefully:*This axe is presented to Firefighter Jacob Higgins, best recruit in 1996.*

Antonella felt her chest swell with pride and her eyes begin to fill with tears. She was so proud of the man she dearly loved. She changed quickly into her pink nightdress and silently slipped under the duvet. She closed her eyes, and in minutes she fell into a deep sleep.

As the day wore on, Mac began to feel tired. The busy night shift had finally caught up with him. Seeing the boys come round he'd found quite moving. It was good to know that his watch held him in such high esteem. He knew that Tony would give his all to filling his boots, but also realised that any new officer in charge often has a big job to do, especially one as lacking in managerial experience as Tony.

'Let's have a quiet night, love. It was pretty tiring last shift, so an early night and maybe I'll be in shape for the do tomorrow night.'

'Yes, I reckon that would be sensible.'

'I don't think young Jake will be having an early night tonight, his girlfriend is coming up from London on the train. He's full of it,' Mac said, smiling to himself, remembering how he used to feel all those years ago when he and Val were beginning to get serious. 'Well, Mrs James, tonight you are sleeping with a pensioner.' They laughed.

The girls had gone back to their flats. Mac and Val sat quietly; the television was playing away unheeded, both were lost in their own thoughts. Today had been the last day of what had been normal for them for the best part of thirty years. A new life was waiting for them and the strange feelings that this had brought about in them had made them both reluctant to say very much.

Val sat staring into space, her thoughts moving from one thing to another. Then her mind focused on the day that Mac proposed to her.

Mac had been at work that night, then had spent a few hours with one of his workmates, cleaning windows close to where he lived. They met up after work. Mac picked her up outside the shop where she worked; she got into the car and Mac kissed her lightly on the cheek.

'I've got to ask you something,' Mac said, right out of the blue.

Val wondered what it could be. She'd felt for some time now that their friendship had developed into a true courtship, they both knew it was a special thing, but neither had spoken about any further developments.

'Go on then, what do you want to know?' Val replied.

Mac was steering the car through traffic, en route to Val's house, where he would drop her off and pick her up later.

'Well, err, well, we've been going out now for a while and, well, you know I like you a lot, err, well, I wondered what you'd think if I asked if you wanted us to get engaged?'

'Stop the car, Mac. We should talk about this with the car stationary.'

'OK.'

187

Mac drove on for a couple of minutes, and drove into the car park at the rear of the shops in the Sheffield city centre.

'So, how long have you been thinking about this?' Val asked.

'About a year, but I didn't want to rush you.'

'Well that's a coincidence, that's about how long I've been thinking about it. I thought you'd never get around to it.'

'Good, so what do you think?'

'I like the idea. We should talk to Mum and Dad first though, don't you think?'

She stirred herself from images of the past and looked across at Mac, who had his head buried in a map of the Dark Peak.

'What do you think, then?'

Mac looked up at Val and wondered, had he missed something?

'Think about what?'

'Oh, I don't know. Us, me and you, everything, our life. Have you been happy with everything?' she said, looking quizzically at Mac.

'What's made you think of that, we've been happy enough, haven't we?'

'Yeah, I've been happy, but sometimes I wondered about you.'

Mac stood up and walked across the room. He sat next to Val and put his arm across her shoulders.

'What's brought this on? Are you OK?'

'Yeah, I reckon, just being a bit daft I think.'

'You're not daft, you're the least daft person I know, and believe me I know quite a few really daft people.'

'I don't know, maybe it's because you've finished in the job. Since we were married you've always been in the job. I've never known anything else; it's going to be strange having you around the house, when I know you loved your job so much. I hope that things will stay the same when we spend more time together.'

Mac gave her a serious look and hugged her tight.

'Now look here, my girl. It's not a problem.' He paused for a few seconds. 'We'll get you a job to keep you out from under my feet.' He laughed.

Val turned and grabbed his ear.

'Oh, so that's your plan is it, mister? Come here and give me a kiss.'

Mac took hold of Val's hand.

'I understand, you know. I've had all those thoughts for a while and I think we've had a really good life. I loved my work; we had the girls with all that goes with that, tantrums, boyfriends, hormones, et cetera. We had Freddie and I'm OK with that now. I still get upset about him sometimes, but having dealt with it, I got a lot of the stress out of my system.' Mac paused again. 'You've been the love of my life, everything we've done and been through couldn't have happened without you and your help. So us, me and you and everything, has been great. I think that now, the future, that will be great as well.'

'I think that's what I think as well.' She looked at Mac. 'Do you fancy an early night?'

Mac laughed. 'I think the television in the bedroom's not working very well.'

'OK, I'll think of something else then,' she said, fluttering her eyelashes.

'The radio still works though.'

She smiled.

CHAPTER 19

Mick Young sat at the side of Paula's bed in the hospital ward. She'd regained consciousness and her condition had improved. Mick was relieved to know that she was no longer thought to be in any danger. She turned her head towards him and smiled weakly at him.

'I'm sorry, Mick. I caused the accident, distracting you the way I did. Are you OK? There wasn't anybody else hurt, was there?'

Mick squeezed her hand gently and smiled.

'Don't worry, it'll all be alright. It was just us, I'm fine. You take it easy and get better.'

'I will, don't you worry. The doctor reckons I'll have a scar, but it shouldn't be too bad.'

'You'll still be beautiful no matter what,' he said fondly.

'Oh Mick, I really thought we were going to die,' she said, her voice cracking. A tear began trailing down her cheek. Mick leaned across her and kissed it.

'Don't be sad; be happy that we both are OK, just a bit beaten up but alive.'

Mick looked at her, her head swathed in a bandage, her skin pale, her hands light and weak. His mind went back to the afternoon when the accident occurred, and a tremor of fear surged through him again as he saw the face of the child in the road, its features stretched in panic as his car screeched, just missing him prior to smashing into the lamp post.

Mac sat up in bed, attempting to read a book he'd had by his bedside for a couple of months. He was determined to finish it. Val lay by his side, dozing. Not quite able to get off too, she rolled onto her side to face Mac.

'Have you got a speech worked out for tomorrow?' she asked sleepily.

'No, I've not bothered. I know I pretty much what I want to say, it will be short and to the point, I don't want to bore everybody to death,' he said.

'People won't be bored, they'll be there to say goodbye because they respect you.'

'Maybe, but I'll keep it short. I've already said enough to the boys on the watch.' Mac closed the book and lay down, attempting to get off to sleep.

Mac's mind was mobile; he had a strange feeling come over him now. Suddenly he was out of work, no commitment to the fire brigade. In the state of half-sleep his mind wandered.

He remembered the sounds and smells of his life as a boy. He could hear Freddie's voice shouting as they careered around the woods close to their house, his voice as yet unbroken. They'd built a den made from twigs and dry bracken in the woods. Freddie had a box of matches, so they decided to light a fire inside the den. Initially the fire was small and controlled, but soon the breeze which filtered through the flimsy wall of the den caused the fire to flare up and the den ignited. Mac and Freddie ran for their lives. There was no thought of putting the fire out, just blind panic as they tried to put distance between them and the burning bracken, which by now had spread. They could hear the crackle of the fire and smell the acrid smoke, see the smoke rising above the trees. Even now, half asleep, Mac felt the fear he had felt then. Soon a fire engine came and the men ran into the woods. Mac and Freddie looked on, their faces covered in guilt.

He remembered the pain he felt when it quite suddenly dawned on him that he no longer had parents. His father had died, just leaving him and his sister. He was bereft; the mother he had loved and relied on so much for all of his young life had gone, and now his dad, his hero. Mac had always believed that his dad was invulnerable; he couldn't even think that one day he would die.

Mac lay almost in control of his thoughts, *remembering the smell of the bread his mother would bake twice a week in the oven on the Yorkshire range. He thought of the times in the dull glow of the gas mantle as they made toast on a long brass toasting fork, the bread pressed up close to the fire, and listening to the radio. Life seemed so uncomplicated back then.* Mac lay still, his head brimming with nostalgia then finally drifted off to sleep.

Jim and Maddie sat in the car outside Maddie's house. The meal had been good, they'd spent a long time over their food, breaking off frequently to discuss the details of their forthcoming wedding. No date had been set but the thought that it was going to happen was sufficient for them to begin the process of wedding lists, venue, photographer, the dress and the suit.

'Well James, it has been a lovely evening but I think that now I must go, my bed is calling and I'm in desperate need of sleep. I think the wine's got to me,' she said theatrically.

'I enjoyed it too,' Jim said, putting his hand on her shoulder. 'I can't believe we're making plans for the wedding. Anyway, you get off, but first give me a kiss.'

Maddie leaned across the car and kissed Jim.

'I love you, matey,' she said lightly.

'Me too, I'll ring you tomorrow. Now off you go before I drive off with you.' Maddie climbed slowly out of the car, turned and waved.

'Bye, goodnight, see you soon, love you,' she called as she walked down the garden path.

Saturday morning

Janet had decided that despite her preoccupation with the Duncan problem she would still go to the station and do her routine patrol, something inside her wouldn't easily let the rangers down. She pulled her car up on the grass outside the station and walked into the briefing room, her rucksack slung loosely over one shoulder. She was the first one in. Jack Gregg came out of the office and saw Janet.

'Heyup Chuck, are you alright?' he said cheerily.

Janet looked at him and smiled weakly. Her eyes were red and he could see the stress in the features of her face.

'You're not, are you, love. What's up?'

Janet looked up at him again. 'Me and Duncan have split up, he's gone. I'll tell you about it later, when the others have gone.'

'Alright my love, are you sure you want to patrol today?'

'Yeah, I'm sure; I need the walk to get my head clear.'

'OK, but we'll have a chat later and you always know where I am if you need a shoulder,' he said in a fatherly fashion.

'I know, Jack, and thanks.'

Just then, the briefing room door swung open and two other rangers walked in.

'Hi Alan, hi Ron,' Janet said, greeting them with all the enthusiasm she could muster.

Ten minutes later, Jack started the briefing. He allocated patrol routes on the blackboard to all of the duty people. Janet wrote her patrol down in her notebook. It would take her along Froggatt Edge on to Curbar Edge, then Baslow Edge. This escarpment was about two and a half miles long, then cross at Curbar Gap, then along to the Wellington monument, cut left down the lane across to Ramsley Reservoir, then the length of Big Moor and back to the station – all in all, about thirteen miles. This was a familiar patrol to her and didn't require the use of the map, except to practise pacing and resections, something she often did when supervising new recruits.

Janet set off, and was soon passing the railway station at Grindleford. She reached the main road, then soon cut right and made her way to the plateau at the beginning of the escarpment. Despite the good weather it was quiet, which surprised her; it was usually busy at this time of the year. She walked and pondered, the miles disappearing beneath her booted feet. Janet was almost oblivious of the walk, her mind churning over her present situation. She had passed the majority of Froggatt Edge when she was startled into sharp focus as she heard a dog bark. She stopped momentarily and surveyed the landscape; to her right the ground, steep and dressed in green bracken with a series of silver birch trees forming a pretty backdrop to the hillside. She looked and noticed the familiar farm buildings, where she had spent the night in a spare bed on the farm. She thought of the kindness of the young farmer who had rescued her from a tight spot. She looked and tried to focus on the farm. She noticed her heart beginning to thump in her chest and she felt hot. She dropped the rucksack from her shoulder and removed a small pair of binoculars from the side pocket. Looking through them at the farm, she noticed a movement, a man coming out of the stone barn. He was carrying a box. He stopped by the side of his Land Rover, opened the back up and put the box inside. Janet looked at the man she knew as Don. She hadn't felt this way for years, she knew; she decided. She picked up her rucksack and continued her patrol, but in those few minutes she'd decided her future, and now she felt a lot better.

CHAPTER 20

Paula was awake, woken by the nurses who would soon be relieved by their counterparts who worked the day shift. The sun beamed in through the window of the ward. There was a bustle about the place, nurses were busy attending to the patients, handing out bedpans and checking the patients' blood pressures. Paula now saw things clearly, she didn't feel ill or injured, seemingly the strong medication was working. She manoeuvred herself into a sitting position and thought of Mick, and the conversation they had had the previous evening. She felt mildly elated. OK, the accident was a problem, and who knows what would happen next. So far there had been nothing from the police. Their intimate conversation had confirmed what she already believed: with Mick it was the real thing, not like the others which had been just casual, temporary flings, there was a permanence about this relationship.

Mick was also awake, and his thoughts were the same. He felt lucky they had both survived; he knew that this was the real deal, and when Paula was well he was going to go for it, ask her to get married, something that he would not have thought about a couple of months ago. Somehow this trauma had focused his mind on what was really important in his life. It was her, Paula, laid in a hospital bed, injured almost fatally, and he had been at the wheel.

Jake was up and about. He hadn't slept very well, he put it down to the excitement of Antonella being in the house with him. The kettle boiled. Jake quickly made three cups of tea, put them on a tray and took them up the stairs. He tapped on his mother's door and stepped in.

'Hi Mum, cup of tea for you.'

'Thank you, son. How is Antonella?'

'I don't know yet, I'll take her tea in now.'

Jake tapped lightly on Antonella's bedroom door.

'Come in, Jacob,' he heard her say.

He stepped in. She was laid flat, her black hair spread across the pillow;

194

Jake's heart thumped and waves of love flowed through his body. She smiled.

'Good morning, Jacob, how are you today?' she said huskily.

Jake could barely speak; he stood and looked at her, feeling somehow detached from reality.

'I've brought you a cup of tea. How did you sleep?'

'I sleep very well indeed, but now that I see you, Jacob, my body is alive. Here, sit by my side,' she said, holding out her arms towards him.

Jake put the two cups of tea on the bedside cabinet and sat on the edge of her bed. She clasped her hand on his, and pulled it to her face and kissed his fingers.

'Jacob, I dreamed of you and me all night. I kept waking up, hoping my dream was true.'

Jake chuckled silently as the blood coursed around his body.

'And just what were you dreaming about?' Jake said, moving his hand and stroking her hair as she sat up in bed and leaned lightly against the pine headboard.

'Oh, Jacob, I could not tell you, I would be embarrassing. I will let you imagine, but I hope that my dream will be soon true,' she said, as she leaned her head against his powerful arm.

Mac climbed silently out of bed, pulled the curtain a couple of inches to one side, and peered out into the woods across the lane. Nothing had changed, everything was as it had always been, with one exception: he was a civilian, not employed. It felt weird, never again to get up in the morning and dress in his uniform and begin the process of planning what he would do with the boys on the watch. Val sensed he'd got up; she rolled on to her back.

'I thought you would have a bit of a lie in this morning,' she said blearily. The night had left her a little tired.

'No; force of habit, I guess. I'll go and make us a cuppa.'

Mac stood with his bare feet on the cool kitchen floor. He leaned against the sink, peering out into the back garden. He could see the sparrows congregating in the trees, the sounds of a new day gently erupting around the house. He could hear the electric kettle begin the task of boiling the water. His mind began to drift.

It was Mac's first year in the job. He'd been given the job of making tea for the watch. His sub officer, Alan Small, nicknamed Tiny Small, had told him that being the new recruit he had to make tea for the watch before the alarm sounded to get them all out of bed. He'd got up early; the wall-mounted gas boiler had boiled the water, which had been poured into the massive aluminium teapot. The tea was brewing nicely. He'd also been told what colour the tea should be when poured. He had a large wooden tray with a plate full of digestive biscuits; the milk was in the cups, and then the alarm actuated. Mac ran along the corridor, his head focused on speed. The tannoy sounded, ordering the water tender to a kitchen fire on the nearby housing estate. He ran across the brown-tiled floor and jumped into the back of the appliance, and quickly got rigged in his fire gear. It was a cold morning and Mac realised that in his haste he'd forgotten to put on his socks and shirt. His leather boots felt too big and his toes began to feel the cold. He pulled on the heavy woollen Lancer fire coat and quickly buttoned it up to his neck, slung the leather belt which held his axe around his waist, and buckled it up; he hung the large battery from his belt and wound the cable across his shoulder, and clipped the lamp onto the tab of his jacket. He was ready. The driver pulled up sharply, close to the garden gate. The two men in breathing apparatus threw their tallies at him.

'Stick them in the board for us, Mac. Cheers,' they said as they dismounted from the machine. Someone pulled off the hose reel as the men ran to the front door of the house. Mac could see smoke issuing from the window of the house.

'Get the bloody hydrant in, Mac; it's just up the road,' Alf shouted.

Mac threw up the locker and pulled out a length of 70-millimetre canvas hose, its gunmetal coupling making it heavy and cumbersome. He reached into the back of the locker and grabbed the standpipe, key and bar before turning and running to the hydrant. He prised up the hydrant lid and was still carrying the BA tallies, which he promptly dropped into the murky water of the hydrant pit. Mac spun the standpipe onto the metal outlet. He fixed the key and bar onto the hydrant valve and flushed it, bringing about an outpouring of stinking brown water which quickly cleared. He slammed the male end of the hose into the outlet of the standpipe, cracked the key allowing water to steadily fill the hose, picked up the hose and ran fast back to the pump. The hose was six feet short of the pump. The pump operator, Alf Smedley, an old hand, looked skyward as he saw Mac's mistake.

'Come on, boy, fast as you like. My water will be done in a minute.'

Mac felt failure for the first time. He controlled the feeling of panic, grabbed another length of hose from the locker and connected it to the female end of the hose, which by now was depositing water across the road. He quickly ran a zig-zag pattern of hose across the back of the pump, then gave the female end to Alf, the pump operator, who pushed it calmly into the inlet to the pump.

'Don't go away yet, young man. Where are the BA tallies, we've got to get them on the board?'

Mac was sweating with effort and stress.

'Sorry Alf, I dropped them into the hydrant pit. I'll go and get them now.'

'OK. When you've done that, get over there and give them a hand at the fire, and take a salvage sheet. And ask Tiny if he needs to send a message.'

'OK Alf, will do,' Mac said, his voice becoming breathless. He ran back to the hydrant and slowly opened the valve. Soon the hose going to the pump was hard as rock, the hydrant pit was filled with freezing water. Mac crouched low and put his hand in. He rummaged around, feeling his way around the metal fittings and stirring up the mud in the pit. He felt one plastic tally. He lifted it out of the water and plunged his hand in once more. He could feel slime and movement. He lifted his hand again, it was filled with huge worms who had taken the pit over as their residence, Mac wasn't squeamish at all, but the site of a dozen worms wriggling in his bare hand made him shudder. He plunged his hand in again and quickly found the other tally. He felt relieved that the chinagraph information on the BA sets' air content was intact; he ran back to the pump and slid them into their wire slots on the entry control board.

Mac grabbed the salvage sheet from the locker and ran across to the house. All of the windows were pushed open and the smoke from the fire was venting

197

freely. A head emerged from one of the upstairs windows and a voice came from within the facemask.

'That's got it all, Tiny, it's all out.'

'Thanks, lads. I'll get a stop off, make it all up. Mac, tell Alf to send a stop, from me. Mid-terraced two-storey house, ground floor severely damaged by fire. First floor severely damaged by smoke and heat, one hose reel and two BA in use. OK?'

'Yes, Sub,' Mac replied, before darting across the garden to tell Alf to send the message.

Mac sat with the crew drinking a mug of tea round the mess room table; he was beginning to feel that he was a part of the team.

'You did well there, young Mac. It was hard work but you did fine, your dad would have liked to see you working like that,' Tiny said as they sat at the mess table, eating their fried breakfast. 'Right lads, you all look a bit grubby. Get in and have a quick shower, but not all at once, don't want to give the other watches material, if you know what I mean.'

Mac laughed.

Even now, all those years later, he remembered how good that feeling of belonging felt.

He was jolted back to the present by the loud bubbling of the kettle. He poured the water into the blue Denby teapot, and was soon delivering the two cups to the bedroom. The day had arrived, the day of his leaving party. Over the years, he'd been to dozens of these, usually those of men that he'd served with. Now it was his turn. He wondered for a moment if young Jake would remember this day when his time came in thirty years. He thought he'd be long gone by then, as were many of his ex-colleagues who had left before him.

'Well, what shall we do today?' Val asked as they sat at the kitchen table, making short work of their bacon sandwiches.

'I need to go to town to get a few things ready for tonight, then I need to clean the car, it's filthy. Then relax a bit before the do at the station.'

The day passed quickly, and soon it was time for Mac and Val to get ready.

'I've pressed your suit, Mac. You just need to polish your shoes.'

'OK. I will do,' Mac called from the bathroom, his face covered in shaving foam. The phone rang. Val picked up the bedroom extension. 'Hello,' she said.

'Hi Val.'

She recognised the voice immediately. 'What can I do for you George? Hang on, I'll pass him the phone.'

'Are you OK for tonight? Just wondered if you wanted a lift in?'

'No, it's fine, George. One of the lads is picking us up and dropping us off. But we're looking forward to it, so I'll see you there.'

Janet had spent the night in a local B & B. She'd spent hours mulling over the situation and the meeting with Don the farmer, whose kindness had provided her with a bed for the night. She decided that for the time being anyway she'd steer clear of any further meetings with Don, but she felt it necessary at least to try to talk to her husband. In her mind, she thought she knew what she wanted, but she thought it important to see Duncan and let him know her thoughts and hear his view on things. She loaded her night bag into the car and headed straight home to the farm.

She manoeuvred the car over the rough ground of the lane leading up to the farm, the familiar track that she'd negotiated so often over the years. The thoughts and memories flooded back. She had never imagined that anything like this would happen to her. She'd always felt that her marriage would be forever, but it had become routine, almost mechanical, there had been no excitement left. Maybe she was partly to blame for not recognising the signs of complacency. She pulled the car into the yard; Justin's car wasn't there. She opened the door of the house. It was cold, the heating was off. It was dark and dull and no longer felt like home. She looked around the large lounge and remembered the many parties they had held there over the years, the happy times and the arguments. She wondered if the absence of children had impacted on them. All she knew was that everything had changed. She noticed a letter on the coffee table and tore open the envelope. The letter was written on a piece of folded notepaper. She wrinkled her brow as she read the note.

Janet, I'm sorry that it's come to this. It's become plain to me over the last months that things haven't been right between us. I have to admit that I've been seeing someone else. It's not your fault that it's happened, and you don't know her. It seems that you are intent on staying here and I will move south, I hope that we can sort this out amicably. I have gone to London and will stay there for the foreseeable future, call me on my mobile if you want to discuss anything. Duncan.

Janet looked at the note and read it again. 'Well, that seems to be that,' she said aloud, surprised at the lack of emotion she felt at reading the letter as she stuffed the note into her handbag. She quickly locked up the house and drove back into town.

Paula was awake early. The nurses had brought her medication and a cup of tea; she felt well, although there was a nagging pain in her leg and she felt the desperate need to scratch it. Her bandaged head was still sore but the best thing was her optimism for the future. She knew she wasn't going to die, she was happy that Mick felt as she did about their future together, the only thing she was worried about was the fact that she had caused the accident that could have killed not only her and Mick, but also the young boy. The guilt of that lingered in her head.

Mick climbed out of the taxi and paid the driver. He didn't like the smell of hospitals, never had from being a young boy, having been in there as a youngster to have his tonsils removed. He walked into the ward and saw that Paula was sitting up and looking much better.

'You look good today,' Mick said, smiling broadly.

'So do you,' Paula replied.

Mick sat on her bed and took hold of her hand.

'I'm looking forward to having you out of here, have they said anything about when you can leave yet?'

'No, but I guess a few more days at least.'

'That's good; don't want you rushing out until you're fit again. And I thought, when you do come out, you could come and stay at mine, so I can keep my eye on you.'

Paula looked at him and smiled a weak smile. 'That sounds like a good

200

idea, but my mum reckons she wants to look after me.'

'Well, I suppose your mum must have first choice, it would only be right,' Mick said, nodding his agreement.

Jake drove Antonella into town and managed to get parked.

'Now, what do you think you would like to see?' he said, as she sat quietly beside him in the car.

'I think to see Sheffield would be very nice. Can we have a drive around it and let me see it in the daytime?'

'Sure can,' he said, pulling out of the car park.

'Mac said an interesting thing to me last night,' Jake said as they drove out of the city.

'Oh yes, Jacob, what was that?' she said, her eyes peering intently at Jake as he drove in traffic along roads which were new to her, but were very familiar to him.

'It was late on our last night shift. It was dark, and we stood looking out over the city, and he said—' Jake paused for a second and looked at her. 'You know, Mac is a very wise man. He said this and it made me look at my town in a new way.'

Antonella put her hand on his arm. 'Your friend Mac is very special to you I think, my Jacob. I am hoping that I will meet him.'

'He is. He said, as we looked over the city, that the lights and hills were like a map of his life, where he grew up and went to school, where he met his wife for the first time and the fires he went to over the years.'

'He is a wise man I think also,' she said, smiling at Jake. 'I am very happy to be with you in your city, I think it is very beautiful and I am exciting to be seeing it for the first time.'

Jake turned to her and smiled, every time he saw her he caught his breath. This was more than he had ever expected from his life. A few months ago he was hauling bricks and mixing cement, going to the pub was his only outlet. Now it was different, he met Mac and Val, he joined the fire brigade, got the silver axe, rescued a girl from a fire, got experience in fires and had seen many things, but meeting Antonella had been the event which was the most important. She had changed everything, and he could see nothing beyond that which could spoil the thoughts and feelings he now felt. All because of the fateful day in London where he instinctively stepped in and rescued her from a man who had just robbed her.

After an hour of driving, Jake had shown Antonella most of the places he thought she should see. He asked, 'Shall we get something to eat?'

Antonella turned her head towards him. Her smile, her black hair ruffled by the breeze, made Jake's heart leap.

'Jacob, you have told me many times about Derbyshire. Can we go there and have something to eat, please?'

'We certainly can,' he said, turning the car at the roundabout and heading uphill out of the city.

Jake drove and soon left the buildings behind; the dark hills loomed on the horizon. Antonella took Jake's hand in hers.

'So this is Derbyshire. It is very beautiful,' she said.

He drove on through Hathersage and Castleton, then up the steep gorge of Winnats Pass.

'Oh Jacob, this is very beautiful,' she said, as Jake changed into a low gear to negotiate the steep, narrow road which bisected the rugged gorge. Jake headed for Mam Tor, where he stopped.

'What do you think?' Jake said, as they parked just beyond the nick in the landscape close to the stone path which leads to the summit of the hill.

'Jacob, it is as beautiful as you have said.'

Jake took her hand in his.

'I'm glad you like it. Shall we go now and get something to eat? I'm starving.'

Jake turned up through a small village built from the local grey limestone, and headed for the high ridge; he drove slowly up the steep, narrow road and soon crested the summit. He slowed to give Antonella the time to absorb the spectacular views. The land stretched for miles to the west, broken into a series of patchwork fields divided by miles of dry-stone walls.

'This is lovely,' Antonella said, as they sat in the old pub with its low ceilings and warm, friendly atmosphere.

'I brought Mum here a few weeks ago and she enjoyed it,' Jake confided.

'It is very, how you say, homely. Just the way I imagined a country pub to be like when I was living in Italy.'

Jake smiled at her and he took her hand in his. 'I would like to go to Italy sometime, maybe we could go together.'

The day wore on, and the time for the retirement party was approaching, Mac had showered and managed to fit into the suit Val had talked him into buying about five years ago. Val was dressing in a full-length black dress. Mac looked at her.

'Well I have to say wife, we're getting there. You still look as good as the day we met, and I bet you never thought you'd be married to a pensioner.'

'I wouldn't have had it any other way. You look OK, and the suit fits almost perfectly.'

Pete spoke to Brenda, his next-door neighbour, who was going to sit in with his boys whilst he was at the retirement party. She had come round early and had decided, without consulting Pete, that she'd cook the boys a meal. She opened the fridge door and leaned forward to look at the contents of the fridge. There was very little in there.

'Pete,' she shouted. She stood up and turned. Pete was there, standing close behind her. She noticed that his face was flushed. He put his hands on her shoulders.

'Thanks, Brenda. You've been very kind and I really appreciate it.'

Brenda knew; understood, she smiled at Pete.

'Don't say anything, just give me a kiss,' she said, just as the boys walked into the kitchen.

'What are we having for tea, Dad?'

Pete pulled away from her, feeling guilty and a little embarrassed.

Brenda smiled. 'Don't worry Pete, there's plenty of time,' she said. Pete mouthed to her that he was sorry, and she smiled a gentle smile. 'Don't worry,

I'll be here when you get back, don't drink too much,' she said in a whisper, and then she winked at him, indicating that what had just started was not yet finished.

The crew of the day shift had spent the day getting the station ready for the function. The fire appliances had been parked on the front of the station. The appliance room had been mopped and polished, then laid out with tables and chairs, a small area of raised staging had been constructed at one end of the room and a microphone had been provided for the speeches. At six o'clock the day watch was replaced by the night watch, who were killing time until the function started by drinking tea and getting the bar stocked, as well as helping the wives get the food and cake set out in the recc room.

Jake pulled his car up outside his house after their trip out into the Peaks. Jake's mum met them.

'Did you have you had a nice afternoon?' she asked, as they walked into the lounge.

Antonella grinned widely. 'It has been a beautiful time for us,' she said. 'You live in a beautiful place, the Peaks are wonderful.'

It was seven o'clock, and Clive pulled his car to a halt outside Mac's house. Helen moved from the front to the back seat of the car. It gleamed; it was Clive's pride and joy, a gift from a grateful man, Hubert Styles, a man who, in a small way, Clive had given moral support to whilst the watch dealt with a fire at his house.

Mac's doorbell rang. Val opened the door. 'Oh, come in Clive. We're almost ready, we'll be two minutes.'

'Hiya Clive,' Mac said, as he walked out into the lounge still fastening his tie. 'How are you both?'

'We're fine, looking forward to your speech, of course.'

Mac grinned. 'I hope you won't all be disappointed, I hope to keep it short.'

One by one, the fire station yard began to fill with the visitors' cars, and the people began to filter into the appliance room where the formalities were going to take place.

As they walked into the station, Mac could hear the buzz of voices which permeated through the station and began to feel a twinge of nerves. Val held his hand and sensed his reaction.

'You OK?' she asked, giving him a wicked smile.

'Yeah, I'm fine; I can't believe I'm nervous though, I think the last time was when I proposed to you.' He laughed.

Mac pushed the double doors which led into the appliance room. It was full, he could see just a monolithic crowd of people, unable to define any individual in the subdued lighting of the room. Then, almost from nowhere, his girls were stood in front of him.

'Hello Dad,' they said together. 'There's a table reserved for you over there,' they said, pointing to a spot close to the stage.

Mick Young stepped out of the taxi which had taken him to the fire station; Clive had offered to pick him up with Mac and Val, but he'd decided that he would come alone by taxi. He pushed the door open with his good shoulder. Immediately he could hear the loud drone of voices. It was awkward, his arm was still encased in a sling, and he still felt restrained by a strong ache across his body. Normally he would feel elated at being with the watch, but somehow the stress of the recent accident, his injury and the worry over the prospects for Paula and her recovery were overshadowing everything, even Mac's retirement party. He walked into the recc room with his head bowed, still overpowered by a feeling of guilt about the accident.

'Jacob, I think that I am the luckiest girl in the world at this moment,' Antonella whispered, as he led her into the fire station.

Jake was proud that she was with him and anxious to introduce her to his friends. Antonella would be looking into his world, just has he had looked into hers at the concert in London; he hoped that she would be as impressed as he had been. They could hear the drone of voices as they approached the appliance room; Jake pushed open the door and led Antonella into his world.

'Watch out, these are my friends coming to check you out,' Jake said, as he put a protective arm across her shoulders.

Brian was the first to approach them.

'Well, Jake, I think you should introduce this lady to us all,' he said, taking Antonella's hand and kissing it.

'Young lady, may I just say you are every bit as beautiful as Jake has so often told us! I'm Brian, and it is a privilege to meet you,' he said, bowing theatrically.

She smiled broadly at him. 'And you, Brian, it is also my privilege to meet you. Jacob has told me all about you.'

Brian stood tall, grinned and pushed his thinning hair back with his hand.

'I hope he only told you the good bits.'

Antonella laughed. 'Of course, from what he tells me there are no bad bits.'

Jake spotted Mick, who had managed to get into the room barely noticed.

'Hiya Mick, how are you? I didn't think you'd be here tonight. How's Paula?'

Mick lifted his head and looked reluctantly at Jake. 'She's OK, she'll recover alright, but I feel lousy. But I thought I should come.'

'Well, it's good that you came. Mac and Val are over there,' he said, pointing them out amid the dense cluster of people in the room. 'Why don't you go over and have a word with him? Then if you need to leave you can go when you feel you need too. It's good to see you, Mick, let us know if you need anything.'

'OK, I'll do just that,' Mick replied unconvincingly.

As Mick approached, Mac could see that there was something not right with him. He turned to Val. 'I think I need a few seconds to talk to Mick.' Val looked at Mick and immediately understood.

Jake spent the next few minutes introducing Antonella to his friends, who were all very keen to meet the girl who had so changed Jake's life.

The day shift had allocated a table for Red Watch, close to the stage where most of the speeches would be made. They were all there with wives and girlfriends. Jake and Antonella were soon being bombarded with questions and being asked about the life of a violinist. It was very plain to see that she had charmed all of the men and their ladies.

'So how long will you be staying, Antonella?' Pete asked.

Antonella looked at Jake, and at the gathered group of strangers who had accepted her into their world.

'Well, I have to go back to London tomorrow, because I have to be at rehearsals on Monday morning.'

'What are you planning to do tomorrow?' Ena asked.

Antonella smiled. 'Since Jacob and I met we have always talked about Derbyshire. He told me that Chatsworth House is very nice, so,' she turned to Jake and looked pleadingly, 'I am hoping that he will show me tomorrow, before I have to go back on the train.'

'Chatsworth is beautiful, I think you will love it,' Ena responded.

Mick slumped down on the chair next to Mac's, his head bowed; this was unusual for Mick, who was normally such a happy-go-lucky person. Mac looked at him; he understood exactly how he felt.

'Hi Mick, thanks for coming,' he said, putting his hand on Mick's shoulder. Mick turned to face him. Mac could see instantly the pain in Mick's face.

'I wouldn't have missed it, Mac. In fact, Paula insisted that I came,' he said, a hint of guilt in his voice.

'I know, and I'm pleased that you came, but I think you would rather be with Paula, so you don't have to stay. I understand, and so will the lads.'

'No, I'll be alright, Mac, I'll stay. I'll be OK in a minute, I just need a bit of time to get myself together.'

'Look, Mick, I really appreciate you coming, I'm glad you did, but please don't feel you have to stay. We all understand.'

'Paula's going to be OK. It will be a fairly long recovery, but thankfully she'll be OK.'

'Well, Mick, you stay as long as you want. I'm glad you came, but you go when you want, OK?'

CHAPTER 21

The background music stopped and the voice of Mick Cork, the station commander, rang out over the microphone. The room became hushed.

'Welcome to Graveton. Tonight, we are here to say farewell to our friend and colleague, Mac. There's a lot to get through, so we have compiled a running order. If you are desperate for a drink or the toilet, go and get it now, the bar is in the recc room.' Mick Cork paused and rattled the sheet of paper in his hand.

'We have a list of people who want to say something, so I reckon I need to say that you should try to keep it as short as possible, otherwise we'll still be here tomorrow. Thank you.'

There was a minor stampede of people for the bar and the toilet, and within a few minutes the room began to settle down. Mick Cork stood up again.

'Right folks, we'll get the show on the road,' he said. *'Obviously we're here to say goodbye to Mac, and as you can see, the turnout tonight tells us a lot about the man.'* He paused and looked at Mac. *'I've known Mac for many years. He was my sub officer some time ago, and in fact he was one of the people who made me realise that there was more to life than beer and women. He told me you can do all that but still do a good job in the fire brigade.'* Mac laughed and looked at Val, who squeezed his hand.

'Mac, I reckon, is probably one of the most respected men in the brigade. Not that he ever tried to be that, it's just that he's been so bloody good at the job, and on top of that his blokes love him. So now, without further ado, let's start on the list. Right, number one on the list is Tony, who will be stepping into Mac's rather large boots on the next tour of duty.'

Tony climbed up onto the low stage and took the microphone from Mick.

'R-r-right, folks,' Tony began, *'I will make this short, you all know why; because even my short speeches can take a long t-time.'* There was a round of applause and laughter. *'I'm very aware that there is a long queue of people wh-who w-w-want to speak, so let me s-say this. Mac, you are and have been my hero for a very long time; in my opinion you are the ultimate fireman. You*

helped me when things got hard, and were it n-not f-f-for you I would probably have l-left the job. I know it's not politically correct to say this, b-b-but I love you, Mac. Unfortunately your time in the job is over and we w-w-will miss you. That's it, th-th-thank you.' The crowd gathered in the fire station gave Tony a loud cheer.

Mick Cork again took the mic. *'Now we have Red Watch, who tell me that they want to say something.'*

The men of Red Watch climbed up onto the stage and lined up side by side. Brian stepped forward and began to speak.

'I've been nominated by the guys to speak for all of us.' He paused and mopped sweat from his brow with his handkerchief. *'We – the watch, that is – have known this was coming for some time, but to be honest it never really clicked that it would happen. Mac has been such a part of the fixtures and fittings of this station and our working lives that you forget that he's only human, and will have to actually retire; I think we all thought it would never really happen. I think, and I know that the guys feel the same, that it's been a privilege to work with him. He's been a great boss and colleague and a friend to all of us. Don't get me wrong, if you step out of line you very quickly know it, but once you've had your balls chewed – metaphorically speaking, that is – he gets on with it, he doesn't hold a grudge. We will miss him a lot, his sense of humour, his knowledge and leadership will be a hard act to follow. So, enough said. We hope that both he and Val have a long and happy retirement, and he knows that the hydrant near his house will be the best maintained in Sheffield.'*

Mick Cork took the microphone again. *'Now Mac's old LF, Ray Swift, has asked to say a few words.'*

He handed the microphone to Ray, who cleared his throat. The last time he'd been in the station was at his own retirement party, and he was nervous. He began.

'Mac, I seem to have known you all my life, and there have been times when I've trusted my life to you and you never let me down. Life in this job is interesting, not just the characters – and by God, there's been some of them – but the job, helping people out, putting their chimneys out, taking a ring off

their finger, digging them out of a car or putting their fire out. We are always there when we're needed. The type of calls we get are too many to list, but that is the essence of the work. I loved it and I know you loved it, and I reckon we were good at it. I loved the job but most of all, Mac, I loved being part of your watch, the friendship, the trust, the sweat and pain – it was all worthwhile. You deserve a rest now, so good luck my friend, and also to Val who is also retiring in her own way. So, that's it from me. I could go on for longer but I must give the others the time. Thank you.'

Pete stepped forward and took the mic. The guys on the watch were surprised, Pete wasn't known as someone who would push himself forward. He cleared his throat and shuffled uncomfortably, light beads of sweat forming on his brow.

'A little while ago I was in another place – another place in my head, that is – and literally a different station. At that time, I had almost become overwhelmed by life. I had two boys and a sick wife, no money, and life was just one long battle to make ends meet. I lost all sense of pride in myself and the job; in short, I had become a waste of space. When I came here my first experience was of meeting Mac. I have to say, that meeting is still burned into my brain. He terrified me almost to the point where I was thinking of asking to leave before I started. Mercifully, I didn't. Coming to Graveton was the best thing I ever did. Mac and the boys on the watch got a grip of me and changed my life, and also the lives of my wife and my boys. The lads on the watch accepted me and helped when things were tough. Sadly, I lost my wife not so long ago. For her it was a release, she had struggled for a long time, but you know when you love someone no matter what, it is still painful, and Mac and the boys were great, they carried me through. So now I look at myself and ponder the past, but look at myself now. I'm proud to be a firefighter, especially on Red Watch at Graveton, and proud now to call them and Mac my friend. Thank you, all of you.'

The audience shouted loud, some very moved by Pete's words. Pete: normally the softly-spoken, quiet man who had suffered in silence for years, but now reborn.

Mick Cork took the mic from Pete. *'Thank you, Pete. It's great that you've settled so well. Now, I think we should let Mac say a few words.'* The audience applauded loudly.

Mac got up from his seat and Val squeezed his hand and smiled. He climbed up onto the low stage and took the microphone. Mac cleared his throat, stood silent for a moment, and looked around the room.

'I'd like to say to all of you that I'm grateful that you decided to come along. It would have been a pretty dull affair if it had been only me and Val here, she's already heard the speech.'

Mac looked around the room. It was full, but he could still pick out many faces that he recognised. In an instant, his mind slid back to the night his father retired from the job. He remembered the speech his dad made. It was short and stumbling, his dad had not been a man to speak in public, but Mac recognised in himself the same feeling for the job as his dad.

'When you join this job, the last thing that is on your mind is retirement. It's only later that it becomes any sort of issue, at least that's how it was for me. I always tried my best to be the best I could be, and I was always lucky to have a wife like Val who has been perfect. She always supported me, but would always tell me if I was out of order, so I believe the marriage I have was a big part of how I did my job.

'Over the years, a lot of things have changed. The gear we use, the uniform – I remember going from black helmets to yellow, that caused a stir. But most of all I remember the people, my colleagues. In the early days, of course, my dad, my hero; old Ray there, a better man you could not wish to meet. I also remember some of our customers. The old lady on her deathbed, with a painful finger because her hand had swollen and we had to cut her wedding ring off. It had never, not once, been off her finger in sixty years. She thanked me and looked into my eyes, and I saw tears. She knew she had little time but still took the trouble to thank me. Things like that have stayed with me. Now, it is my intention to make this a short speech, so let me say a few words about my watch. The Reds are not the best-looking blokes you will ever meet. In fact, they're a pretty ugly bunch, but I love them, like a dad or brother that is. Let

211

me tell you about them. Brian: big, going bald, funny and brave, devoted to his mates. Jock: what can I say, he's Scottish. You know what that means. Yeah, despite reputations he isn't tight – well, not very. He once lent me ten bob and didn't ask for it back, so I have it for him later when he buys me a drink. Taff: the Welsh republican. Despite that, he is the best driver I have worked with, if only he knew where he was going. He did say he knew his way back to the station from anywhere on the station ground. So we never got lost coming back from a job. Mick: Mick is a wonderful man to have by your side; he always has mints in his pocket, as you can see he took the time to be here tonight despite his injuries and the need to be with his girlfriend Paula. So thanks, Mick, you are a good bloke. And we have here, young Clive: Clive was a boxer, not a man to argue with, but also he has a heart of gold, he would do anything for anyone. He is also a very, very good fireman. Then there is Pete. Pete has been a revelation. Despite all his problems, he has never fallen short with Red Watch, I have to say, Pete, that you have my great admiration. And young Jake. I met him when we were out in the Peaks. He helped me with an old guy who had collapsed, he carried my rucksack, thinking that someone of my age probably needed help. But fortunately for us, and the job, he joined the job and has settled in well. Tonight he's brought with him his lovely lady friend, who has travelled up from London.

'The young guys today are tomorrow's old sweats; they'll carry forward the standards that we set for them. I've got no worries at all about the future of you all in the job, despite everything, all the changes, health and safety, et cetera. The changes in our duties. When it comes to the crunch, we do it, and I'm sure that when it gets tough you will all grit your teeth and do the job we are paid for.

'So what will I do after today?'

Mac stopped, paused and looked around the room. He'd been to many retirements, and now this was his.

'What will I do? Well, for one thing Val and I will be spending more time together. But I will also be joining the ranger service, so I'll be getting out and doing quite a bit of walking around the Peaks. But also I'll be thinking

about you all, doing the job that I've loved for all these years. I'll probably be envious, and maybe I'll be one of those old fogies who says it was much better in my day, but I will always love the job and the men who do it – so thank you, and good fortune to all of you.'

Mac bowed to the cheering crowd, and was soon joined on stage by Mick Cork.

'*Well, Mac, thank you for those kind words. Now, there are still a few formalities to get through. So first, Red Watch has something for you as a parting gift.'*

Mac's watch climbed back onto the stage, and Jock came forward carrying a large parcel.

'*Mac, we thought we should get you something from all of us, something that we hope you will find useful.'*

He passed the parcel to Mac. He read the card which was attached to the wrapping. It read: *To our Friend and boss Mac, you were the best and we will miss you.* Mac tore open the paper wrapping and smiled broadly as he realised what his boys had got for him. Still enclosed in its plastic wrapper was a coat, dark blue with yellow trim. Mac grinned. 'Do you mind if I put it on now?' he said, smiling at the men. He slid on the coat, undid the hood and pulled it over his head.

'*This will do very nicely, thank you boys.'*

The crowd of people gathered there laughed as Mac strode back and forth across the stage.

'*This will be great if it rains tonight,'* he shouted over the laughter in the room. Next came a presentation from the men of the station. He was given a pewter mug, emblazoned with the brigade badge and an inscription: *To mark the retirement of Sub Officer Malcolm James. 15th June 1966 to 12th June 1996.*

John Blain climbed onto the stage and presented Mac with his axe, which had been chromium plated and mounted on a dark mahogany plinth. He shook Mac's hand and paused. He took the microphone from its stand.

'*It had not been my intention to speak tonight, but now I feel I should. I've moved around brigades quite a bit since I joined the service. When I*

213

moved to South Yorkshire, I had little idea of what living and working here would be like. I guess I was an archetypal southerner, you know, the world ends at Watford sort of thing. I moved around quite a bit. I have to say that now both my wife and I are very settled. Some time ago, I met up with Mac and his watch at a job, and something occurred that gave me a new perspective on my career. I now feel that South Yorkshire is our home, and believe that this is where we will settle. Mac is an exceptional fire officer, and more than that, he is an exceptional man. He does it all in an understated way. He is good at his job and he runs a good watch. I wish him all the good fortune for the next phase of his life, which I'm sure will be just as successful. So thank you, Mac, for your service to the people of Sheffield. You are right, things will carry on after you, we will grit our teeth and do the business – but that is down to the example you and other officers have shown. You leave a strong legacy for others to emulate.'

Mick Cork again took the mic, and asked Val onto the stage. He then presented her with flowers, which she graciously received. Then, to everyone's surprise, Sub Officer Henry from Billing Fire Station came onto the stage. He offered Mac his hand, then turned and spoke.

'Tonight I've surprised myself. I can't say that Mac and I have always got on, in fact the opposite is probably true. I know what a good fire officer he is and his reputation around the brigade tells you that. He is very highly thought of. I've watched and listened tonight to the kind words offered to Mac by his many friends, and I have to say I am envious. I've learned the meaning tonight of respect. So, to Mac and his watch I say, thank you for the many times you've come along and helped Billing at jobs, and I wish, Mac, that both you and your wife have a long and happy retirement. I had a collection at Billing, and I have to say I was surprised at the result'.

He lifted a large bag from the floor and passed it to Mac. Mac was surprised, he hadn't expected anything from Billing. He unwrapped a large, heavy box. Mac was startled. In the box were several bottles of expensive wine.

'That is very good of your station. We love Italian wine, thank you very much.' Mac took Henry's hand. *'To all the guys at Billing, thank you, we will*

enjoy drinking this wonderful wine.'

For the next thirty minutes there was a series of minor speeches and presentations, then the formalities were over. Mac relaxed, loosened off his tie and drank another bottle of lager. Various people came to their table to shake his and Val's hands and to wish them well. Jake sat at his table with Antonella by his side. Mac looked at them and smiled.

'Do you know, young lady, your young man is a very good man, and it's good to meet you. We can now all see why he's been so keen to have you visit us all.'

Antonella smiled as she looked at Mac and Val. 'Jacob has spoken so much to me about you, I feel almost that I know you already. I think that he is a very lucky man to work with such nice people.'

Val took her hand in hers. 'Well, we think that Jake's a lucky man to have you. You are beautiful, and from what we've been told you are a very talented lady. Maybe we will come to see you at one of your concerts.'

'Thank you,' she replied. 'Jacob as told me much about his life and how he loves his fireman being. It has been my great pleasure to meet Jacob and his mama, and now to meet all of his friends and for you all to be so kind to me, it is a wonderful feeling you are giving me. I am very proud to be the girlfriend of Jacob; I hope that I will be welcome to come again soon.'

Val leaned toward Antonella and put her arm around her shoulder.

'I have a very strong feeling that we will be both hearing a lot about you, and seeing you a lot more.'

Antonella flushed, and her eyes became filled with tears of happiness.

'I do hope so, Mrs Valerie and, as Jacob says, Sub,' she said, dabbing her eyes with her handkerchief. 'I love Jacob a very much more than I can tell.'

Mac stood up and stood behind her. He leaned forward and put his head close to hers.

'I think, young lady, that your feelings for Jacob are mutual. And please, call me Mac.'

Mac sat looking around at the many people in the room. It felt surreal. He was saying a final goodbye to the world he had known for most of his life. He felt a tinge of sadness that it had come to an end. He knew that he would still visit from time to time, and that the many friends he'd made over the years would still be a part of his and Val's life, but he found it hard to tie down in his mind that this was the end. Val could see the process his mind was computing; she leaned against him and squeezed his hand. Jake stood close by him and looked at Mac, and their eyes met. Jake came in close.

'You know, Mac, I've been very lucky to have spent time with you, lucky that we met up on White Edge. Thanks so much.' Mac took Jake's hand. 'Young Jake, I'm the luckiest one of everyone in this room. It's been a privilege to do the job with so many good, dedicated and brave men, you among them. Bring Antonella to our house tomorrow before you take her to the station. We would both like to see her away from this, if you have the time.'

Antonella had been listening to the conversation. She leaned against Jake and put her arm through his. 'That would be very nice to visit you, I'm so proud to be here tonight, it has been for me very interesting and exciting.'

As the night passed, Mac and Val were visited by many friends and colleagues, all wishing them lots of luck. Slowly the crew of Red Watch and their partners congregated around Mac's table, which was rapidly becoming filled with empty glasses and bottles. Antonella and Jake sat side by side, holding hands and occasionally turning their heads to look at each other and smile. Brian and Jane sat together chatting to Taff and Ena, Clive and Helen talked with Tony and Mick. As the night wore on, Mick's demeanour improved. He relaxed and talked about how he felt and how Paula was improving, and their hopes for the future.

People began to drift away, the hour became late, and it was time to leave. The watch stood up to allow the night shift to begin the process of restoring the station back to normal. They began shaking Mac's hand. Mac's body stiffened, he felt the hairs on his neck stand up. 'Fire call coming,' he said.

Two seconds later, the lights came on and the call out alarm actuated. Then a swirl of activity, as the night crew ran out to the fire appliance and in seconds, in a cloud of diesel fumes and flashing blue lights, disappeared into the night.

'Well, you've still got it, Mac,' Brian said, smiling broadly. 'I've never understood how you do that.'

Mac returned a subtle smile. 'I don't know, it's something I've always done. Right from the early days, I've had this sense when a call was coming.'

Antonella squeezed Jake's hand and looked into his eyes. 'Oh Jacob, it is so exciting for the fire call to send your friends to their fire, I feel I am still trembling.'

Mac stood up. 'Well lads, we can't leave the station in a mess while they're out on a job. Why don't we set to and put it straight. It'll save them a lot of time when they get back.'

Val laughed. 'I don't know, Mac, we should go home.'

'Nah, come on, it'll be fun. My last job on my old station.'

And so Red Watch, and the last of the stragglers, cleared the tables. Val and Antonella did the washing-up, Jake and Brian swept and mopped the appliance room floor, and soon it was done.

'Thank you all, for making this pensioner very happy. The night shift will be very pleased when they get back to see there's nothing for them to do,' Mac said.

Mac and Val drove slowly from the station, Mac reflecting on the night. He felt a warm glow over his body. The good things that people said had left him with a sense that it had all been a worthwhile life.

Val took his hand. 'Well now, young man, we really are retired. What a good night it was.'

Mac drove slow, his mind flooded with happy thoughts of the past, and now the future was there to be explored.

Jake and Antonella sat quietly in the car. It was dark, and the roads were quiet.

'So, how did you like my fire station?' Jake asked, as they sat hand in hand.

Antonella looked at Jake and pulled his hand up to her cheek. 'It was beautiful, you have so many of nice friends, they were all lovely. I had a very nice evening, Jacob. It was so exciting when the alarm rang; it made my heart beating very fast.'

'You make my heart beat very fast,' Jake said. 'I think we will have a nice day tomorrow.'

Antonella pulled Jake's hand to her chest, leaned into him and kissed him. 'I am very looking towards visiting Chatsworth tomorrow, my love.'

Mac lay quietly, unable to get to sleep. Images from the past flew across his mind.

He was sitting on the back of his dad's motorbike; they were going on his first fishing trip. He was eight years old. Then a picture came into his mind of Janet falling off her new bike, and cutting her chin.

The first intimacy he and Val shared, he felt the same tremble of excitement he felt then. The birth of their children and the early nights, afraid to go to sleep, lying awake, listening for their babies' breathing.

The sound of the church bells at his wedding and their honeymoon in Scarborough.

He was standing next to Freddie, with his arm across his shoulder, laughing at some corny joke.

The warmth of his mother's bosom as she pulled him close when he was five years old, and kissing his forehead.

Then his dad was sitting on his bed and ruffling his hair, telling him about the fires he had been to that day.

Mac sat up in bed. The clock showed twenty past six, he hadn't slept. But he felt good. He could hear the traffic in the distance, then the faint sound of a siren. Mac knew, he'd felt it, the fire call coming in to the station. He also had a premonition of what and where the fire was. *Car fire on the parkway,* he said to himself.

Jake woke himself; the daylight had disturbed him, his mind instantly fixed on the girl in the bedroom next door. He climbed quietly out of bed and slipped silently out of his room. He opened the door of the spare room where Antonella slept. The house was silent; the only sound was of the occasional car passing the house, its occupant off to work on the early shift. He stood next to her bed and looked at her as she lay on her side, sleeping quietly. He sat on the chair and watched her, sad that she would have to go back to London later in the day. But he was happy, he now knew for sure that both he and Antonella felt the same and he knew that this was a love that would last. He sat for several minutes, listening to the sounds of her breathing. He dozed, and was soon asleep in the chair by her bed.

Mac climbed silently out of bed. He looked around the bedroom, which was still in semi-darkness, then made his way into the lounge. He reflected on anything which came into his mind. It had been a good thirty years; he'd shared many things which he would treasure. His picked his way through his life with Val and the girls. His work, life in the job, had been a journey that he could never have imagined. The friends he'd grown to love and trust, the friends he'd lost to the job. His mind was tinged with both happiness and sadness. Happiness that he'd spent the whole of his working life doing something he loved. Sadness that now it had ended; excitement that the future would be as interesting and challenging as his past had been. It had been a good journey.

He heard the water in the kettle boil; he made a cup of tea, sat and drank it slowly, savouring the first cup of the day. He heard more sirens in the distance. *Police or ambulance,* he thought. Then more sirens. He swung open the curtains of the lounge. It was going to be a nice day. The trees sat unmoved in the early morning sunshine, barely a breath of wind. His eyes focused on the sky above the trees in the wood across from his house, and he saw what looked like a plume of smoke rising gently in the sky. Then there were more sirens. Mac felt the hairs on his neck stand up and the old familiar sensation, like a small rush of adrenaline. He could see the smoke cloud rising higher in the sky and then a loud explosion. Mac wanted to know what was happening, his curiosity had been roused. He went back to the bedroom and slipped into his clothes. Val turned over in bed, opened her eyes and looked at Mac.

'I heard the bang, but you don't have to worry. It doesn't concern us now.'

'I know,' Mac said, 'don't worry. I'm just curious. I may just pop down and have a little look. I won't be long,' he said as he slipped out of the room.

Jake felt the warm lips on his. He woke instantly.

'Jacob, why are you in my room?' she said, smiling.

He sat up. 'Sorry, I came in to see you, but you were asleep so I sat and waited and fell asleep. I just wanted to be near you.'

Antonella smiled a sleepy smile and brushed her hair back with her hand.

'Last night, Jacob, was a wonderful night. I loved meeting your friends, I see now why you love your job.'

'I do love it, and I'm glad that you were there with me, just as I was glad and proud to be with you in London. We are lucky to have found each other,' he said, without even the slightest sense of self-consciousness.

'It wasn't luck in my opinion, Jacob, it was fate. I believe that we were sure to be together. I always wondered, from being a small child in Italy, who I would have as my husband and be the father of my children. When you came to my rescue in London I knew then that it was you. Fate: I know it was meant to be, that we would be together.' Just then there was a light knock on the door. The door opened slowly and Jake's mum poked her head around and looked into the room.

'Hello there, you two. I didn't want to disturb you, but I wondered if you would like a cup of tea in bed?'

Antonella smiled shyly. 'We were just conversing about us, and fate. Do you believe in fate, Mrs Higgins?'

Jake's mum smiled a knowing smile. She knew; she realised that her son and this girl were meant to be together.

'Well, Antonella, I can't say it was something I ever thought about before we went to London; but when you were attacked and Jacob knocked the man out on Oxford Street, and then I saw you, I just knew then – just something, I think instant chemistry. So yes, I do believe in fate now.' She stood by Jake's side and tousled his short hair. 'I think that you are both very lucky people. Now, let me go and make that tea.' She turned and left the room, closing the door quietly behind her.

Mac drove the car the mile to the industrial site just off the bypass. He parked the car and walked around the office buildings, and could see the pall of smoke closer now. He could hear the shriek of the appliance pumps and he caught a glimpse of men running, setting the hydrant into the water main. He stopped and thought. *This is daft. This is what I was, I'm not that now. Nothing sadder than an ex-firefighter who won't let go.* He turned and walked back to the car, he didn't look back. He knew now that his past was behind him, and his focus should now be on his and Val's future.

He pulled the car into the drive. Val was up and she'd drawn the curtains. He opened the door; he could smell the bacon cooking in the grill.

'Well, you weren't away long,' he heard Val call from the kitchen.

'No, I just had a quick look; I won't be doing that any more, it's time to move on.' He walked into the kitchen. Val had her back to him; he stood behind her and put his arms around her waist. 'Thanks for being my wife, and looking after me all these years,' he said.

Val turned around and put her arms over his shoulders. 'It has been my pleasure, Malcolm James. You've terrified me, worried me, made me laugh and cry, but I wouldn't change a thing. Your mum and dad would both be very proud of you now.'

'Well, Mrs James, I think that when the dust has settled we should sit down and decide where we go from here.'

Jake's mum sat on a chair and Jake sat on the side of Antonella's bed as they sipped their cups of tea.

'So, Antonella, what have you decided to do today?' she asked.

Antonella looked up at Jake; he sat with his arm across her shoulder as she leaned against his body. 'Well, Mrs Higgins, I think that Jacob and I will try to go to see the Chatsworth House. I have heard so much about how beautiful it is, so that is what I hope we will do.'

'Well I think that is a good idea, it is very beautiful. Now, I'm going to get changed and I will get the breakfast going. Will bacon and eggs be OK?'

Antonella smiled broadly. 'Of course, it will be lovely, so English. Thank you.'

Pete turned over in bed. He felt the warm body next to his and, for a second, thoughts of Trudy, his now dead wife, came flooding back into his mind. One of his boys had crept into his bed during the night, something that happened often these days; even now, they still missed their mum and talked about her frequently. Pete had pangs of guilt still, especially now that his neighbour had made it clear that she liked him a lot, and he had reluctantly allowed his deeper feelings to show. She had kissed him and he had felt all the old feelings that he'd hidden for a long time, since his wife's illness. His mind slipped back to his arrival home from Mac's retirement function. He'd parked the car, opened the front door; he could hear the soft tones of the TV playing in the lounge. The room was almost in darkness, illuminated only by the glow from the television. Brenda sat on the sofa.

'Hi Pete, how did it go?' she asked.

Pete stood and looked at her; she wore a tight blouse which amply demonstrated her well-developed body. Pete's eyes were drawn to her; she knew, she could see.

'Come and sit here with me, Pete,' she said, patting the sofa cushion next to her. Pete moved unsurely and sat beside her. They said nothing. She turned and looked at him. She put her hand behind his head and pulled him to her, locking her lips on his. Pete gasped, his heart pounded, his body quickly, overtaken by desire. Her hands searched him out.

'I've wanted to do this for a long time,' Brenda said, as she undid buttons and zips.

In a few minutes it was done. Pete lay back, exhausted; a feeling of happiness and gratitude filled his being.

'Thank you, Brenda, that was great.'

'It was. Now I'll get off home. You get some sleep, and maybe we can do this again sometime.'

Brian woke early. Jane was by his side, and he could hear Jill playing quietly in her room. He crept out of bed, so as not to disturb Jane. He went quietly into Jill's bedroom; there she was, sitting up in bed, reading one of her many books.

'And how are you today, young lady?' Brian asked.

'I'm fine, Dad. Shall I go and make us a cup of tea?'

'No, you go and slip in beside Mum. I'll make some tea, and we can all sit in bed together and drink it.'

'OK, Dad,' she whispered. 'I'll be as quiet as a mouse.'

Jock sat in his new conservatory, with his face buried in the sports pages of the newspaper. His team, The Blades, had managed to scrape a win against Birmingham and were now lying in third place in the league. He was a happy man. Fraser had played for the reserves away at Bolton, and had scored the equaliser against an experienced back four with a header from a corner.

In the dressing room, the coach, Jack Bevan, was full of praise for the team's work ethic and singled Fraser out for special praise. It had been tough against bigger more experienced players, but he'd done well. Jock sat quietly mulling things over in his mind's eye. He imagined his son to be soon in the first team squad. He was so proud. He tapped lightly on Fraser's bedroom door and pushed it open. Fraser stirred.

'Good morning, Dad.'

'Morning son, brought you a cuppa. How do you feel this morning?'

'Yeah, I feel OK, just a bit stiff. Their centre-half kicked me up in the air a few times.'

'Yeah well, it was a tough game, you did well.'

'Yeah. Terry Jenkins, the centre-half, he shook my hand and said I'd done well, which was nice of him.'

'Yeah well, he's been a good player in his time, a lot of experience. A few years ago he was in the squad to play for England; never got on, but he was a good player, not too far off retiring now though.' Jock smiled.

'What are you grinning about?' Fraser said.

'You make me happy, son, I'm proud of you,' Fraser smiled.

'I'm proud of you, Dad.'

Jock turned to leave the room. 'Right son, I'll go and get your breakfast started, it'll be ten minutes.'

Taff and Ena were up and dressed. Shopping was on the list of jobs for the day, but first their usual trip to chapel. The one thing in their lives that had been a constant, it had given them solace when things got tough in their marriage. They were both brought up to go to chapel from an early age in the Rhonda valley.

'It was a nice night last night, don't you think?' Ena said, as she sipped her glass of orange juice.

Taff looked at her and nodded sadly. 'Yes, it was, but I feel sad that Mac has gone. It won't be the same, no matter how good Tony is. But what did you reckon to Jake's girlfriend?'

'Well, I thought she was beautiful; young Jacob has struck gold there, she seems to be a very nice girl.'

Taff smiled to himself, remembering when Jake first came to the watch.

'You know, he has changed a lot. He's always been a good lad, but the past few months he's become a man. We've seen it happen in front of our eyes, and I think this girl is part of the reason.'

'I think you're right, they seem perfect together.' She drained the juice from her glass. 'Right, boyo, let's get off to chapel,' she said, her face beaming with happiness as she slipped her arm into the sleeve of her coat.

Mick paid the taxi driver the fare and walked painfully into the hospital. The corridors were quiet. He glanced carelessly at the pictures on the walls as he walked, he could smell the food cooking from the canteen; he heard the chatter of the nurses at their stations as he made his way toward where Paula would be waiting for him to arrive. As he walked, he met a porter pushing a clearly very sick elderly lady in a chair, and something clicked in Mick's mind. *Was this to be their future, forever looking back at the bad things that happen in life?* He decided in that instant that it wasn't going to define their lives. There may be physical scars and some tough memories, but life was precious and now he could see it, life is good. He straightened himself up and forced a smile onto his face, and walked into the ward. Paula was sat up in bed, held up by a large volume of pillows. The wooden cabinet at the side of the bed was filled with get well cards and a bottle of orange juice. She looked up as Mick walked into the ward and smiled.

'Good morning,' she said, her voice now sounding much stronger.

'Hi,' Mick replied. 'You look better today, how are you feeling?'

'I feel really good; I think they'll let me home in a few days. The doctor had a look at me this morning and he says he's really happy with the way I'm getting on, so hopefully I'll be home soon.'

'That's good. I went to Mac's do last night, and all the lads send you their love, it was a good night.'

'I'm glad; Mac deserved a good send off.'

'Yes, it was a really good night. You know, things have got me thinking. When you're up and about, we need to have a chat about things, the future. Life is too short to waste it, so let's have you back fit soon.'

Mick sat quietly by her bed. The ward was beginning to get busy with visitors; they held hands, but said little, sure in the knowledge that some sort of inevitability had risen out of this bad experience. *Yes, we'll talk soon,* Mick thought. Paula dozed on and off, the effects of the drugs making her drift off, then suddenly she'd be awake again.

Jake changed gears and the car climbed steeply, soon leaving the city behind. The high moors were golden and green, illuminated by the early afternoon sunshine.

'It is very lovely, the countryside, Jacob. It is very different to London, I love it.'

Jake turned and smiled at her. *Well, aren't I lucky,* Jake mused, *the place I love and the girl I love sitting with me, it's perfect.* Jake took the roundabout at the Owler Bar roundabout and turned, heading south towards the village of Baslow. Soon, Chatsworth House came into view through the trees.

'Oh Jacob, it is such a lovely setting, I can't wait to go inside.'

Jake drove slowly over the bridge, which gave a view of the house set in the bottom of the valley, fronted by a tree-lined river. He paid the parking fee and pulled into a space. It was busy, the park bustled with families; some intent

225

on visiting the gardens, some just came to wander in the grounds, families, children, people with dogs. Sheep meandered around the park, oblivious to the visitors. They walked hand in hand to the entrance of the house, then up a tree-lined drive to the main entrance.

'Jacob, I am so excited, I think that we will bring our children here to see this house.' Jake felt a rush of blood to his head. He hadn't thought that far ahead, but it seemed to him that it was as he had hoped, Antonella was serious about them. Sure enough, he was serious about them. He squeezed her hand.

'That would be really nice,' he said, turning and putting his arm over her shoulder.

'So, Mr James, what is on the agenda for today?' Val enquired.

Mac sat looking at the paper. He lowered it and smiled.

'Well, I think a day of doing not a lot would be nice. It'll give me a bit of time to get used to the idle life.'

'That sounds good to me; I'll go and make us a cup of tea.'

'Good, no sugar for me, I'm going on a diet.'

'Oh yes? I've heard that before,' she laughed.

Mac grinned. 'I'm serious. If I'm going to be trudging around the Peaks doing my rangering, I'll have to get myself fit. You know, Janet won't want to be dragging me around on the patrols.' Val walked out and into the kitchen. 'Oh, and we did say to Jake that if he had time, to pop round with his young lady before she left for London?' Mac called.

'Right Mac, let's sit out in the garden, it's a nice day for it. You get the chairs out of the shed while I make the tea.'

Mac sat in his T-shirt and shorts, a peaked cap sat firmly planted on his head. He mulled over the last tour of duty and the leaving party. It had been great but he had no regrets. The last tour would stay with him forever, as would many things that had occurred over the years. So many thoughts and memories like a mental scrapbook, to look into whenever the fancy took him. Val brought the tea and a plate of digestive biscuits.

'I enjoyed last night,' Mac said.

'So did I,' Val replied. 'I was proud of you, as were the girls. It was so nice to see the people who you have helped and influenced over the years.'

'Yeah,' Mac sighed. 'Jake's dropped lucky with his girl, she's even nicer that he'd said, and very intelligent with it.'

Val sighed. 'Yes; young love, it makes me think of us when we started going out, you can see it in them. I think the way they met, it being so intense, helped secure the bond.'

Mac looked at Val. 'Now, don't you go getting all sentimental, we'll have that to deal with when our two decide it's time for them to think about getting married.'

'Yes, I don't know when that's going to happen; they don't seem to be in too much of a hurry.'

Mac sat and dozed in the sunshine, his mind gently drifting about randomly focusing on things from the past. He remembered the guy Edgar at the garage, who he'd had the confrontation with, and wondered what he was doing now. He thought about Freddie's mum and dad. Freddie's dad had died but his mother still lived nearby, Mac made a mental note that he and Val should visit soon. Mac was brought out of his dreamlike state by the sound of the doorbell.

'I'll get it, Mac,' Val called.

'Hello Dad, how are you doing now you're an official old man?' Lucy said, with a chuckle in her voice. Mac turned his head; his eldest daughter had come to visit.

'Hi Luce, so you managed to creep out of bed this morning alright?'

'You are a cheeky thing,' she replied, 'I've been up ages, I just got bored so thought I'd come and see how you were.'

'I'm fine, thank you for that. What have you got planned today?'

'I plan to spend the day with you and Mum; I've got it on good authority that Mum's doing a roast dinner.'

'Well, it's good to see you. Sit down here and I'll get you a drink, do you fancy a Pimm's?'

'That would be lovely, Dad, thanks,' she said, lying back in the reclining garden chair.

Clive stirred. It was late. They'd overlaid, tired from the previous late night. Helen lay, still asleep. As he climbed out of bed she stirred and opened her eyes. Clive looked at her.

'I was just going to make some tea, do you fancy a cuppa?'

'Yes please,' she said, as she stretched and yawned. 'After that I have something else on my mind, which you may be interested in.'

Clive guessed what she was implying. 'OK, I'll make the tea and be back in a flash,' he said, grinning.

They sat up resting their heads against the headboard.

'Do you think we should try for another baby?' she asked.

Clive gripped her hand. 'Well, we tried yesterday and the day before, but if you want to try again, count me in,' he laughed.

Helen slid her pillows down and lay back, pulling the duvet up beneath her chin. 'Right mister, what are you waiting for then?' she laughed.

Clive laughed at her and pulled the duvet up over both their heads. 'OK then, where shall I start?' he growled.

Janet turned the car off the road and onto the dirt track. Above and to her front sat the grey-brown rocks of Froggatt Edge. Her mind wondered about the things that had brought about her present situation with Duncan. She mulled it over and over, and finally concluded that they shared the fault for the breakdown. He'd become immersed in work, his mind focused on expanding the business; she had allowed things to drift. Somehow, almost invisibly, they had become different people, wanting different things. Having come to that conclusion it became easier to deal with, the bitterness began to fade and a light appeared at the end of the tunnel that a new life could be hers. The car jolted and bumped its way up the track. Ahead she could see the farmhouse. She felt she needed to see the young man who had been happy to help her when she needed it.

Don was having trouble catching a sheep which was in need of some attention. He heard the car pull to a halt close by and turned. He saw the car, and when he recognised it his heart leapt. For a second he wondered what had brought her back, and then the wonder turned to hope.

228

'Hello,' he said, his voice breathless, unsure whether it was caused by the struggle to subdue the sheep or just plain pleasure at seeing Janet again. 'What brings you back here?' he said, his sweat-covered face broken by a broad smile.

She climbed out of the car and looked at him. He was breathing heavily and his face was red and damp with sweat.

'You look as though you've had a fight,' she said.

He grinned. 'Well I have, and I think so far the sheep is winning,' he chuckled.

'Well,' she said, 'I thought about your offer of dinner, and being as you've been so kind, I've decided to take you up on it.'

Jim was up early; he'd taken tea for him and Maddie back to bed. After a late night out, Maddie had stayed at Jim's flat; an occasional arrangement, Jim didn't like the idea of her being out on the roads late at night on her own.

After breakfast, they packed the rucksacks and were soon on the road, heading for the Peaks.

'So, what's the plan today?' Maddie enquired. It had become custom and practice that Jim would make all the arrangements for their weekend walks.

Jim looked across the car to Maddie and smiled. 'I was in town the other day and heard a girl talking about a little walk below Stanage Edge. It sounded pretty interesting, so I looked it up on the map. I thought that was what we could do today.' He smiled and turned to look at their newly acquired companion. 'It's not too long for Henry and his arthritic legs,' he said, looking fondly at the Labrador who had settled very easily into his new life. Maddie smiled back.

'Good, we've not done much up there.'

Jim drove steadily into the countryside; every time they came out this way he sighed, somehow the hills made the everyday stresses of his life evaporate. He had Maddie at his side and the sun was shining, what could be better. He steered the car off the main road and drove up a steep, narrow lane. To one side were pretty houses, with lush gardens lined with dry-stone walls. Soon the long, grey ribbon of the rocks of Stanage Edge appeared; already, they could see that there were climbers draped across the escarpment. He pulled the car into the car park.

'This is it, we've arrived,' he said as he climbed out of the car and opened up the boot. He helped Henry to get out of the car and attached the lead to his collar.

Soon they were on their way, cutting around the back of the ranger station and descending a steep, wet, stony track through the woods. After a few minutes a large stone building appeared to their left.

'That looks like a nice place, Jim,' Maddie said, peering over the stone wall which surrounded the property.

Jim looked at the map. 'Yeah, it's North Lees Hall. I seem to remember something about one of the Bronte sisters visiting it when she was in this area.'

'That's interesting,' Maddie said. 'I've read most of the Bronte books; do you reckon this is where she got some of her ideas for the locations in the books?'

'I wouldn't be surprised,' Jim replied.

They continued downwards, crossing smooth green open land, the landscape opening up before them. Across to their left were trees which lined the edge of a deep gorge. As they descended along the cropped green meadow, which was a patchwork of bracken and grey rocks, a small ruined building appeared in the middle of a field.

'It's sad to see these old buildings falling down, don't you think?' Maddie said, squeezing Jim's hand.

'According to the map it's a derelict chapel, probably hundreds of years old.'

'It always makes me imagine the people who went to the place, maybe got christened or married there. Wouldn't it be interesting if you could look back and see things as they were in the olden days?' Maddie said wistfully.

In the bottom of the valley a small wood nestled in the sunshine. As Jim and Maddie approached, a small swarm of goldfinches erupted from a thorn bush, causing a startled cry from Maddie.

'Oh Jim, look at that, aren't they beautiful.'

Jim had become accustomed to her regular outbursts of enthusiastic comments about a pretty flower or a statuesque tree; it was one of the traits which he loved most about her. Until he'd met Maddie his life had been dark, boring and grey; since they'd met, she'd changed his whole view of life. Now there was excitement, colour, and not least something to look forward to. The addition of the dog, Henry, had given Jim a whole new incentive, someone or something to be responsible for, and providing that Jim filled his bowl with food regularly Henry was one happy Labrador. Jim had never felt so content with his life, these past few months had seen seismic changes in his life. He'd gone from being a scruffy no-hoper, with nothing in his life other than to look at other people and stare in envy as they went about their lives. Things now were so different, most of all he had Maddie, the love of his life, the person who, almost without trying, had caused him to re-evaluate his perspective on everything he had ever thought: his attitudes, his work, his future. He felt truly blessed.

They crossed a shallow stream which flowed gently over rocks, amid a small group of hawthorn; they stopped to look around them. It was as if they had stepped into a film set, the land was positioned perfectly. Behind them the ground climbed, the ridge beyond had the ramparts of Stanage Edge sitting like a huge grey castle wall protecting it; to their left, in the distance, was the outline of the Burbage Valley. They stood in the centre of a bowl, the ground covered in a blanket of fresh green grass; it gave a sense of remoteness, almost as if they were the first people ever to set foot there. In the centre of the bowl was a raised grassy bank. They walked slowly, taking in all the images of the place. As they climbed to the top of the steep mound, Jim gasped out loud.

'Come and see this, Mad woman,' he called.

Maddie walked up towards him, and as she surmounted the low hill she came upon a surprising sight. There before them was a hidden pond, surrounded by heavily leafed trees. The water was clear as crystal, and lying beneath its surface was a sponge-like bed of luminescent green weed, which almost glowed in the bright sunlight.

'Oh Jim, do you think we could have a little swim in it, it looks so lovely?'

Jim looked at her and smiled. 'You can if you want. Count me out. I'll stand guard just in case anyone comes along.'

'Right, OK. I'm going in, just for a quick splash.' Maddie gave Jim a cheeky smile as she stripped off her T-shirt and shorts.

Jim looked around, there was no one around. 'Off you go then, don't be long, you never know if we'll get visitors.'

Maddie sat on the grassy bank and dangled her feet into the water. She recoiled. 'Brrrr, it's freezing,' she laughed. 'I'd best get in quick,' she giggled as she launched herself in. She swam smoothly across the water, then turned onto her back and floated. Jim smiled to himself, he was so happy. He looked at her; her body glistened in the sunshine. Maddie laughed out of pure pleasure.

'Come on Jim, its lovely once you get in.' Jim was shy, and not one for displaying his skinny frame. 'Come on, my man, I'll give you a kiss if you do.'

Jim laughed. 'Oh OK, but just a quick dip, alright?' Jim climbed out of his shorts, took off his boots and socks, and walked into the water.

'Whoooah, it is freezing,' he squealed, hunching up his narrow shoulders.

'Come on, don't be a wuss,' Maddie shouted.

Jim launched himself across the pond towards Maddie. Maddie swam away from him, then turned and splashed her hand in the clear water. Jim blew the water from his mouth and wiped the hair from his eyes.

'Right, I'm in. Where's the kiss?' Jim said, smiling.

'Well James, you have to catch me of course.'

Jim was not a strong swimmer, so after a minute of him trying to catch her she stopped and waited for him.

'Your reward, sir,' she said, as she put her arms around his slim waist. She kissed Jim and pulled him over, so they were both momentarily submerged; she held on to him and kept her lips locked onto his. They both emerged from beneath the water blowing out sprays of water from their mouths. Jim laughed out loud.

'You really are a mad woman,' he blurted as she launched herself at him, and pushed him beneath the surface again. Jim's head bobbed up again and Maddie swam close to him. She grabbed his hands.

'Aren't we lucky, Jim. A few months ago we hadn't even met.'

Jim grinned wildly. 'Dead right, who would have thought.'

Maddie swam to the pond's edge and pushed herself up and out of the water.

'Right, I'm going to dry off. Are you coming out?'

Jim splashed inexpertly to the bank. He raised his arm, and Maddie took hold of his hand and pulled him up. They dried off and sat in the warm sunshine. They ate their sandwiches and drank their tea, and Henry chewed contentedly on a stick. Jim leaned across and put his arm over Maddie's shoulder. 'This is heaven, wife to be.'

CHAPTER 22

The sun beat down on the rocks above the farm. Don looked at Janet and mopped his face with his handkerchief.

'Well, it's nice to see you. Sorry about the state of me. Do you fancy a drink? Tea, coffee or water?'

'That would be nice. It's pretty warm, you must be boiled.'

'Yep, I am. Shall we go indoors, it'll be cooler in the kitchen?'

They sat opposite each other at the large pine kitchen table.

'Well, it's nice to see you again. What brings you back?' Don asked.

Janet looked at him and a semblance of a smile crept across her face.

'You were very kind giving me a bed for the night and rescuing me from the lane, so I thought you deserve to know what it's about.'

'I was a bit curious, but you know you don't have to explain.'

Janet sipped on the mug of tea. 'I was in shock, really. Right out of the blue Duncan told me he wanted us to move to London.' She paused and took another sip from her mug. 'I was shocked. We had a real barney, something we haven't done very often in all the years we've been married. Then it transpires that he's been having an affair, so that's it really, he's gone, and I'm now on my own with the prospects for the future a bit up in the air. That's it in a nutshell.'

Don massaged his chin. 'Well, that must have been painful. What now?'

Janet ran her hand through her hair and shuffled on her seat.

'I don't know. I'm always busy, I guess the rangers will occupy me, and the house is pretty big so that will also keep me busy; but beyond that, I haven't yet thought about it.'

Don looked at her. 'Well you know that if you need anything, give me a call or pop up. And if you need any help with the house, let me know.'

'Thank you, I'll let you know. I just wanted you to know that I'm grateful for your help.'

Mac sat in his garden, chatting with Lucy about his retirement function and his thoughts about the future. He smiled to himself. He felt good. It had been busy; there had been a number of telephone calls which had taken his time, mostly from old friends wishing him well.

'So, Dad, what now do you reckon?' Lucy asked. 'You've been busy all your life; will you and mum have a holiday?'

Mac took off his cap and wiped the perspiration from his head.

'We're not sure yet, probably a holiday somewhere. I've a few jobs to do around the house, and of course I'm hoping to start with the rangers soon. To some extent I'll let Mum decide what she wants to do.'

Lucy leaned across and grasped Mac's hand. 'I was very proud of you last night, Dad; it was lovely hearing all those people saying such nice things about you.'

Mac smiled as memories of the evening came into his mind. 'Yes, it was nice, it was good to see so many old colleagues and the boys of the watch did well.'

Lucy looked at Mac. 'You know Jake, Dad? Well, he is a nice young guy and I thought his girlfriend was great, very pretty and clever. I chatted to her a bit and she told me about how Jake had rescued her in London. She's very smitten by him.'

'I think Jake is smitten by her also,' Mac replied. 'I hope it works out for them. The distance could be difficult, and work patterns; I believe she has to tour with the orchestra sometimes, so fingers crossed that it all works out.'

Val came out into the garden with a tray of drinks and a plate of biscuits.

'So, what are you two plotting?' Val asked, as she laid the tray on the table.

'Not plotting at all just, having a natter about things; last night, Jake and Antonella, what I'm going to be doing next, et cetera.'

Jake and Antonella climbed the short flight of stone steps from the entrance lobby into an ornate corridor; the floor was of highly-decorated coloured stone, a series of small Dutch oil paintings decorated the walls and ornate chairs were placed against the walls.

'This is a very pretty area,' Antonella said, her face split by a broad smile.

They moved slowly on. They entered a large, high room, whose ceilings were covered with paintings.

Antonella gasped. 'This is such a beautiful room, Jacob.' Close by, a smartly dressed, bearded guide whose blazer was adorned with the Chatsworth emblem emblazoned on the breast pocket asked if he could be of any assistance.

'Can I tell you anything?' he enquired.

Jake looked at the man, who appeared to be someone who had a lot of knowledge of the house.

'Yes, can you tell us something about this room? It's beautiful,' Jake said.

Antonella hooked her arm through Jake's and listened intently as the guide described the room. He spoke about the Glorious Revolution, when King William and Queen Mary were invited to England to usurp James II, and the paintings about the life and demise of Julius Caesar. They climbed a wide, ornate staircase to the top of the building and entered the state rooms. Antonella noticed a large, beautifully sculpted vase. A young woman guide stood nearby, and she noticed Jake and Antonella studying the ceramic creation.

'Would you like me to tell you about it?' she asked.

'Yes please,' Antonella responded enthusiastically.

The guide told them that it was a tulip vase from around 1700, made in Holland. At the time, tulips were very valuable and were a sign of wealth, and the vases were made to enable the wealthy to display their position in society. She continued to talk about the ceiling paintings by an artist called Antonio Verrio, and spoke about one of the figures depicting the head housekeeper, Mrs Hackett; having not got on well with the artist, he had painted her on the ceiling as a witch – like the figure Atropos, one of the three Fates, the one who decided the death of everyone and lends her name to *Atropa Belladonna*, deadly nightshade. They moved on through the drawing room the music room. On the wall of the music room there was a door on which hung a violin. The elderly room guide, who was a little rickety on his feet, stood close by as they peered at the violin.

'That looks like my violin,' Antonella said.

The guide stepped up behind them, and with a gentle smile asked, 'Do you play the violin, madam?'

Antonella turned to look at the guide; he was short, with a head of grey hair. Immediately she thought that he looked like her grandfather.

'Yes, it is my job; the violin looks like it is a good one.'

The guide touched her arm gently and smiled. 'It isn't really a violin, you know.'

'Oh, well it looks very much like my instrument.'

'Look very closely.'

They peered hard at the violin.

'Well, it looks like a violin to me,' Antonella said. 'I play one every day.'

The guide smiled again. 'It's actually a painting, done by a painter called Jan van der Vaart,' the guide confided.

Antonella was surprised. 'Thank you very much, it is a wonderful. I would not have thought,' she said.

They moved on, holding hands as they descended a flight of stone stairs, and soon stepped into a magnificent chapel with a beautifully carved altarpiece and yet more paintings on the ceiling. The walls had complex carvings of fruit and wildlife adorning the timber walls. Jake put his arm across Antonella's shoulder.

'This is beautiful,' Jake said, and looked at his girl.

Antonella smiled and crossed herself. 'Yes, Jacob, it is very beautiful; I wish we could be married in a place as beautiful as this.'

Jake laughed silently and pulled her towards him. He kissed her on her cheek.

'Maybe I'll have a word with the duke and see if the chapel would be available for us; when would you like us to use it?' he smiled.

She put her hand on Jake's bottom and squeezed it.

'Now would be perfecto,' she replied, giggling aloud.

'OK, I'll see what I can do,' Jake said. 'When I next see the duke, I'll ask.'

They walked slowly, absorbed by the building and the fine pictures and furniture. They entered a room completely furnished in wood, ornate columns and dark wood panels. Antonella studied everything, she was fascinated. Jake looked on.

They climbed an oak staircase, and entered a room which had walls that were filled with books. The guide, a young woman, pointed out to them the main library, which they thought to be the most beautiful room they had ever seen, with its decorative plaster ceiling and beautiful furnishings. The walls lined with thousands of books made them stare in awe. The guide spoke quietly about the family's love of collecting books. They moved along into a wonderful dining room with its curved, decorated ceiling, the room almost filled with a huge table set for a meal and filled with fine silver. There were magnificent paintings by Frans Hals and Antony Van Dyke adorning the walls. Antonella took many pictures, most included Jake posing by the table or close to the beautiful curtains. They moved into the sculpture gallery with its high stone walls and ceiling, built especially to house the pieces. Naked men and women stood or lay in poses the sculptor had captured. The overall impression was of something very special.

'Jacob.'

Jake didn't reply. Suddenly, he was lost in his own thoughts.

'Jacob,' she repeated.

'Oh, sorry, I was daydreaming,' he said apologetically.

'Oh, that is alright. I just wanted to tell you how delighted I am that you have brought me to this beautiful place.'

Jake squeezed her hand. 'It is my pleasure, the house is lovely. I was just thinking about what we said earlier.'

'Oh, what is that?' she asked.

'Well, about us getting married. It got fixed in my head and I can't get it out.'

Antonella turned and put her arms around his waist.

'Oh Jacob, the thought of you and me being married makes me tremble.'

'Well, I know it's very early days, but I'm sure we'll stay together. It's been so good having you stay with me and Mum.' He paused. 'I don't look forward to you going back to London.'

'I know, I will miss you again very much, I hope that we will be able to see each other again soon.'

'Well now, I think we should drive back to town and call in to see Mac and Val, before you go back to London.'

Antonella hugged Jake. 'I think, my Jacob, that you love Mac as much as you love me.'

Jake pulled her to him and kissed her neck.

'Well, I reckon I do love him, but don't tell him that. I would never live it down,' he laughed. 'But I don't love anyone as much as I love you; except maybe my mum, and that is different.' He smiled.

Soon they were back in the car, heading slowly through the countryside to Sheffield.

Val was in the kitchen, preparing food. She was certain they would have visitors today, so she was making sausage rolls and scotch eggs and egg and cress sandwiches. Lucy came into the kitchen.

'Can I help, Mum?' she said as she dipped her finger into the mayonnaise.

Val looked at her. 'No, you just talk to Dad. He's so glad to see you, we haven't had much of a chance this past few weeks. It will be nice for you to have a bit of time with him on your own.'

'Well, I wanted to have a chat with you before I spoke to Dad.'

Val looked at her. 'Is there a problem?' she said.

Lucy looked sheepish. 'Well no, but there is something I need to talk to you about. I keep getting fellas coming on to me when I go out and, er, well I don't find them interesting at all.'

'Well that's OK love, you're still young. There's loads of time for someone nice to turn up.'

'Well, er, that's it really. That's what I wanted to talk to you about.' She moved up to Val and put her arms around her. 'I've met somebody.'

'Well that's good, isn't it?'

'Well, yes, I think so but, er, well they call her Louise.'

Val gulped silently. 'Oh, right. Yes well, mmm. So you're friends, have I got it right?'

Lucy squeezed herself tight to Val.

'Well. Yeah, we're just friends so far. I like her a lot and she likes me, but…' She paused.

Val saw her struggle and kissed her on the cheek. 'You know, love, that it's not such a big deal these days.'

'I know, Mum. What do you think Dad will think?'

'If I know your dad, and I do, it won't faze him at all. All we have ever wanted is for you and Ruth to be happy. All I would say, sweetie, is don't go rushing in, and don't be pressured into anything. It's your life and we'll always support you.'

Mac walked into the kitchen.

'I need a cold beer,' he said.

'Well, you know where they are,' Val chided. 'Just because you're retired, doesn't mean we have to wait on you.'

'Oh right, getting militant are we? And what are you two plotting in here, chatting away?'

'We were just discussing ways of getting rid of you and running off with your pension,' Val laughed.

The doorbell rang.

'I'll get it,' Lucy said, as she turned to get the door.

'So what were you two up to?' Mac said. 'I could tell you were up to no good. I'm perceptive about things like that.' He laughed.

Val half smiled, Mac noticed.

'Is there a problem?' he asked.

'No, forget it. I'll talk to you later.'

Janet climbed into the car. Suddenly she felt better, calmer. Don leaned forward and put his hand on the door.

'Well, thanks for coming. I'd better get back to sorting the sheep out.'

'No, thank you for the help. Just to say, I'll take you up on the offer of a meal, once I've got my head sorted out.'

She drove off down the lane, the tyres kicking up dust behind her in her wake. She looked in the mirror and saw that he'd turned away and was heading back to the sheep pen. She smiled. She liked him, liked him a lot. Quite without thinking, she pulled the car to a halt and reversed back to where Don stood. She wound down the window.

'You know, if you offer me the use of the bed again sometime, I may take you up on it.'

She smiled, pressed the accelerator on the car and drove back down the lane.

Don stood with his arms loose by his side. He shook his head, and wondered if he heard her correctly. He smiled to himself, thinking, *I hope so.*

'Come on in, nice to see you again,' Lucy said, as she gave Jake and Antonella a peck on the cheek. 'Dad's just through in the kitchen, he'll be glad to see you both.'

'Well hello, young lady,' Mac greeted. 'You look lovely again today.'

'Thank you, Mr Mac, I am so pleased to be seeing you also and Mrs Val, you look beautiful today.'

Val grinned widely. 'Well thank you, Antonella, so do you. Remind me to have a word with my husband, will you? I can't remember the last time he said I look lovely.' She grinned.

'So how are you both today?' Mac asked.

Jake leaned back against the doorframe, allowing Antonella to speak.

'I am thinking that I am very happy to be here in Sheffield. Last night at your fire station was wonderful, to have all of those people say such wonderful things is a, how you say it, a very big complimento.'

Mac smiled. 'It was very nice for me too, to have friends and family and people that I have worked with over the years come to say goodbye.'

'It was also very exciting for me to see where Jacob works, and I think it was a lot of exciting when the siren went and the men ran out to the engines. It made me shake.'

Val began pouring out several cups of tea. 'Now, I know you'll be ready for something to eat, so I've got a few things ready. Shall we go and sit in the garden?'

They moved out of the house. Mac had arranged the garden chairs around the table, which was filled with plates of food.

'So, Jake, what have you been up to today?' Mac asked.

Jake shielded his eyes against the sun as he looked at Mac.

'We went for a look around Chatsworth; I never knew it was that good.'

'It is lovely, we've been loads of time, and they change it around a lot so it's different every year. Did you see the violin?' he asked.

'Yes, we did. I thought it was real, the guide told us it was a painting.'

'So – you've had a look at Sheffield and Derbyshire, what do you think?' Mac asked.

Antonella smiled. 'It is all so beautiful. Sheffield is very interesting, it has many nice buildings, and I liked Derbyshire very much. I think when I visit again I will ask Jacob to do a walk in the hills.'

Val came out into the garden with a tray of cold drinks.

'OK, let's get stuck into the food while it's fresh,' she said.

Mac looked mischievously at Jake.

'Well, Jake, I have to say your young lady has met our expectations. Do you know, Antonella, Jacob walks around in a dream most of the time and he talks about you all the time. We all felt that we knew you before you came to Graveton.'

Jake sat sipping a glass of lemonade and squirmed.

Antonella grinned. 'You know how Jacob and I met, I think.'

Val laughed. 'Yes, we heard. He was very gallant.'

'He saved my life, he was my instant hero, and I knew then that I would love him.' She paused and smiled. 'I, how you say in England, fancied him immediately.'

Mac chuckled. 'Well, Antonella, I can say that from the way Jake has been since he met you, he seriously fancies you too.'

Jake smirked, embarrassed by these comments. 'Aww, come on, Mac. Are you trying to kill my credibility with the boys on the watch?'

Mac grinned. 'If I'm a judge, they already know. It's been obvious for some time that this young lady figures very strong in your mind; and I reckon I can see why. She is beautiful, clever and talented; you know, Jake, all the things that you aren't.'

Antonella laughed at the banter.

'I think Jacob is the most handsome man, and he is also clever and brave. Just the type of man I dreamed and hoped I would fall in love with.'

'So you go back to London today?' Val said.

'Yes, I have to be at practice tomorrow at nine, so I have to go home and sleep.'

'And when will you and Jake see each other again?' Lucy asked.

Antonella creased her forehead. 'We are not certain yet, I have some concerts in the future and I believe we will tour parts of Europe also this year, so I hope not very long.'

Jake looked up and put his hand on Antonella's shoulder.

'I think I'll be going to see her in a couple of weeks in London. I got a taste of it when I was there with Mum at the theatre, so hopefully we will be together again soon.' The hour passed quickly, and Jake looked at his watch and noted it was time to go. 'Well, I think we have to leave. Got to get back home and get her bags sorted, then down to the station. Her train leaves just before seven o'clock.'

'Well, Antonella,' Mac said, 'it has been nice meeting you.' Mac put his arms around her and kissed her cheek. 'I hope that you will come back to visit us soon.'

'I hope so, it would be very nice for you all to visit in London,' she added. 'It has been lovely; I enjoyed greatly your party and my visit to the Peaks and Chatsworth House. I am very happy here.'

'It's been a pleasure to meet you at last,' Val added.

'If you wish to come to London you must let me know. I can meet you and I can arrange for you a visit to a concert,' she said.

Jake backed the car out of Mac's driveway, and they both waved as they disappeared down the lane. Mac put his arm across Val's shoulder.

'She's a nice girl,' he said wistfully. 'Do you remember how it felt to be that young and that committed to me?'

Val shrugged. 'Well it was a long time ago, but yes, I remember a time when being together was all that really mattered too.'

Mac twisted his lips, as if thinking what to say.

'Yes, me too. I do envy them that feeling now, new love, all to live for. I think that they'll make it, she is clever and Jake is very grounded. The only worry is the distance, but these days it's just a couple of hours by car.'

Jake drove slowly back home, almost as though to delay the moment when he would have to take Antonella to the station. They drove in silence, neither able to speak, not wanting to break the spell, both feeling something that neither had felt before. The weekend was coming to an end and they knew it, but were trying not to think about it. Jake pulled the car to a halt on the road close to home, and he noticed a tear sliding slowly down Antonella's cheek.

'Jacob,' she said tearfully.

Jake took her hand in his and looked at her. He could see that she was upset. So was he, but he was determined not to show it, certainly not to the point of allowing tears to run.

'Jacob, it has been the best time of my life and I am so not wanting to go back to London, but I have to. I will be missing you even more now.'

'I know, it has been perfect. You met my friends, who have all fallen for you, and it has all been even better than I imagined,' he said. 'We must try to get to see each other again more often. I'll come to London very soon, in about two weeks.'

Antonella stroked Jake's leg as he sat behind the wheel of the car. Every nerve in his body responded, and she could tell.

'Oh, two weeks. Can I wait so long? I will arrange for a hotel for us to stay, so we can be alone,' she said, looking Jake in the eye.

Jake's heart pounded at the thought. 'That will be great. Come on, let's go in, see Mum, get your gear, and then we'll have to think about getting to the station.'

Mick sat by Paula's bed. He was pleased to see that she was improving fast, and the prognosis from the hospital was good. The scarring to her face would, they suggested, be minimal. This had buoyed him up after a period of guilt and worry. He held her hand and they sat silently reflecting on everything that had happened over the past few months. He smiled to himself, remembering the occasion when he jumped in the river to rescue her from her fears as she stood on a stepping stone in the river.

'And what are you smirking at?' she said light-heartedly.

She herself was feeling upbeat about their situation, the news had all been positive. Her injuries, whilst not trivial, were not life-threatening and somehow over the past hours and days she seemed to have matured from the happy-go-lucky girl to being something slightly more serious. Mick found that aspect of her very attractive. He himself had undergone change in many ways, no longer feeling the need to prove himself; he was content in his skin and convinced that he and Paula would go the distance.

'Nothing special, just glad you are on the mend and looking forward to the future with you and the guys on the watch. I've got a lot to smile about,' he said, reassuringly.

'So, tell me about Mac's do, and about Jake's girl. From what I hear she is nice.'

Mick grinned mischievously. 'She's more than nice, she's gorgeous,' he said.

'Yes, so I hear. You be careful, I'll be watching you,' she said laughingly.

Mick squeezed her hand. 'It's going to be strange without Mac, you know.'

Paula looked sympathetically towards him, realising that Mac's leaving would be a big hole to fill on the watch.

'I know it's obvious, but Mac is just a bloke like the rest of you. He was a young fireman once and did well for himself.' She paused and thought for a second. 'You do know; if you applied yourself, you could be a sub officer, what with your army experience.'

Mick pondered the thought.

'You're right, but Mac was special. He just knew how to deal with stuff, people respected him.'

'Yeah, I know that, but that doesn't just happen. He's obviously done things to earn that respect.'

Mick scratched his head. 'I know, you're right. Maybe I will take the exams and see what happens.'

'Good, that makes me happy that my man has some ambition and wants to better himself.'

Mick picked up a magazine from her bedside cabinet.

'Here,' he said, 'get your nose into this. I have to get away, things to do.'

'OK. Give me a kiss and I'll see you tomorrow.'

Mick leaned across her bed and kissed her. 'Now you behave, no chasing those handsome doctors, alright? I'll see you tomorrow.'

Mick walked slowly along the polished corridors, his mind dwelling on what Paula had just said. *It makes me happy that my man has some ambition and wants to better himself.* He thought about it all the way to the car, and all the way home, it even interrupted his sleep. He'd never really contemplated promotion, he'd always been happy being a fireman in the back of the machine and doing what he was told, enjoying the buzz he got from the close contact with danger. Now he was thinking maybe there was another way.

Brian got up from the kitchen table. 'Come on, girl, let's get the pots washed up. It'll save Mum having to do them, then we can get out in the garden.'

Brian wasn't really much of a gardener, mainly grass cutting and the heavy stuff. It was Jane who did the pretty things, planting flowers and plants, talking about grit and compost, none of which excited Brian at all – but he saw it as a duty to help keep it tidy, and it did please him to see it looking nice. Jill had followed in her mother's footsteps; she also liked weeding and edge trimming, partially driven by the inevitable couple of pounds extra pocket money Brian would secretly pay her for the help. 'Don't tell your mother, she'll skin me alive if she finds out,' he told her. 'OK Dad, I promise,' she said. Little did he know that she had negotiated a similar arrangement with her mother, who similarly had told her it was a secret and Dad should be kept in the dark. Jill promised to keep the secret and crossed her heart.

'Oh, Mrs Higgins, it has been wonderful being with you in Sheffield, I have had a wonderful experience.'

'Come here,' Alice said. 'It has been our pleasure; it makes me very happy to see Jacob so happy. I'm glad you have enjoyed your visit, come again soon,' she said, her face beaming as she wrapped her arms around Antonella.

Antonella stood back, and said, 'I hope that you will not be offended if I invite Jacob to come to spend a weekend with me in London soon?'

Alice smiled, realising the inevitability of it. Before, the thought of her son being this close to a woman had not entered her mind, but now it was all too clear to her that there was a serious relationship brewing. A tear welled up in her eyes, with the realisation that now, for the first time, she wasn't the only woman her son loved. In a way she was relieved, even pleased, but there was also a sadness that her little boy, whom she had nurtured through everything for the past eighteen years, was changing – becoming a man, with everything that goes along with that.

'Of course he should come, I am happy that you want to be together. I'm sure that Jacob will be with you at the first opportunity.'

'OK, Mum,' Jake said. 'We have to go, the train won't wait.'

The drive to the station was the hardest Jake had ever done. It was a drive he didn't want to do. He spent so much of his waking and sleeping hours thinking about this girl, and here he was taking her to the station, where she would get on a train and leave him 150 miles behind. It was hard, but inevitable; it would be something that they would have to get used to, because this would be their life for the foreseeable future until a more permanent arrangement could be made. They dawdled through the station, Jake pulling her suitcase behind him, his other hand firmly attached to Antonella's.

'I don't want to go, Jacob,' she said, her face a mask of sadness.

Jake stopped and put his arms around her. He pulled her close, her black hair covering his face.

'I don't want you to go either, but you have to. Ring me when you get home and we will talk every night.'

'I know, but I shall think of you every minute until you come to London.'

'And me too, I'm already looking forward to that. It has been a lovely weekend, and we'll have many more.'

They turned as the train pulled slowly into their platform.

'Well, I'll miss you, lovely lady. I've put something in your case, don't open it until you get to your apartment.'

Jake opened the door and carried her case into the carriage. She stood silently, wiping tears from her eyes. Jake put his big hands to encase her face and kissed her.

'You have a good journey, get a good sleep, and have a good rehearsal tomorrow.'

'Also you, Jacob, have a good sleep. I miss you even before I leave you.'

Jake stood on the platform; his heart ached as he watched the train pull away out of the station. He waved to Antonella as she peered out of the window, then she was gone, away, back to her other life in London.

'Hi Ruth. It's Dad.'

'Hi Dad, how was your day?'

'It's been odd,' Mac said to his daughter.

'Oh. How?' she replied.

Mac scratched his head. 'Oh, just funny, knowing that I won't be back at the station for the next tour. I've not had to think that for years. But I'll soon get my head round it.'

'Sure you will, Dad,' Ruth said lightly.

'Anyway, Mum, me and Luce are off out, do you want to come?'

'Yeah, where are we going?'

'Don't know yet, I thought we'd just drive out somewhere and stop off for a meal somewhere.'

'Sounds good to me,' she said enthusiastically.

'Right, we'll pick you up in half an hour.'

'OK, I'll be ready, see you then. I'll go and put some clothes on.'

'That would be a good idea,' Mac laughed, aware that his daughter often wandered around her flat half-dressed.

Pete sat comfortably on the sofa, the TV played to itself. The boys were in their rooms with their Playstations. Brenda had called round. They sat opposite each other, both aware that the occurrences of the previous night had changed things between them. Now, not just neighbours, but lovers or potential lovers. Pete still harboured some guilt, still felt like a cheat, but at the same time he realised it was possibly a good thing to happen. It would help his recovery from the torment of the loss of his wife, it would make him happier, thus a better parent to his boys, who had suffered enough over the past few years. And who knows, maybe a more permanent arrangement could give him and the boys some stability in their lives.

'So, Pete, how was the retirement party last night?' Brenda enquired.

'Well, Mac has left, he's the one who gave me my pride back and both he and the boys on the watch have been fantastic through all of the hard times since I went on to Red Watch.' He thought for a minute. 'Mac going will mean changes, but I think I'm OK now. He'll be missed, but that's life, people come and go. I've changed, I'm sure for the better. And now, of course, we are good friends,' he emphasised, looking at Brenda. 'I'm happy about that.'

Brenda leaned forward and grasped his hand. 'I think we are and will be more than just good friends. It will be good for both of us, and the boys.'

'You're right; we've got a lot to look forward to.' Pete smiled inwardly; a few months ago he was a different man. Now he was happy; happy with his work, his kids, and his life settled with a future to look to.

The old pub sat out in the darkness of the Peak landscape. The lights and decorations on the outside were a welcoming sight. Mac pulled the car to a halt in the sparsely populated car park. The pub was old, with low, oak-beamed ceilings. A log fire crackled in the Inglenook fireplace. The bar was decorated with a mixture of bottles, the tables were spread through the area and were all illuminated by candles. They sat at a table and picked through the menu. Twenty minutes later, they ate and drank. Mac sipped at a glass of orange juice.

'Well, ladies,' he said. 'Here's to us, the James family.'

Jake lay quietly on his bed, his mind wandering randomly through the past few days that he'd spent with Antonella. He felt warm, the thought of her and the way she had adapted to his home and his friends made him happy. He was glad that his mates from the station liked her. Brian hadn't been able to take his eyes off her, he's said to Jake that he thought she was beautiful, something of course that Jake didn't need to be told, but he was happy to have his opinion affirmed.

'You know, Jake,' Brian said, his lips slightly slurred after a couple too many beers. 'Jill's just given me a right telling off, she said I should stop banging on about how gorgeous your girlfriend is. She said I was embarrassing her.'

Jake smiled to himself; he knew what Brian was like: he was a proper ladies' man, but also knew that he was no risk to his friends. There was a tap on his bedroom door.

'Are you conscious yet, Jacob?'

'Yes, come in, Mum,' he replied.

'How are you, son?'

'I'm OK, Mum, just thinking about the weekend.'

'Well, it went well I think,' his mum said. 'She's a lovely girl, and she seemed to have really enjoyed the weekend.'

'She did, now we have to wait a couple of weeks before I go down to London to see her.'

'It'll be worth the wait, Jacob. I think your feelings are mutual, but no need to rush things. I think you're there for the long haul. Anyway, I'm off to bed; see you in the morning, sweet dreams.'

'Goodnight Mum, love you.'

'And I love you too, son.'

Antonella hauled her case into her flat. The journey from Sheffield had overrun due to problems on the line, so now at 11.45 she was tired and ready for bed. She sat on the bed, not bothering to unpack her case, and ran the events of the weekend through her mind. She had loved the weekend with Jacob and his mum. Previously her life had revolved around her life in Italy, then moving to London and her time being consumed by work, with little chance of expanding her knowledge of England; but now she knew more, she had visited Yorkshire and Derbyshire and was amazed at the beauty of these places. Her very mistaken view of the northern parts of the country was that they were dull, dark places full of grimy people, and that the real English were around the south. She now knew differently. Her man Jacob, the man who, to her mind, had saved her life, was from the north. When she had been attacked there were plenty of men from the south who stood and watched and did nothing. Jake did something, so she knew the stereotype of the north was inaccurate. Her experiences of the weekend confirmed that the people were funny, friendly, loyal, brave, bright and the countryside was beautiful, and all the money in the south couldn't buy those qualities. She loved Jacob and she loved the north and was sure that it would not be too long before she was there again, hopefully walking among those lovely mountains with her man Jacob.

Val finished drinking her cup of tea. 'Right, I'm off to bed, are you coming?' she said. Her voice was relaxed and cheerful.

Mac folded the paper he'd been browsing through and slid it into the paper rack.

'Yes, I'm with you. It's been a tiring day, it's hard work being a civilian and a pensioner.'

Val laughed. 'Well, don't think you'll be taking it too easy, there's plenty of things need doing around here.'

Val lay in bed, her glasses perched precariously on her nose as she started to read the book she'd been trying to finish for weeks. Mac lay back on top of the bed, his hands tucked behind his head.

'Why don't I book us a break at the coast somewhere for a change tomorrow?'

Val peered at him through her glasses. 'You mean we can go away to the seaside? Yippee,' she laughed. 'That would be nice.'

'Well, I thought we can get off somewhere and get a bit of sunshine later, when we've got ourselves sorted out. Spain or France, maybe.'

'Yeah, that would be nice. Maybe take the girls with us if they can make the time.'

Mac slid into the car. The luggage was safely stowed in the boot.

'Right, gal, let's go. Scarborough here we come.' He pulled out of the drive. It was 10 o'clock and the coast was waiting.

Red Watch were on duty. Tony had taken the watch on his first parade. Jock was the nominated driver, Brian and Jake were riding BA and Pete was middle man in the back. They sat round the mess table, drinking tea. Tony wanted to talk to them; it was his first day as the officer in charge.

'Right guys, I have to tell you that I never imagined that I would one day be doing this job here. I never imagined a time when M-Mac wouldn't be here, if I'm honest. I want to say that I'm pleased and proud to be with you, and I will be doing my best to fill Mac's very large boots. Bear with me, you can be sure that I will do anything to make this watch, Red Watch, maintain what Mac and you achieved. I hope you will help me in that.'

Just then the lights came on, the shrill beeps reverberated around the station, their chairs were scraped back and in seconds the mess deck was empty. The diesel engine roared into life, the station doors swung open, and Pete jumped aboard with the message on a sheet of paper.

'What have we got, Pete?' called Jock.

Pete read out the message. 'Shed on fire, 22 Fleming Street.'

'OK, let's go,' Tony called. Jock hammered down the throttle, the appliance lurched into the traffic and sped towards the city in a cloud of blue diesel smoke with the horns blaring.

Mac pulled on to the Parkway. He heard the sirens in the distance, then he glanced in his mirror and saw the appliance gaining on them fast.

'I wonder where they're going?' Mac said to Val.

Pete saw them first. 'Hey, is that Mac's car?' he shouted as they approached fast from behind.

252

'Yeah, give him a blast,' Tony said, a grin stretching his face. Jock pushed the button and the horns blared as they came up behind Mac's car and then moved out to overtake. Jake looked out of his side window and saw Mac looking up at them, grinning. Mac gave them the finger and laughed.

Mac saw Jake laugh. He noticed Jake was wearing the BA set, and wondered where they were going. In a second they were past. Mac watched as they moved away, heading for the city. He took in a deep breath. *No regrets*, he said to himself as he pressed the accelerator.

'Right, Scarborough here we come,' Mac laughed.

EPILOGUE

Brian and **Jane** were married, Jill was their bridesmaid. Mac was his best man. The watch sang to him at the reception. Brian transferred to the training school as an instructor, and was quickly promoted to the rank of sub officer.

Jock remains on Red Watch and has been promoted to leading fireman. He has moved house and now lives in Chesterfield. His son Fraser played in midfield for the Blades, and subsequently transferred to Birmingham City FC, where he is a first team regular.

Taff remains at Graveton. He and Ena adopted a little girl. They call her Madeline, they are in the process of adopting a second child.

Mick and **Paula** are now engaged; both have recovered well from their injuries and are planning to get married. Mick is studying hard for his promotion exams.

Tony has settled well onto Red Watch. He is undergoing a remedial course to rectify his stammer, and is doing well; he often rings Mac for advice.

Pete continues on Red Watch, he is also studying hard. He and Brenda have moved in together and live in Pete's house, the boys have both accepted her.

Jake is studying for his exams and continues to burst with enthusiasm. He and **Antonella** see each other regularly, and the talk is of an engagement in the near future. They have talked a lot about the future, but as yet how they will overcome the problem of the distance between them is undecided.

Mark Devonshire and Jake meet up regularly; Mark has adapted well to life in the north and is studying for promotion.

Ian is still the divisional commander and has no plans to push for further advancement, but there is the possibility that he will move into Brigade HQ as a staff officer in the future.

Jim and **Maddie** are still not married, but their relationship continues to grow, they are expecting to be married within the year. They are saving hard to put down a deposit on a house. They still walk in the Peak most weekends.

Janet and **Duncan** still live apart, but their relationship is calm and a divorce will happen. Janet and Don continue to meet and go out socially but nothing formal has happened yet.

Doris and **Ernie**, the old couple. Doris has recovered well from her illness, she and Ernie continue their trips into the Peak, but their walks have become shorter. Ernie has bought a new, second-hand car. The heater works, so Doris is happy.

Mac has adapted to life after the fire service. He has qualified as a volunteer ranger and enjoys his life. He spends much of his time with his girls doing DIY. Ruth has told Mac about her sexuality; Mac, as expected, brushed it off with a smile and a hug. The hydrant close to their house is tested most weeks.

The South Yorkshire Fire and Rescue Service continues its work, saving life, protecting property and rendering humanitarian services.